PE:

The Confession Room

Lia Middleton is a barrister who specializes in crime and prison law, and lives with her husband and two young children in Buckinghamshire. You can find her on Twitter @liamiddlet0n and on Instagram @liamiddletonauthor.

By the same author

When They Find Her
Your Word or Mine

The Confession Room

LIA MIDDLETON

PENGUIN BOOKS

PENGUIN BOOKS

UK | USA | Canada | Ireland | Australia
India | New Zealand | South Africa

Penguin Books is part of the Penguin Random House group of companies
whose addresses can be found at global.penguinrandomhouse.com

First published 2023
002

Set in 12.5/14.75pt Garamond MT Std
Typeset by Jouve (UK), Milton Keynes
Printed and bound in Great Britain by Clays Ltd, Elcograf S.p.A.

The authorized representative in the EEA is Penguin Random House Ireland,
Morrison Chambers, 32 Nassau Street, Dublin D02 YH68

A CIP catalogue record for this book is available from the British Library

ISBN: 978-1-405-95454-9

www.greenpenguin.co.uk

For my big sister and brother, Eva and Kyriacos.
Thank you for a childhood bursting with happy memories.
And for a life of support, love and friendship.

It will be the smell that wakes him.

At first he was perfectly still, but now, he is stirring. His nostrils are flaring. His reaction is fascinating to watch. Cautious sniffs transform into abrupt intakes of breath and his eyes fly open, wide and childlike. Humans are all the same; all animals reacting in the same instinctive way to a stimulus. In this case: the realization that something is incredibly wrong.

And something is very wrong. He is not in his bedroom, as he should be, but instead in a room made up of four cement walls, a grey ceiling, no windows . . . and the overpowering smell of bleach.

He sits up and rocks forward. The room will be tossing violently back and forth, the after-effects of falling unconscious without warning. He clamps his hand over his mouth . . . That will be the nausea.

After a few minutes, his rapidly blinking eyes lift. He looks around, forcing himself to take in the strangeness of the situation.

Why am I here? How did I get here?

He brings his knees up towards his chest and —

There it is. The moment of recognition I've been waiting for. He stares down at his leg, his mouth dropping open as his eyes take in the shining steel cuff wrapped around his ankle, attached to a chain, tethering him to the wall.

'Hello?' *he calls out, trying to keep the panic from his voice.* 'Hello?'

His face slowly falls as he waits for a response that won't come.

I

He won't even find comfort in the echo of his own voice. The room is too small for that. The walls and ceiling both too close.

There is nothing but silence.

He forces himself on to his knees and then groans as his body rights itself, chest heaving with the effort. He is shaking. Shaking with adrenalin and nerves and the confusion that is keeping him from screaming out, from crying for his mother, from calling for someone, anyone.

This is fear. This is the moment he understands how fear really feels.

He steps forward, one small step into the room, his eyes darting around as he tries to make sense of his surroundings. He frowns, turning slowly in a circle, tangling his legs in the chain.

He focuses first on the corner of the room to the right. There is another bolt fixed to the wall, for another person to be chained to. But it is empty. So instead he turns his attention to the objects sitting innocuously in each of the room's corners.

Four boxes, painted black.

How long will it take him to brave opening one? Some people would launch themselves directly at the boxes, scrambling in their haste to crack them open, like overeager children at Christmas. Others would cower, shrinking away from the unknown.

I had anticipated that he would be the former. But by his reaction to the room, I'm guessing now that he might be the latter. Not so big and brave, after all.

His eyes shift away from the closest box and look up to where a stop-clock is hanging in the centre of the ceiling, its red digital figures ready to begin counting down.

00:60.

Sixty seconds.

He stares helplessly up, his thoughts written across his features.

What will happen after sixty seconds?

And when will the countdown begin?

Before

We look before and after,
And pine for what is not;
Our sincerest laughter
With some pain is fraught;
Our sweetest songs are those that tell
of saddest thought.

Percy Bysshe Shelley

4th November, 7 p.m.

Emilia slams the door, leaning against it as she briefly closes her eyes, relishing the feeling of finally being at home. Another day spent in a car, watching a house, waiting for a man to visit somebody's wife, has made both her body and mind ache. The unrelenting ache of boredom.

But being paid to see if somebody's wife is having an affair is better than nothing. It is better than the first six months after she left the police, when all she did was eat into her small amount of savings and vegetate on the sofa, waiting for the anxiety to settle to a level where she might be able to go for a walk, or visit her parents. Back then, the dread had been all-consuming. But now it is out of sight. Hidden in a place where she can at least attempt to push it so deep inside that she can no longer feel it.

She opens her eyes at the sound of Mimi barking, her feet clipping down the corridor towards her.

'Hello, darling,' she says softly, before walking to the kitchen at the back of the house and turning on the tap, waiting a few moments for the water to run cold. She gulps thirstily from the glass and then refills it, sighing loudly, as if she can breathe out the day.

Heading to the living room, she walks directly to the rosewood desk that is tucked into the corner by the window, just as she does every day. She places the glass beside her keyboard and nudges the mouse. The screen brightens and comes to life, the documentary she was watching last night still paused, a message box pinned to the centre of the screen.

'Are you still watching Can Women Kill?'

Emilia clicks Yes, and the programme buffers for a brief moment before it continues, the narrator telling the tale of Mary Ann Cotton in his low, gruff voice.

She turns to a second screen and begins to scroll through various sites. She does this every night: listening to the documentary, her mind occasionally becoming fixated on the drama before turning back to the forums which she always consumes in the same order. First, *The Fun Lovin' Criminals* chat: an open group for people who used to work in criminal justice and who miss the thrill and satisfaction of working on a case, but they can't return to work – for any number of reasons. Sometimes they discuss the reasons. And sometimes they don't. None of them knows why Emilia left the police. She wants to tell them, she knows that all it would take would be to type the words, *I'm Sophie Haines's sister,* but every time she's tried, she couldn't bring herself to do it. It's as if her fingers became immobile, her brain unable to comprehend how to even spell out the words, let alone type what happened into existence. And she couldn't bear the questions. Nor the inevitable moment where one of them would suggest they work together to solve the mystery of what happened to Sophie. Emilia has already tried. The police have tried. Going back there would only drown her, after a year of thrashing against the current to fight her way to the surface and take that first life-saving breath. She fought with everything she had to solve what had happened.

6

And, after she left the force, the police had tried their best too. But there were no leads. No clues left behind by whoever had been following Emilia's sister.

After a while, the investigation began turning quiet; still juddering along but never gaining momentum. And the heartbreak was simply too much. Every time she had the urge to push herself to investigate, the grief washed over her all over again, the wound open and fresh. She couldn't do it. Maybe nobody would ever know who killed Sophie. And that's something she'll just have to live with.

After catching up with that group, she always turns to *Websleuths.com*. Then the Reddit Bureau of Investigation, followed by *lipstickalley.com*. And then finally, the Confession Room.

There are so many places for confession now: countless websites that offer a place for anonymous atonement. When Emilia first visited the Confession Room, she didn't expect to find anything new. Surely there were only so many times you could read about someone cheating, or lying, or stealing from the corner shop, before you glazed over. But that hadn't been the case ... not at all. She returns there, night after night, her eyes glued to the screen as she takes in each day's new confessions. As the months have passed, the confessions have darkened.

Emilia clicks in the address bar and types the first few letters and the address appears automatically.

theconfessionroom.com

She slams one finger down on to the keyboard. Enter.

The window turns black and the image of a door appears, metallic and cold. A creak leaks out from the speakers as it swings open and Emilia smiles, just as she did the first time she went on the forum and was surprised by the effort that had been put into the experience. Most other forums were plain and simple. But this one was different.

Behind the door, lying in the centre of a room, on a plain grey floor, is a box. Black and solid, its lines clean. The lid lifts and a piece of paper unfurls in the foreground. Calligraphy appears slowly, the writing dark and slanted, as if written with ink, which seeps lightly from the letters, like blood leaking into the clean white page.

You are about to enter . . .

It hangs there for a moment, perfectly still. But then it curls in on itself, into a scroll, and lowers itself back inside the box which closes suddenly, the lid slamming shut with a heavy finality. There is a low swell of music, violins, and a rumble of drums as the box begins to rotate, spinning faster and faster. It finally comes to a stop, a corner pointing towards the screen. And then words begin to appear, letters etched into the surface of the lid and two visible sides.

THE CONFESSION ROOM.

The word *Enter* shimmers into view.
She clicks.
The box opens, a bright white light emanating from inside, growing brighter and brighter until it has consumed the entire screen.
The title hangs at the top of the page, its letters ashen

and black. The forum is designed like a room, cold and clinical: a wide horizontal mirror fixed to background, light grey walls and exposed pipes wrapping their way across the top and down the sides of the screen. And written in the same calligraphy as before:

Welcome to the Confession Room.

A safe space for atonement and confession without consequence.

Beneath that: line after line of confessions. Emilia's eyes widen. It's growing. Exponentially. Every day she is shocked by the increase in the number of posts; the number of active users suspended in a box on the top right of the screen.

How many of them are merely reading the forum – and how many have confessed? Actually revealed a piece of themselves for the world to see?

Emilia understands the compulsion – the urge that pulls you in as you read other confessions, the feeling that it would be so good to spell out in words the very darkest of your thoughts. It's what she did, all those months ago when she first found the website. She allowed herself to type it out, letter by letter, the secret that had been with her like a constant toxic companion ever since Sophie had been killed.

I could have saved my sister. It's my fault she's dead.

And she hadn't stopped there. Some deeper impulse had churned inside her, dark and volatile, spilling out breathlessly.

9

> If I knew who he was, I would kill him.

Emilia jumps at the sound of a slamming door, heavy and final: the signal for a new post. The first time she had been on the forum it had scared the life out of her: she had jolted so suddenly that her tea had swelled out of her mug and sloshed all over her pyjama bottoms, turning the skin beneath a violent red.

Her eyes dance over the newest confession, widening first and then narrowing as her brow lowers into a frown.

> No matter how badly he treats me, I'm not sure I'll ever be
> brave enough to leave. I hate myself.

Emilia shakes her head, reaching for her glass. She gulps loudly, The confession, so simple, but with so much left unsaid. Just one sentence had set off a cascading line of questions, like dominoes, one falling after the other. Even though she is no longer in the police, she is still the consummate detective. But she can't get this drawn in by every confession on this page – especially as more and more are like this now, dark and chaotic. She has to switch off, like she used to in the police. Not every case can be let in. Not everyone can be saved.

Her stomach turns – *not everyone can be saved*. Not even the best of us. Not even –

No. She mustn't think of Sophie.

Blinking rapidly, Emilia scrolls upwards, and then stops at random. She reads quickly, her toes curling, ready for another emotional torrent, but her face breaks into a smile.

> Apparently my husband is leaving me for a woman he's fallen
> in love with online. He doesn't know that it's me. I'm sure he'll

be heartbroken when she doesn't meet him at the airport and falls off the face off the fucking planet. Surprise, you lying bastard.

Emilia reads it again, lingering on the final sentence. She laughs out loud, full and raspy at the back of her throat. It feels good. She moves up the page again, scanning the words, taking them in voraciously. Enjoying this place where people can admit their secrets and keep them safe. Get them off their chest, with no consequence at all except for relief. There are admissions of affairs, screwing over colleagues, stealing, hatred of partners, regret over having children – then Emilia's hand falls still as she takes in a post a third of the way down.

I sometimes follow a woman home from the station. She's so beautiful. I would never hurt her, or any one, but sometimes I wonder how it would feel to just reach out and grab her.

Emilia's vision clouds over, her heart thumping in her chest, her fingers tingling.

I wonder how it would feel to just reach out and grab her.

That's how it begins. That's how it always begins. That must be how the man who killed Sophie felt. At first he just watched her – she had told the police she was sure she was being followed. Stalked. But there's always the first time – the time that they stop being satisfied with wondering, and start needing to *feel*.

Who is the woman this man is following? Is she safe? His post feels like a warning – a blaring signal of impending danger. But a signal for who? The person who posted this can't be found.

Emilia's phone rumbles, the vibration loud and jarring. She jumps, then picks up the phone.

'Hi Dad,' she says.

'Emi! Just checking in. Are – are you okay?'

'Yes.' She clears her throat, trying to rid her voice of its adrenalin-fuelled high pitch. 'Why?'

'You . . . You sound strange.'

'No, I was just watching a documentary and the call made me jump . . . Everything okay?'

'Yes – just checking in.' He sighs. 'I don't know why you watch that kind of stuff, Emi. Crime and unsolved cases . . . Why don't you watch something relaxing? Something fun? What's that show you always used to watch with Sophie? The baking one?'

Emilia sighs. She hasn't been able to watch *Bake Off* since – not without her sister. They had watched it together every week, without fail, curling up on the sofa together underneath a thick blanket, cups of tea balanced on their laps, commentating on each episode through mouthfuls of shortbread.

'I'm not forcing myself, Dad. You know it's what I'm passionate about. It's what I love –'

'Well, if you love it –'

'Don't say it, Dad.'

'If you love it so much,' he continued, ignoring her warning, 'why don't you go back to the police? You know they'd have you back in a heartbeat.'

Emilia scoffs. 'Not so sure about that.'

'You're a brilliant officer –'

'*Was.*' She begins to chew on the edge of her thumb, on

the piece of loose skin she's been trying to ignore. 'I *was* a good police officer. That was before.'

'You can still do it.'

'No, Dad. You know that isn't true. You know that after . . . after everything, I was not a good officer. I could hardly function. And I just . . . I just couldn't. I can't go back.'

'Emi, your mum and I really think –'

'Please don't say it again.' She inhales deeply as her voice breaks, her eyes stinging. 'Please.'

He pauses. He doesn't know what to say. He never means to hurt her but he does. Every time he tells her to go back to the police, every time he tells her that she can still do it, it is a burning reminder that she can't. It isn't in her any more. The love for it is. The passion for it. But not the ability. Nor the stability. Mentally, emotionally . . . She just can't. It's too difficult now. Everything feels too personal. After Sophie, it was impossible. She felt as though her colleagues were treading on eggshells around her, assessing how each case might make her feel, whether she could cope. And the truth was, she couldn't cope at all. She went to a therapist, she saw a psychiatrist – she did everything she could to find her footing. But every moment was like wading upstream, the current ready at any moment to sweep her feet out from beneath her. And then she started making mistakes. Her doctor diagnosed her with post-traumatic stress disorder. She only lasted a few days beyond that.

'I'm sorry, Emi. But doing private investigation just seems like such a waste.'

'I'm good at it,' she insists. 'I can find anyone. And it makes me money. Good money. Better money than being in the police, that's for sure.'

'You know we just want what's best for you.'

'I-I know.' She gulps, blinking away tears, trying to push the swelling emotion back down deep inside her. 'I really wish I could, Dad. You know that . . . right?'

Silence.

'Dad?' Emilia pauses, listening to his breathing, knowing that he is trying to think of the right thing to say. 'Are you still there?'

'Yes, I'm here, love . . . So you're definitely not going back?'

Emilia closes her eyes, pressing her lips together to stop herself from crying again. Her hand rises to her mouth, her teeth finding that loose piece of skin once more. She winces. The taste of blood hits the back of her tongue, iron and salt. The taste of what it is to be alive.

'No,' she says with finality as she lowers her hand and watches a drop of blood trail down the side of her finger and pool in her nail-bed.

He sighs again, his tell-tale exasperated exhale. 'Well, of course it's your decision. And we're here for you. You know that, right?'

'I know.'

He pauses. 'Love you, Emi.' He blurts his affection out quickly. They are out of practice. She pushed them away for so long, unable to face the guilt that stirred inside her when confronted with their grief. Did they blame her too?

'I . . . I love you too.'

She ends the call and presses the side button, turning

the phone black. She places it back on the desk, lost for several minutes in the dark reflection staring back at her from the screen.

She slumps in her chair, rolling her head backwards, the nape of her neck resting awkwardly against the headrest. The sudden rush of emotions has dissipated, leaving her empty. A drained battery – all energy siphoned away.

Her eyes slowly move to her computer. She reaches out her fingers, slowly, stretching them to gently nudge the mouse.

The forum is there, the confessions suspended on the screen. She scrolls slowly upwards, taking them in, smiling at some, rolling her eyes at others. But finally she reaches the top, the most recent confession highlighted in bold: someone stealing two fifties from their mum's purse. Emilia shakes her head. Glancing at the clock, she yawns loudly. It's 7:45 p.m. Time for dinner.

The sound of a slamming door bursts from the computer and Emilia jolts.

There is a new confession at the top of the screen.

She leans forward, her eyes travelling quickly over the words. But she frowns, re-reading the post, her mind whirring as it tries to process, like a child sounding out new words.

Anonymous 01

Here's a confession: Murder. London. Hayley James. Luca Franco.

The Room

Ryan stares blankly at his reflection in the mirror.

What is happening? How did he end up here?

The face gazing back at him is pale, almost grey under the harsh fluorescent lighting; his hair wild and falling into his eyes. He tears his eyes away and looks back up at the clock – its figures poised, ready for the countdown.

'Hello?' he shouts up to the ceiling. 'Can anyone hear me?'

Panic is stirring in his chest, his stomach churning. His eyes dart around the room, from the boxes in the corners, back to the timer hanging above the mirror, and finally to the door. It's just a normal door – wood and a latch. Even if it's locked, he can break through it, he's sure. He darts towards it, holding his breath, but is pulled violently back by the chain around his ankle.

He screams loudly, frustration and anger bellowing out of him. 'Somebody help me! What the fuck is going on?'

His vision is wavering, the small room rocking from side to side, his hands clammy, sweat seeping through his T-shirt. He staggers backwards, collapsing against the wall and sliding to the floor. He presses his forehead against his knees and tries to draw in deep breaths, but instead the oxygen comes in jagged snatches and his heart races faster.

Take yourself out of this room. Think. You somehow ended up here. What's the last thing you remember? Think.

He had been at home. In front of his computer. Waiting for his mates to message with plans for that evening. The screen had blurred before his eyes, the words morphing into each other. He leaned backwards in his chair, his neck cracking as he rolled it in a circle, closing his eyes for a moment.

'Ryan!' His mum's voice echoed up the stairs, shrill, like a bird, the sound going straight through him.

'What?' he called back, trying to keep the tinge of annoyance out of his voice. No matter what she said or did, and no matter how much she bent to accommodate him, just the sound of her calling his name sent a flurry of frustration through him. He loved her, but her love was claustrophobic.

He pulled open the drawer of his desk and Fiona's photograph peered back up at him. He kept her hidden. His mum would just ask questions if she saw. But the photo was pocked with holes from when it had been on the wall, marked from every time he had decided to take her down and then put her back up. Sometimes it was the sight of her that was too much: her smiling face, almost cruel, as if she was laughing at him.

'Ryan?'

'Yes!' he yelled, no longer showing restraint.

His mum's face appeared through a small opening in the door, her nose scrunched up in disapproval as her eyes roamed over the bedsheets tangled at the foot of the bed; the clothes he was wearing yesterday in a pile on the floor.

'There's no need to shout, love,' she said, a nervous smile twitching across her mouth. 'Did you want a sandwich? You should eat something.'

'I'm not really hungry, Mum.'

'Are you sure?'

'Mm-hmm,' he nodded, not looking at her.

'Okay.' She stepped backwards, almost disappearing from sight, but then paused. 'Are you . . . are you going out tonight?'

'In a bit,' he nodded.

'Okay, love . . . Do you fancy coming to church with me tomorrow?'

He twisted his mouth, wanting to turn her down, but he couldn't do it. It meant so much to her. 'Sounds good . . . depending on how late I'm back tonight.'

'Perfect,' she said with a smile before stepping out into the hall and closing the door.

He sighed again, lifting a hand to rub his forehead. He never meant to be cruel to his mum. But all he felt when she was around was strain. Their once-close relationship bending under the weight of too much pressure, too much misplaced hope, too much proximity. Just too much . . . everything. They were a branch, ready to snap.

His phone vibrated. It was the group chat:

Pub?

Yep – let's get on it.

See you there.

'Finally,' he said, standing up and grabbing his keys and phone from his bed.

Be there in ten.

Leaving the house, he walked down the alley at the end of the street to get to the corner shop on Bridge Road. He went into the shop, chatted to Dave for a few minutes before buying his cigarettes and then went back to the alley to cut across to Woodgate Road and the pub . . .

He frowns. Did he get to the pub? Yes . . . he did. He can picture the rowdy shouts of his friends as he walked through the doors, he can feel the wooden bar beneath his fingertips, tacky with old beer and heat. He can hear the landlord, his familiar voice asking if he wanted another. And there was a couple sitting two stools down, a man and woman, laughing together at something on her phone.

But then everything goes dark – until he woke up here.

Now, all he can do is wait. Wait for someone to come into the room, wait for the countdown to begin.

But no – that isn't true. He doesn't just have to wait.

The boxes.

They must be here for a reason.

He inches closer to the nearest box, his hand reaching out before him, his fingers trembling. The chain around his ankle pulls tight, but he can just reach it. He turns quickly to look over his shoulder at the timer. But it is still frozen. He looks over to the door, his pulse thrumming in his temples, but nobody is there. No one is coming.

He narrows his eyes as something in the corner above the door catches his eye. How did he not notice that before?

A camera. The light glowing red.

A camera. The boxes. A countdown.

He knows where he is.

This is the Confession Room.

4th November, 7:50 p.m.

Murder. London. Hayley James, Luca Franco.

Emilia reads the confession over and over again. The words are there, as clear and bold as any headline on the front page of a newspaper or along the bottom of the ten o'clock news.

Someone has confessed to murder. And not just one victim. Two.

But it can't be real. It can't be.

Emilia opens the browser, navigating quickly to the search engine. Mimi trots towards her, manoeuvring herself to the space beneath the desk, her body warming Emilia's bare feet. She smiles – who would have guessed Mimi would be such a faithful companion, even if she can only fill a tiny part of the huge hole left behind by Sophie? Emilia has never been a dog person before, but after leaving the police, Mimi has helped the loneliness. Her life is so different without Sophie: her days empty, as though all of the colour in her life, in her, has faded away to black and white. She lives in a new place, moving about fifteen minutes further out of the city than the house they had shared. Out of the buzz and into the quiet suburbs. Life feels so different. So she tries to fill it with any small pieces of joy she can find. A walk in the woods with her puppy. A podcast. Visiting her parents. Coffee with Jenny. But it isn't the same.

Turning back to the screen, she types in 'Hayley James', her stomach turning. But there is nothing about a body being found or a missing person with that name. The confession has only just been posted – it will take some time for the media to discover it, verify, publish . . . But surely their families have realized that they're missing?

Emilia grabs her phone and opens Instagram. She searches again, frantically typing Hayley's name. The accounts load – countless profiles. No – she'll never be able to find anything on Instagram. She clicks out of the app and opens Twitter. Her fingers fly across the screen as she searches again.

Hayley James, Luca Franco, London, Murder.

No results.

Soon enough, the users of the Confession Room will spill out, leaking the confession on to social media and out into the wider world. But for now, it seems, it's still a secret locked inside the confines of the forum. Emilia shivers. She could be the first person in the world to have seen it.

She throws herself back in her chair and rubs her eyes frantically, her breath wavering.

It's okay. It must be a joke. It's just someone messing around.

She turns back to her phone, opening Instagram again. The search results are still there – the many faces of Hayley James beaming out at her from their various happy locations – a mum cuddling her small baby; a teenager playing volleyball on the beach; a young woman raising a glass of champagne, her head thrown back as she smiles. Looking through those profiles would take too long, the name too common. But the man . . .

Luca Franco. *Yes.* He might be easier to find.

Emilia types his name into the search bar. A list of results appears, and she begins to click through them, her eyes scanning the locations.

The first is a man in his early forties, with greying hair and bright blue eyes. But he posted less than an hour ago from Rome.

The second profile is a young boy in his early teens – America. And she clicks away quickly from the third – Australia.

'London', the post said. She needs to find a Luca Franco in London.

She clicks on the fourth profile down and images of a young man in his late twenties at the most smile back at her, his teeth gleaming inside his open-mouthed laugh. And there, in his most recent image – Annabel's. He was in Mayfair just yesterday.

Emilia clicks on his followers. She searches for the name: *Hayley James.* They must be linked somehow.

A single profile appears.

They *are* connected.

Her breath held, Emilia clicks. She is there – hair tinged pink. Pretty. But there are no recent stories. And her last post was six days ago.

Emilia goes to her followers list and clicks through, searching profile after profile, watching their stories, looking at their most recent posts – but none of them are showing any indication that Hayley is missing or has faced some kind of danger. She does the same for Luca . . . Nothing.

There is nothing.

Nothing that she can find, anyway . . . But if these people have been reported as missing, the police would know.

Maybe Ciaran would know.

Emilia looks down at her phone, still cradled in her hands. She can't contact him. Not now, after all these months of not speaking. She could call Jenny. But she wouldn't know: she works in custody, not investigation. She should just call 999 and report the post: show them the website and let that be the end of it. But she needs to know that it isn't real – that it's just another hurt or sadistic person playing at a sick kind of make-believe. Or even one of Hayley and Luca's friends, thinking for some deranged reason that this would be funny.

She should call Ciaran.

Her stomach flips at the thought of speaking to him again. The last time she saw him, he kissed her on the forehead, the same way he always did, and told her that when she was ready, he'd be waiting. But she hasn't spoken to him since. Just a week before, he had helped her move to her new house – he had comforted her as she closed the door of the house she had shared with Sophie for the last time.

He might not even answer the phone. He might see her name on the screen and wait for the ringing to stop.

With shaking fingers, Emilia navigates her way to his name in her contacts. She never would have had to do that before – he would have made up all of her most recent calls and messages, their incoming and outgoing communication taking up the entire screen without interruption.

An all too familiar sadness stirs in her stomach. She has missed him with the aching that only comes from *truly* missing a person. But she had forced herself to forget.

Maybe it's time to remember.

She jabs the call button and lifts the phone to her ear, her heart beating faster and faster with each long ring.

'Emilia?' His surprise sends chills down her arms.

'Hi Ciaran . . .' She waits, hoping he will say something, but he remains quiet, his shock palpable. 'How . . . how are you?'

'Um . . .' He pauses, clearing his throat. He has always done that when he doesn't know what to say; biding his time to formulate a response. 'I'm good, Emi. I'm good . . . How are you?'

'I'm okay.' She chews her lip, trying to detect a hint of a smile in his voice. 'I . . . Are you on shift? I'm sorry for calling you like this –'

'No, it's okay. It's good to hear from you . . . I'm just at the station. When I saw your name on the screen, I thought you'd sat on your phone or something.'

She smiles, her heart warming at the sound of his soft laugh. 'I'm sorry I haven't reached out to you sooner. I just . . . I didn't know how –'

'Please, don't apologize.'

Emilia nods, squeezing her eyes closed. How did she let him go? How did she push a man like this away? A man who would have done anything for her, a man who loved her in the way that most people can only ever dream of being loved.

'There's something I wanted to ask you about.'

He sighs quietly – so quietly that if she knew him less well, she would have missed it completely. He's disappointed. Disappointed that she was calling him because she wanted something, and not because she wanted him. 'What is it?' he responds.

'Have you heard of the Confession Room?'

'Um . . . I can't say I have.'

'It's a forum where people can post confessions anonymously. It started around a year ago but it's been gaining a lot of traction recently. It's got thousands of confessions now –'

'Okay –'

'Anyway, I was on the forum just reading through the confessions, and one just came through . . . Someone has confessed to murder and left two names.'

He doesn't respond. His breathing rattles through the receiver but he doesn't say a word.

'Ciaran?'

'Sorry, I'm here . . . What exactly does it say?'

'It just says, "Here's a confession. Murder. London. Hayley James. Luca Franco." That's it.'

Emilia waits, chewing on her thumb nail as Ciaran taps on his keyboard. She can see him now, his dark brow lowered over his green eyes as he squints at the screen, pushing a soft curl of hair from his vision.

'Do you see it?' she whispers.

'Yep . . . When did this appear?'

'About fifteen minutes ago. I searched for the names on social media and I'm pretty sure I've found them. I can send you their profiles but I thought you might have heard something about missing persons?'

'Uh, not off the top of my head. Let me check . . .'

Emilia listens as he taps away on his keyboard. 'No.

Nobody with those names.' He sniffs. 'How long have you been on this forum?'

'Months now . . .'

'But have you looked through it? Have you read other confessions?'

'Mm-hmm.'

'And are they serious? Or is it a joke?'

'Some of them are serious. And some of them seem . . . I don't know, more like jokes. Dark humour.'

'Well, we haven't got any investigations out for anyone with those names. No missing persons. Nothing . . . So unless it's all happened very recently, my gut instinct would be that it's a hoax.'

'You think?'

'Yeah . . . I'll look into it though. And Cyber Crime will be able to trace the IP address.'

'Okay. Thanks, Ciaran.'

Emilia falls silent, unsure of what to say, or whether she should say anything else at all.

'Emi? Are you still there?'

She nods, even though he can't see her. 'Yes. Yes, I'm still here.'

'It's . . . it's been good to hear your voice,' he whispers, his words tinged with a smile.

'Yours too,' she whispers back. Anything more than a whisper feels too loud, but their shared quiet fills her with a sudden bout of bravery. 'I've missed you.' She listens to his intake of breath, then his silence. 'Sorry. I didn't mean to make you feel awkward —'

'No, you didn't. I've missed you too. Maybe we could meet up one evening. Have a drink?'

'That sounds great. Thanks again, Ciaran.'

'Cool. Well, you're welcome. I'll call you . . . Night, Emi.'

'Night.'

The phone call ends, but Emilia remains completely still in her chair, the phone still fixed to the side of her face, his voice still echoing in her ear.

She turns to look back at her screen – he's right. It must be a sick joke. Somebody stumbled upon the forum, and thought it would be hilarious to confess to the most violent crime that exists.

Emilia nods decisively and stands, making her way back to the kitchen. She pulls her dinner – a macaroni cheese – from the fridge and places it in the microwave. But as it rotates, her mind begins to wander, navigating its way back to the Confession Room.

It must be a hoax. Nobody would publicly confess to murder.

Would they?

6th November

Emilia watches the house on the corner, her eyes narrowing as the front door swings open.

Is this finally it? Is she finally going to catch him leaving?

She has been staked outside this house in Hampstead for three days, waiting, assured by the man paying her that if his wife is having an affair, it's happening during the day, while he's at work. But she's yet to see the man he's concerned about. Every day she has seen her, the wife, leaving the house, closing the pale rose-coloured front door behind her, and descending the three white stone steps to the pavement with such grace it's as if she's floating. Her chic bob is always styled to perfection, her clothes classic and streamlined, large sunglasses placed just so on the end of her nose. And Emilia has followed, taking photographs of her going for coffee with friends, going to yoga. Having lunch. But no affair. Not one that is visible, anyway. Her life seems perfect, *she* seems perfect. But her husband tells a different story. The story of a manipulator, a woman who will smile to your face and then stab you in the back. Maybe it's all in his head. Maybe his judgement of her is blinding him, convincing him that she must be doing something wrong, that her change in behaviour must be because of another man and couldn't possibly be because of him. It wouldn't be the first time.

She leans forward, her camera poised, her vision focused

down the lens, ready to capture the secrets that are hiding behind the flawless facade of this Hampstead address. The door slams and—

Emilia slumps back in her seat.

It's their son, Harry. Eleven years old, rucksack almost the size of him strapped to his back, on his way to rugby.

Emilia lowers her camera, setting it down on the passenger seat. This job has been more challenging than most, the boredom more prevalent as her mind is consumed with thoughts of the Confession Room.

She has continued checking every day, but there have been no more posts. The morning after the confession, as she staked out this house for the second day, she checked it on her mobile, but became quickly frustrated as it glitched and buffered. She had only ever looked at it on her computer before as part of her nightly routine. But the temptation is so high. And no matter what she has done to distract herself since, it has been there, the words like an echo in her ears.

Murder. London. Hayley James, Luca Franco.

What if it is real? What if it has actually happened and their bodies are lying somewhere? What if their families, their partners or children, woke up this morning with worry in their stomach, with a creeping unease that they haven't spoken to Luca in a while, or Hayley hasn't called like she normally would? What if it wasn't a joke?

A car door slams and Emilia lifts her chin. She reaches again for her camera, lifting it quickly and then snapping several photographs in succession.

A man is walking up to the house, throwing his arm behind him casually to lock his matt-black Mercedes. He trots up the steps to the house. But he doesn't knock. He simply stands there. Within seconds, the door opens narrowly and he slips inside.

He was waiting for the son to leave. That Mercedes has been parked there for close to half an hour. He's been biding his time until he could go inside. How didn't she notice him before? She's too distracted.

Emilia rolls her eyes and sighs. She had so wished that this was a case of a paranoid, controlling husband. She had so wished that this time her client was wrong. But in her time as a private investigator she has come to realize that there is usually truth in suspicion. Smoke. Fire.

She notes down the registration plate – now is her favourite part, the part she truly excels at: finding out who he is. Turning a stranger into a fully formed person. Without the confines of the police, there is so much you can find out about a person. And she's good at it.

Emilia can find anyone.

'Are you sure I can't get you anything else, love?'

Emilia's mum sets down a large mug of tea on the table in front of her, a bony hand squeezing her shoulder.

'No, Mum, thank you.' She reaches for the mug, relishing the heat burning through the porcelain. 'This is perfect.'

'I can get you some food together – if I'd known you were coming I –'

'No, don't be silly. I just wanted to pop in to see you.'

Her dad reaches out, placing a gentle hand on her forearm which rests on the table. 'Quiet day today?'

'I found what I was looking for sooner than I thought.'

'Another affair?' her mum whispers with a raised brow.

'Yes,' Emilia nods. 'Another affair . . .'

'Will you take a little break now?'

'No, Mum.'

'You could teach – what about that training job that your old Inspector mentioned?'

'Teaching was Sophie's thing, Mum,' Emilia says, trying to prevent the words from biting. 'That was her – she wanted to help people –'

'And so do you –'

'Yes, but in a different way.'

Her parents share a glance across the table: so subtle that they think she won't catch it. But she does.

'I spoke to Ciaran a couple of days ago,' she whispers.

The brief glimmer of tension in the air instantly evaporates. Her dad restrains his reaction, responding with a gentle tilt of his head. But her mum's face is brightening by the second, a grin slowly stretching across her face. She had loved Ciaran. So had her dad. But it was her mum who was devastated when Emilia told them that she had ended their relationship. Three years over – just like that. She just hadn't been able to comprehend it. But her dad seemed to understand in his own way. He could see that anyone being too close was just too painful for Emilia. That the sudden absence of Sophie in her world had created a gaping vacuum – a black hole which was ready to destroy everything.

'How is he?' her mum asks, blinking rapidly. 'What's he been up to? Is he with –'

'Marie, for God's sake, let her speak.'

Emilia lifts her mug to her mouth and sips, peering at

her parents over the rim, enjoying the warmth of their back-and-forth, even when they are poking at each other, her mum insisting that it's just an innocent question, her dad responding with the fact that no question she asks is ever innocent.

'Oi, you two, stop it. It's not a big deal . . . I just reached out to him because . . . because of this thing I saw online. And we had a chat and that was it.'

'Is he still in your old team?' her dad asks.

'Yes . . . he's a sergeant now.'

'Good for him.'

Her mum wrinkles her nose, glancing uneasily at her dad. 'How long has it been, love?'

'Since what?'

'Since you last spoke to him?'

Emilia blinks down at her lap. 'Nine months, I think,' she whispers. 'We split a week or two after I left the police and we haven't talked since. He . . . he tried at first and I just ignored him . . .' She shrugs, forcing the casual gesture as her eyes sting with tears. 'If he never spoke to me again, I'd have deserved it.'

'Don't say that, Emilia,' her dad says, his voice stern. 'You were going through so much. It was such a huge loss and in such a violent way –'

'It was a loss for him too. He loved Sophie. And he was there when –'

The words falter. Her head collapses into her hands, her shoulders shaking. She shouldn't talk about it – not that day, the day it happened. Not the way she was found.

*

They had been on the way to an arrest when Sophie tried to ring her. Her personal phone had vibrated, but Emilia had glanced at it and pressed the side button, sending her sister to voicemail. It wasn't until an hour or so later, when she and Ciaran returned to the car, that she saw that there were six missed calls. One after the other. But still, she thought nothing of it. She and Sophie spoke all the time, calling each other about the most banal events that made up their day. And they had plans for that evening – a friend's hen night. She was probably just calling over some emergency with a costume. Sophie had always been that way, forgetting the details and looking to Emilia for the answers.

But then the call came over the radio. A break-in. A lone female. The phone call to the emergency services ending abruptly.

And then the address came through in a muffled blur. Their address.

Her sister. It was her sister.

And she had tried to call Emilia.

Ciaran raced them to the house, weaving through traffic, the tyres screeching, Emilia screaming at him to go faster – but they were too late.

The front door was ajar.

They had pushed into the home she and Sophie had shared. The floor lamp in the living room had fallen on to its side, into the hallway. The pile of washing that Emilia had placed on the bottom step this morning, was now scattered. They had darted around the downstairs rooms before Ciaran had tried to stop her from bolting upstairs, but she threw herself past him, launching herself up them two at a time.

And there she was. At the threshold of her room, her feet sticking out on to the landing. A pool of blood beneath her, soaking into the carpet. It was too late. She was gone.

Ciaran had dropped to his knees with Emilia, catching her before she hit the floor. He cradled her to his chest, his arms wrapped tightly around her shoulders, rocking her as the wails burst out of her, the sound of sirens tingeing the distant air.

And every so often, her strangled cries: 'I could have saved her . . . I could have saved her.'

The music starts and Emilia presses the button on the side of her phone, blaring the volume until it is echoing around the bathroom, bouncing off the dark green tiles. She steps into the shower and turns it on, rotating the valve until the water is so hot it turns her skin pink, her cheeks flushing – anything to burn away the guilt that the memory of Sophie has brought to the surface.

She shakes her head, then forces herself to sing along to the music and scrub herself with her favourite body wash – the expensive one her best friend Jenny bought her. It smells like lilies. *Look after yourself*, Jenny said. *Self-care, and all that bollocks. It's important.*

I really need to call her, Emilia thinks. *It's been too long again.*

She pauses as the music from her phone suddenly fades away, a low vibration humming from the basin.

Someone is calling her.

She tilts her chin up towards the water and lets it spray on to her face for a few seconds, her eyes closed, breathing in the scent of lilies. The buzzing ends and the music begins again.

Opening the shower door, she pulls her towel around her, walking towards the mirror as steam swirls around her. She wipes the glass with her arm and picks up her phone, tapping the screen with her wet fingers.

Three missed calls: Ciaran.

She catches herself in the mirror – there's a faint smile with a hint of something she hasn't seen in a while. He said he would call. And he has.

She dresses quickly, wondering what Ciaran might have to say.

She stops the music, her flat falling quiet except for the serious voice of the news reporter on the six o'clock news floating in from the other room. She inhales deeply through pursed lips, holding her breath as she navigates to his name. But her fingers still as the newsreader's voice catches her ear with two familiar names.

'. . . Hayley James and Luca Franco.'

7th November, 1 a.m.

Emilia's eyes strain under the weight of her tiredness, but she can't go to sleep. Her body won't let her – even though it's 1 a.m.

She glances back at the television which is still playing the news on an endless loop. Every so often, the report repeats, and chills run down Emilia's arms all over again as she listens to the stoic voice of the reporter.

'Police are investigating the case of two missing persons. Hayley James, twenty-three, and her boyfriend Luca Franco, twenty-five, have been named in an online confession to murder on an internet forum. The Confession Room, which describes itself as "a place for anonymous atonement", contains thousands of confessions to wrong-doing, and on the 4th November a confession was posted to murder with Hayley James and Luca Franco named as the victims. They were last seen by their friends at lunch in Clapham Common on that same day.

Hayley, a nurse who lives with her parents in south London, was due to return home on the 6th November after a shift at St George's hospital; however, her parents received a phone call from her employer stating that she had not turned up for work. In a statement, Hayley's family have said: "It is very unusual for Hayley to not turn up to work. We thought she'd just stayed at Luca's, but she loves her job and is a highly responsible and thoughtful person. It's entirely out of character that she would skip a shift without informing the hospital or telling anybody why." Luca Franco lives by himself in Clapham, but has not been seen since the lunch and his phone is no longer connected. If you have any information regarding either Hayley James or Luca Franco, or any information in connection to the Confession Room and tracing the authors of the posts, the police have asked that you contact them using reference 22MIS007134 . . . '

Their photographs flash up on the screen. Hayley James, young and vibrant, her dark blonde hair tinged pink at its ends, her leg popped coquettishly, her eyes lined and heavy. And then Luca Franco, his olive skin and beaming smile. Their faces like a light being switched on in a dark room, turning Emilia's stomach. She had found the right people on Instagram. And now their faces are on the news.

She glances at her phone. She called Ciaran back as soon as she finished watching the report for the first time but he didn't answer. Since then she has been waiting for it to light up with his name, hoping that he'll know something, be able to tell her anything. But there has been nothing.

Instead, she has spent the last few hours, without eating or removing herself from her chair, scouring the internet.

She began with Luca's Instagram profile. She scrolled back through his photos: with friends at a festival; at the gym; holding a young baby. She checked the comments of that one – it was his niece. Click after click, photo after photo, until finally. There they were, together, her cradled with her head in his lap, her hands raised up to her mouth as she laughed, him gazing down at her. The caption beneath: 'my girl' and a heart.

Emilia tapped the photo: Hayley was tagged.

She clicked on her name and was transported, as if through a portal, into the world of Hayley James. She hadn't paid attention before, she had been too rushed, too desperate to find out what was going on. But Hayley's feed is curated, the colours all uniform, the filter faded and pink, as if you are looking at her photos through rose-coloured lenses. Straightaway, Emilia noticed a very obvious difference between Hayley's profile and Luca's. On Luca's page, she had clicked through multiple pictures before finding one of him with Hayley. But on her page: he was everywhere. In almost every photo, he was there, smiling at the camera, Hayley's hand gripping his arm, or head resting on his shoulder. Every so often there was a selfie, Hayley staring wide-eyed with lips parted at the camera, and even less often there was a photograph of her with a small group of friends. But Luca was her world. Anyone could see it.

What did someone want with them? And why both of them?

Emilia had scoured their profiles, searching for anything that could have led to someone wanting to target them. Searching for clues. But all she saw was two young people, working through life together, having a relationship similar to millions of other people in their early twenties. They were unremarkable.

Next Emilia had turned to social media. It hadn't taken long for people who frequented the Confession Room to put the pieces together and hold up the completed puzzle for the whole world to see. There was already a hashtag on Twitter – #The ConfessionRoom, and even more horrifying, #TheConfessionRoomMurders – the mentions growing exponentially. She had watched as it grew from posts in the tens, to the thousands, to entire threads discussing the forum.

And it's still there, on her second screen. The number of active forum users growing all the time. Is this what the person who posted the confession wanted? Attention by any means? Even infamy?

Emilia refreshes Twitter but her mouth drops open slowly – the mentions have grown by thousands in a number of seconds.

Have you seen the video?!!!!

**OMG THAT
FUCKING VIDEO!**

**That video that's just been posted
on #TheConfessionRoom is so wrong.
What the hell?!**

**So they're definitely
dead? I thought it was a
joke until now.**

Emilia navigates quickly to the forum, her fingers trembling, her mouth dry.

The page loads and her stomach twists.

There it is: a link to a video at the top of the page. No accompanying words or confession. Just the link.

She moves the mouse slowly towards the link, her heart hammering, her pulse buzzing in her ears. She shouldn't look at it, she knows she shouldn't. But there's no way she can't.

She clicks quickly and the page redirects. A black screen loads, the circular symbol whirring as it buffers quickly.

Emilia's chest squeezes, as if her heart is shrinking, as she reads the title of the video.

THE CONFESSION ROOM: HAYLEY JAMES AND LUCA FRANCO

This is real. It's actually happening.

Somebody committed murder. Filmed it. Confessed to it . . . and then uploaded it to the internet for the world to watch.

Emilia hesitates for a moment – then presses the play button, holding her breath.

The video shows a room filmed from above, a camera hanging in one of its corners. CCTV. But the view is zoomed in, close to a young woman's face. Hayley. She is chained to a chair by her torso. Her breaths are ragged, her shoulders heaving up and down as she tries desperately to snatch some oxygen into her lungs.

Then –

'You're running out of time, Hayley!'

Emilia frowns. The voice is low and hoarse. Who is that? Is that Luca's voice? Or the killer's?

'I can't!' Hayley whimpers from between her fingers, the nails painted red, the polish chipped. She looks up, her gaze intent, as if she is looking directly at somebody. 'I can't do it!'

'Just do it! For fuck's sake! We don't know what will happen when the timer runs out!'

Hayley manically shakes her head faster and faster, her high-pitched wails turning into guttural sobs.

'Hayley! Just say what you've done –'

'I've been cheating on you!'

The video falls silent for a moment, the only sound the almost undetectable white noise of the camera.

'What?' the other voice says.

I've been cheating on you.

It's Luca.

'I-I'm sorry.'

'Tell me what happened. How long?'

'I can't –'

'You have to, remember? You're meant to confess!'

'I . . . I . . . It's been going on for almost a year. And it isn't because I don't love you,' she cries, her eyes now wide and pleading. 'It's because I know that I love you in a way that you will never love me. And I just wanted to know what it felt like to have that power over someone: for them to be so in love with me and for me to feel nothing.'

'What the fuck are you talking about? I do love you.'

'Maybe you think you do. But you don't. Not the way you're meant to love someone. I think you loved me in the beginning, but you've changed. Those people you spend time with, they've changed you! What you do isn't love. It's control. And I'm sorry . . . I'm so, so sorry.' Her eyes move from his face to somewhere above her and she gasps. 'I'm almost out of time! What's going to happen? Please! Somebody help me!'

The footage cuts suddenly to black.

Emilia waits, her breath caught in her mouth, shallow and stale. Is it over? She nudges the mouse – there's still a minute of footage left.

After a few moments, Emilia's stomach drops again as the room returns. Hayley's face, full of fear, has also returned, but it isn't the steady view of the fixed CCTV footage. The camera is shaking, moving around, as if filmed on a hand-held.

'Please, don't do this,' Luca says, his gravelly voice choking him.

'Please,' Hayley whispers, her gaze looking upwards. 'Please don't –'

Emilia gasps in horror as the barrel of a gun appears to one side of the camera. Then, a gunshot sounds, heavy with finality.

And Hayley's head flops forward; her eyes wide open, but still.

7th November, 9:37 a.m.

Emilia snaps open a small compact and frowns at the dark circles under her eyes — even under the make-up they are showing through. She hadn't imagined seeing Ciaran for the first time in months on three hours' sleep and a stomach full of anxiety. She had dragged herself to bed at 3 a.m. but the video had played over and over in her mind, Luca and Hayley's desperate pleas echoing in her ears as if she was reliving a distant memory. As if she had been there.

'Emilia.'

She snaps the compact closed and shoves it back into her bag. She would recognize that voice anywhere — in a crowded room or at nothing more than a whisper. She had missed it.

'Hi Ciaran,' she says, standing up as he closes the door of the café behind him and approaches. He smiles widely at her, but his face is pale, his eyes looking smaller than usual. He must have been up all night at the station. But he is still beautiful, his eyes full of warmth, dimples pressing under his cheekbones.

'Hello, stranger.' He stops in front of her. She feels an awkwardness she didn't expect.

Luckily, Ciaran has never been awkward. He reaches towards her, his arm wrapping around her neck, his lips pressing into the top of her head. She clutches his waist, her fingers curling around the wool of his coat. But tears prick her eyes. She can't cry . . . she mustn't cry . . . but – he smells the same. This is the man she loved. The only man she has ever truly loved. She is such a fucking idiot.

'It's good to see you,' he says, holding her by her shoulders and meeting her gaze.

'You too,' Emilia says, gesturing nervously to the table. 'Here, I got you a coffee.'

'Thanks. I'm so sorry I can't stay long. I've literally got under an hour before I have to be back at the station. I just went home to shower and eat something when you called.'

'Has it all gone mad?'

He glances around at the other mostly empty tables and takes a seat before speaking, his voice lowered. 'The FLOs have been with the families all night. We . . . once we realized that the people named in the confession you told us about had actually gone missing, we knew it was likely they were dead, but that video . . . Whatever we're dealing with: this isn't a run-of-the-mill murder.'

'Glory chaser?'

He tilts his head. 'Seems like it . . . or –'

'Or what?'

'Or, the boyfriend's behind the whole thing.'

'I don't know . . . I mean – why would he do that? If he wanted to kill his girlfriend because she'd been cheating, why would he announce it on a forum? And the confession was about him too.'

'The video didn't show him being killed. Only she was forced to confess. Only she was held at gunpoint.'

44

'But you could hear him. He was distraught. And he kept saying, "Please, don't" –'

'Maybe that was to throw us off. Maybe all of it, naming himself, making sure he "went missing" too, being distraught on camera – maybe it was all to make people believe it was someone else.'

They stare at each other for a moment.

'That room they were in – any ideas?'

'Well, you used to be a detective: do you think there's anything in that footage that could lead you anywhere?'

Emilia sighs, shaking her head. The CCTV was zoomed in all the way, so that you couldn't see Hayley's surroundings. And the hand-held camera was the same. All that was visible was the cement floor beneath her. It could be anywhere. 'No,' she mutters. 'But the confession and the video – have they been traced?'

'No. Whoever's done this knows what they're doing. It seems like they used several programmes to scramble the IP address and it was also uploaded through the dark web. It just leads nowhere if you try to trace it. Brings up a different IP address every time, all over the world. They keep scrambling it.'

'And the website – is it being taken down?'

'Wild wants to keep the forum live – if someone is going to name victims, it's a vital piece of evidence. They've tried to go to the host and order a take-down of the video, but so far it's still up. And it's been shared, thousands of times. Even if we get it taken down, it's out there now.' He shrugs and then shakes his head, his eyes darkening for a moment. 'Look at me . . . I'm talking to you as if you're still my partner.'

Their eyes meet, tension radiating in the air between them at the word 'partner'. They had been partners in every sense of the word. And now they are . . . what? Friends? Strangers? Do they know each other at all any more?

'I've been following it ever since the confession first went up, Ciaran,' she says. 'I've been doing everything I can. I know I'm not an officer any more, but I want to help –'

'But you can't, Emi,' he says, softening the harsh truth with a soft whisper. 'Leave it to us. Please.'

'I won't compromise anything –'

'It isn't that,' he says. 'It isn't good for you to get involved, to linger over something like this.'

Her lips part, ready for her rebuttal, for her assertion of, 'I'm fine.' But that won't work with Ciaran.

'It makes me feel like . . . I feel like if I can help with this, maybe I can –'

'It won't bring her back.'

His words sting, another quick lash of honesty.

'I know that,' she mutters. 'Don't you think I know that?'

His gaze softens, his mouth turning downwards at the corners. 'I'm sorry. I didn't mean it like that, I just . . . I don't want you getting caught up in this. The police are searching for bodies, the families are being prepared. They're still trying to trace the video, we're talking to everyone who saw them last. It's all we can do for now. But . . . this isn't for you. Not any more.'

She nods, not wanting to argue with him. It won't lead them anywhere. The only place it can lead them is away from each other. And she doesn't want that – not again – not now when they're within touching distance. 'I know. I'm sorry . . . What's going on with you otherwise?'

He smiles, acknowledging her deft change of subject with a tilt of his head. 'Not much. Always so busy with work now . . . Sam is having a baby.'

'Really?' Emilia says, her face breaking into a beaming smile. She had always liked Ciaran's brother. 'I'm so happy for them. Joanna must be so pleased.'

'They were both over the moon.'

'That's so lovely.'

'And Pete has a new girlfriend –'

'Oh, thank God. I thought he'd never get over Francesca!'

'None of us did! I've only met the new one a couple of times, but she seems really nice. And he seems happy, so . . . '

Ciaran's voice fades away. Emilia blinks slowly, unable to look away from his arresting gaze. But an awkwardness soon takes over and she glances down, staring at the wood of the table, her nails subconsciously scratching at the surface.

'What about you?'

She lifts her head, her heart racing. 'No, I . . . I'm not seeing anyone.'

'No, I meant, what's going on with you –'

'Oh shit,' she says, her cheeks flushing pink. 'Sorry, I –'

'Seriously, Emi, it's fine.' He sighs. 'I haven't been dating either.'

Her face is hot, her chest slick with sweat under her

three layers, but the look in his eye is like a rush of cooling air, like stepping out into the snow.

His phone buzzes loudly on the table.

He closes his eyes, sighing deeply.

'So sorry.'

'It's okay —'

'Jones,' he says, answering the call.

He pauses, listening, and then his eyes dart towards her. Emilia frowns as he angles his body away from her and responds with one word: 'Where?' He nods as the answer comes. 'I'm on my way.'

Tingles spread up Emilia's arms, the hairs standing on end.

They've found something.

'Emi, I'm so sorry. I wish I could stay here longer and we could actually catch up but —'

'You have to go.'

'Yeah. I really am sorry.'

'No, it's fine,' she says, smiling at him. She wants to ask him what's happened, what's been found, and where? But she can't. Not after his speech about this not being for her any more. 'Thank you for seeing me.'

They stand and he pulls her into another hug, lowering his head to rest his chin on her shoulder. 'I'll call you, okay?' he says, his breath fluttering her hair.

'Okay.'

He squeezes her waist and then releases her, his smile spreading across his face, a warm glow in his eyes. 'Don't leave it months again, okay stranger?'

She smiles. 'Bye, Ciaran.'

He walks away, looking over his shoulder one final time

as he opens the door before waving goodbye with a familiar salute.

But he wants her to stay out of something that she simply can't stay out of. She needs to know what they've found.

She stands quickly and strides out of the café, dashing across the empty road to her car. Ciaran has just pulled away. If she hangs back just far enough, she can follow him. At least being a private investigator has taught her how to stay hidden.

She stays two to three cars behind him at all times, her eyes scanning traffic but always keeping him in her line of sight. She can't lose him. She needs to know what's happened.

He has driven north from the café for fifteen minutes. But he doesn't turn left when they reach the crossroads to head towards the station. No – he has carried on straight, eventually driving past the turning for Emilia's flat. After ten minutes on the main road, she mirrors his turns – right, then right again, and then left. Ahead is the park. Emilia walks there all the time. At this hour on a Saturday, it'll be empty, occupied only by the odd jogger or dog walker.

But as they drive closer, Emilia's eyes widen. There are several police cars just outside the entrance to the park, uniformed officers lining the pavement.

Ciaran pulls up abruptly, swinging into an empty bay. Emilia slows, leaving more distance between herself and the car in front of her, which is also braking to gawk out of the window. But Ciaran doesn't look over his shoulder or glance around at all. He strides straight towards the gates, his pace quickening, pausing only to nod at the officers and duck beneath the crime scene tape that is stretched across the entrance.

Shit.

Emilia drives past, following the road around, her fingers drumming against the steering wheel. As the hedge line lowers, tapering away behind black railings, she can finally see inside the park.

The frost-covered grass is dotted with the monochrome of police. Some are maintaining the police barricade and sending away curious onlookers; others stand in conversation in small groups, their faces stern. And behind them, not too far from where Ciaran entered the park, others are erecting a white tent.

Emilia's heart slows, her breathing slows, as if she and the car are moving through time at half-speed, watching the world swim past. She indicates and pulls over quickly.

Reaching towards her glove box, she pulls out her binoculars. Ciaran would think she was crazy if he could see her now. Who does she think she is, sitting in her car and spying on people with binoculars?

But they've found someone. They've found Hayley or Luca. Maybe both of them.

She lifts the binoculars to her eyes and turns a dial.

The scene comes into sharp focus.

There on the ground, the tent being erected around her fluttering gently in the early morning breeze, is a woman.

Pink tinged hair. Blood splattered clothes. Red chipped nail polish.

Hayley.

He has finally summoned the bravery to approach the first box.

I placed it just so, in the corner of the room, its edge perfectly parallel to the concrete wall. The chain that is tying him to the wall is stretched, but not all the way. This box is easy to reach — much easier than the one on the opposite side of the room. His eyes have darted across to that one a number of times, his mind weighing up if he will be able to reach it. But that isn't the question he should be focusing on.

He stares down at the box. I wonder how long it will take him to reach down, his hands outstretched and trembling. It took him far longer than I had expected to even approach it in the first place. Maybe he thinks that if he doesn't acknowledge its existence, if he doesn't open the lid, the process of being in this room will stall. Because he knows where he is. He must do. Or maybe he thought he would never end up here.

Foolish, really.

Anticipation swirls in my chest as he continues to gaze down at the box, his eyes wide — a deer gawping at the long beams of light stabbing down the road towards it. What will he make of the first photograph? What will he feel? A rush of fear? Of panic? Or the slow, creeping fingers of realization?

I lean in, watching intently, desperate to see every minute detail of his reaction.

Open it.

Open the box.

The Room

Ryan stares down at the first box.

Looming over it, his gaze fixated on its dark lid, he tries to imagine what could possibly be inside. And what will it mean? The four black sides of the box are holding something inside, like this room and its four walls keeping him captive. Is it something he'll want to see? Does it want to be seen? And is it meant to help him? Or is it designed to be a burden?

He reaches down, the tips of his fingers tingling with a heady mixture of anticipation and dread. Gripping the edge of the lid, he pauses and gently closes his eyes, slowly drawing in a steady measure of air. He has always done this — a forced reset to some sort of calm. And it usually works, even in the worst situations. But has there ever been anything as bad as this?

His eyes flicker open. His heart is still racing.

Just do it, Ryan.

He lifts the lid. It slides off the box smoothly, with ease, as if it was designed to be opened and not shut. As if what was hidden was always meant to be set free. But . . . there's nothing inside . . . Is there?

He crouches down, staring at the bottom of the box.

Frowning, he traces a finger around the side of the

base. His eyebrows rise: the white rectangle – which at first glance he had assumed was part of the box itself – is a sheet of paper. And now that he looks closer, he can see the outline of the image on the other side, but he can't make out what it is.

He picks up the paper slowly and flips it over. As he takes in the photograph, his hands begin to shake violently, the picture blurring before his eyes.

It's her. The only woman he will ever love.

But this isn't just any photo of her. It's the one he has hidden away in his drawer at home, marked with holes.

His chest tightens, his breath shallow and quick.

How do they have this photo?

And why is it here?

8th November, 10 a.m.

'And from the Homicide Investigation Unit, Detective Chief Inspector Holden and Detective Inspector Wild gave the following statement: "Detective Inspector Wild and I offer our deepest condolences to the family of Hayley James whose body was identified after being discovered yesterday morning. Luca Franco, Hayley's boyfriend, is still missing and enquiries are being made to locate him. If anyone watching has any information about Luca Franco or his whereabouts, please contact the police immediately."'

Emilia takes in Inspector Holden's tired face, his bloodshot eyes. She had always liked him. He was the life and soul of the unit, always offering kind encouragement and clear direction. And when her sister was killed, he did everything he could to help her. But she has never met Detective Inspector Penelope Wild. She has heard of her, through Ciaran and through the low whispers of her ex-colleagues. She has a fierce reputation. And now, standing there in front of the station, she looks immaculate, her clothes and make-up pristine, her posture straight, chin lifted.

The news report ends and Emilia taps immediately on Ciaran's name, holding the phone to her ear. She couldn't call him about Hayley's body being found until after it was announced on the news. If she did, she would have to admit that she had followed him yesterday.

The ring tone repeats, over and over again, and then is answered.

'Ciaran?' she says. But she is interrupted by an automated voice.

'You have reached the voicemail of – Ciaran Jones. They are not available to take your call at the moment. You can leave a message after the beep, or hang up.'

BEEP.

'Hi Ciaran . . .' Emilia says quietly. 'It's me, Emi. I just saw the news about Hayley James's body being found. And I . . . I know you said I need to stay away, and I will, but I just wanted to talk to you. I know you'll be absolutely slammed with everything but . . . call me when you can. Okay? Bye.'

She ends the call. Her eyes glaze over as she stares into the empty space in front of her. Was that a mistake? The last thing she wants is to push him away. Why can't she just leave it alone?

She darts to her computer, typing *Luca Franco* quickly into the search engine.

The page fills with article after article, their titles highlighted in bold, photographs of Hayley and Luca shining out in bright technicolour.

THE CONFESSION ROOM MURDER: HAYLEY JAMES FOUND

HAYLEY JAMES DISCOVERED IN PARK, LUCA FRANCO STILL MISSING

BODY OF THE CONFESSION ROOM VICTIM FOUND – BUT WHERE IS LUCA FRANCO?

It won't take long for the focus to shift – away from Hayley James, away from her body and the bullet to her head, and towards Luca. The missing boyfriend.

A loud knock comes from the front door and she drags herself away from the computer.

'Oh hi, Jenny,' Emi says as she pulls open the door and is greeted by her friend's smiling face.

Jenny bounds forward and draws Emilia into a hug, buzzing with her seemingly endless high-octane energy. She's so serious at work – behind her desk as the Custody Sergeant she is the consummate professional – but outside, in the real world, she is outrageous and wild. Always the life of every room she enters.

'It's been too long again, Emi. I don't like having to stalk you like this,' she laughs.

'I know,' Emilia says, as Jenny releases her and steps into the flat. 'I'm sorry.'

'Stop that now,' Jenny responds as she strides inside to the living room. 'It's my fault too. And anyway – it doesn't matter.' She flings herself casually on to the sofa. 'I'm here now . . . this is an okay time, right?'

Emilia smiles. 'Of course.'

Jenny glances at a photo on the side table – Emilia's parents with their arms around each other, posing on the Brooklyn Bridge. 'How are your mum and dad?'

Emilia folds herself into the corner of the sofa, tucking one leg beneath her and bringing the other knee up to her chest. 'They're okay. Doing pretty well. We're planning a surprise for Mum's birthday – Dad wants to take her away somewhere.'

'Ah, how lovely!'

'Yeah, well her birthday is so close to Sophie's, so Dad thought it might help distract her . . .'

Sadness sloshes deep in her stomach, that familiar feeling of the world shifting beneath her. She and Sophie had never spent birthdays apart. Even as grown-ups, even when both of them had partners, they always celebrated together. Sophie's last birthday, Emilia and Ciaran went out to a bar with Sophie and her friends, Emilia's face stretching into a beaming smile as her sister stood in the centre of the crowd, her eyes glowing, feeding off the attention. She was so happy. So alive. She sighs, shaking her head. 'Anyway . . . Is everything okay with you?'

'Yea, I'm okay . . . I just . . . Well –'

'Jenny, what is it? Come on . . . it isn't like you to struggle with your words.'

'Ciaran's worried about you.'

Emilia's chest tightens, her breath catching in the back of her throat. 'Ciaran?'

'He said you saw each other for the first time the other day? Which is great – and don't get me wrong, I know he was over the moon to see you, but –'

'But?'

'He's just worried that you're going to get too caught up with his new case. You know, the Confession Room . . . Especially now . . . I worry about you too, Emi. I know how hard hearing stuff like this must be –'

'It isn't the same,' Emi says, her chest tightening even more as she spits out her lie. 'I'm fine.'

Jenny frowns. 'Really?'

'Really. I promise. I just . . . I want to talk about it. I want to help, because that's the way my brain is hard-wired. Same as yours. Same as Ciaran's. That instinct doesn't just leave you because you've left the police.'

'I know. But just . . . don't let it suck you in. Okay?'

'I won't.'

'Promise?'

Emilia nods, chewing on the inside of her lip. 'What do you think about the whole thing?'

Jenny sniffs and glances up at the ceiling. 'I think if the boyfriend doesn't make an appearance soon . . .' She shrugs.

'You think it might have been him?'

'Don't you?'

'Are the police treating him as a suspect?'

'Of course. You know they will be – come on, Emilia.'

Emilia nods but her brows knit together. 'So do you think that he released the video to shame her?'

Jenny nods vigorously. 'She cheated on him – for a long time. You know the type he'll be – the sort that can't cope with any kind of rejection. I think he found out, forced her to confess, filmed it, and then killed her.'

Emilia pulls a cushion on to her lap and clutches it to her chest. 'It just doesn't make sense to me.'

'Why not?'

'Because why name himself?'

'To cover his tracks. Even the video was filmed to make it seem like another person was in that room with them. But I don't think there was. And he named himself on the forum to make it seem like he's a victim too. Otherwise, where is he? Why was her body dumped to be found in broad daylight but he's been hidden? Why isn't he protesting his innocence? Why disappear?'

'But why confess? Why confess at all?'

'Well, that takes us back to the beginning, doesn't it? He thinks it will help him evade suspicion. I mean . . . it's working, isn't it? On you?'

Emilia nods. 'I guess . . .'

'You know the truth, Emilia: the most simple answer is most often the right one. There isn't always some underlying story. Sometimes it's just a bad man who does a bad thing. Sometimes –'

'Don't you think I know that?'

Silence falls between them. Emilia's breathing is heavy, her bottom lip wavering.

'Emi, I'm so sorry. I should have thought before I spoke –'

'No, I know. I'm sorry. I didn't mean to snap.'

They gaze at each other, forgiveness slowly dissipating the tension in the air.

'Anyway . . . we shouldn't even be chatting about this,' Emilia says. 'Really, I'm okay. I'm not getting obsessed, I promise . . . What's been going on with you? How's Adam?'

Jenny begins to speak, her face spreading into a wide smile, her words forming and flowing out into the air. But her voice is blurring in Emilia's mind, as if time is slowing down, like a finger pressing down an old record. Because her promise to Jenny was a bald-faced lie. Her thoughts are still there, like they have been since the beginning. With Hayley James. With the missing Luca Franco.

With bad men.

And bad things.

8th November, 9 p.m.

'Ciaran?'

'Emilia . . . hey.' Ciaran's voice sounds muffled through the phone, as if he is cupping his hand around his mouth, the background noises loud and relentless. 'So sorry it's taken all day to call you back.'

'Are you at the station? It sounds loud.'

'Emi . . . Emi, I can't really hear you. I'm going to head outside. Just a second.'

She waits, the phone pressed to her ear, listening to the sound of Ciaran's footsteps pounding down the hall. The station ripples into her mind, and as a door slams, and then another, almost immediately after, she can picture exactly where he is – on the long stretch of corridor between the serious crime unit and child protection at the other end. Soon he'll be turning right and making his way down the stairs to the exit. And yes – there it is: his rhythmic trot as he bounds down three at a time. One final slam and the air around him seems to clear. He is outside.

'Hey, sorry about that.' He sighs heavily. She can hear scratching – that'll be him rubbing his jaw, the day-old stubble rough under his nails.

'Heavy day?'

'Yep. Heavy day . . . Are you okay? Jen said she saw you earlier . . .'

Emilia's cheeks flush. She knows they talk about her – Jenny has been their mutual friend for years, and they've always been close – but the thought of it makes her skin crawl.

'Yes, I'm fine . . . absolutely fine. I just . . . I saw that they'd found Hayley and I wanted to check on you. Are you okay? Were you there when it was called in?'

He sighs again. 'No . . . I went straight there after I saw you.'

'Who found her? Was she hidden?'

'A dog walker. And . . . no. She wasn't hidden. She was just left out in the open. It was so eerie seeing her lying there, no attempt to hide her at all.'

'Any CCTV?'

'Emilia –'

'I swear I'm not getting too attached, I just want to help in any way I can . . . Was there CCTV?'

'There's CCTV of the entrance on the south of the park, but the camera at the east entrance looks like it was tampered with. We're looking at the streets nearby but haven't found anything yet.'

'And Luca?'

'We're looking for him.'

'No trace of him in the park?'

'No. Nothing.'

'Is he . . . is he the main suspect?'

'You know the answer to that. Look, Emi, I really need to go back in now. But I'll speak to you soon, okay?'

She bites down on her lip, his abrupt ending of their conversation sending a sting down her spine. 'Mm-hmm.'

'It . . . No, never mind.'

'What were you going to say?'

'It's so good to hear your voice again . . . I've missed it.'

She smiles softly. 'Yours too. Speak soon.'

'Bye, Emi.'

'Bye,' she whispers.

She pulls the phone away from her ear. For a moment she simply sits, staring down at her phone, her body thrumming. Everything inside her is telling her that she needs to be involved, she needs to help. But why? Why is this different to any of the other cases that her old team has dealt with since she has been gone? None of them have sucked her in like this one – a swirling vortex pulling her towards its centre. Is it because she was there, in the forum, when the first confession was made?

No – deep down she knows the truth. She wasn't able to solve what happened to Sophie. She couldn't get her justice. And this case is so public, so much of the information out there for anyone to investigate. Maybe if she can help, the guilt for failing her sister will begin to fade. Whoever did this deserves to be punished. And she'll do anything she can to make sure that happens.

Emilia gets up from the sofa and darts across the room to her desk, quickly turning on her computer screen. The forum is there, waiting. It's always there now, fixed to her second screen. She's been unable to click away.

And it would seem that others are trapped just the same.

The website is swimming with activity, the number of anonymous users fixed at the top of the forum in bold.

120,483 active users.

Over one hundred thousand people, all on the website, all watching, waiting to see if whoever did this – Luca or someone else – will post again. But what are people waiting for? Another video? Another opportunity for them to watch as a woman lives out her final moments in fear? Is her horror entertainment now?

Emilia pushes against the desk, her nails digging into the wood, and slides away, the wheels of her chair squeaking. She stalks to her kitchen and reaches for a glass before turning on the tap. She gulps thirstily as the water thrums down on to the steel of the sink. She refills the glass and drinks again, trying to quench the rage that has begun to burn inside her chest.

A door slams – a notification.

Emilia turns slowly, the water still running from the tap behind her, her heart pounding. She walks towards her computer, her feet suddenly cold against the wooden floor.

Focusing on the screen, her eyes fix on the new confession, highlighted in bold.

Her stomach drops.

Anonymous 01

Another confession for you. Murder. London. Gregory Weiss. Isabella Santos.

9th November, 9:40 a.m.

The cordon is still up around the park, the tape pulled tightly over the entrance. Emilia drives past slowly, peering over the hedge. The white tent is still up even though her body will be with the coroner now. Her death written up as a report: stark facts and findings. All humanity gone.

She shouldn't have come here. It isn't on the way to the job she has today, but she felt drawn to the location, pulled towards it like a magnet. And it seems like many others felt the same. The pavement is lined with people, leaning against the tape, some clearly from the media, with professional equipment, microphones attached to their lapels. But others are simply normal people, their curiosity getting the better of them. The police will widen the cordon soon.

She turns away from the park, navigating her way through residential roads before meeting the dual carriageway which will take her north. Today she's in Highgate – her investigative work taking her, as usual, to the wealth of North London. Another suspicious partner: a wife today, certain that her husband is planning on leaving her.

Emilia sighs as she parks down the road from the stone mansion. Every case she is asked to investigate is just another bout of jealousy or possessiveness or betrayal. Mostly affairs. To them it is the most important thing in their lives. But it all seems so pointless. So insignificant.

She narrows her eyes, staring over at the house in all its beauty. Double-fronted, bay windows, a gleaming dark green front door with a brass knocker. Supercars parked on the sweeping drive. The front door opens and a woman steps out, pulling her fine wool coat close to her body. That's Emilia's client, leaving her home, knowing that her private investigator will be parked somewhere close, staking out her house. Staking out her husband.

Emilia pulls out her laptop, connecting it to the internet on her phone. She usually doesn't bring it with her – she knows she should focus on the job at hand – but God knows how long it'll take for the husband to emerge or for anything to happen. She could be here all day without any sighting of a mysterious woman at all – so better to spend the time being productive. Helping in any way she can. And squinting over her phone simply won't cut it.

She opens the internet, the pages from last night still there. It hadn't taken her long to find them. It was much easier than last time, their names far more unusual, their connection instantly clear.

Gregory Weiss and Isabella Santos: together for two and a half years before they split a few weeks ago. But seemingly no communication between them since. At least not on social media.

She had searched the internet for any connection between them and Luca Franco. If he is behind all of this, there must be a motive. There was a motive for him killing Hayley. But could he be behind Gregory and Isabella too? And if not, then where is he?

Emilia opens Instagram, tapping Gregory Weiss into the search bar again.

When she had first started investigating, she had quickly realized that Instagram could be her most powerful and effective tool. People give so much of themselves away online. Their photographs can be used to pinpoint locations, their stories monitored to discover plans, places where that person will be, or where they are, right at this very moment.

Gregory Weiss's feed loads. His photos are all of himself, at the gym. There is nothing else. Nothing that can send her towards him. Nothing that reveals anything about where he might have been. Or how they might have disappeared.

She shakes her head. Rubbing her eyes with the back of her hand, she looks up at the house again. Nothing.

She switches back to Isabella Santos's profile. She scrolls, her eyes lighting up as she takes in the feed. Isabella's is a different story. Many of her photos – a few remnants of her relationship with Gregory, others with friends, some with family – all have their location tagged.

And here – there are several photos all outside the same house. A red-brick terrace – the end of the row. In some she is sitting on the front steps, the sage-coloured door behind her; in others she is standing on the pavement outside, the Victorian black-and-white tiled path leading up to the house, visible in the background.

Emilia scrolls again, her eyes scanning the locations. A number of photos are all taken at the same pub – the Wolf and Hound.

Like so many people, Isabella hasn't realized how simple she is making it for anyone at all to find her. Getting this far has only taken Emilia a few minutes. A minute or so more, and Emilia is sure that she will have her address. And her intentions are only good. What about others? What about those who would mean her harm?

Emilia opens another window and navigates to Maps, quickly typing in the Wolf and Hound. The map zooms in on a pub, set on the corner of a road in Enfield. She scrolls on the trackpad, the image zooming outwards, and focuses on the roads around the pub, eliminating those which are clearly not residential. But just two streets away from the pub, there are a few roads seemingly lined with terraced houses. Emilia clicks on street view and begins methodically making her way down each road, turning the camera in all directions, searching for a flash of that distinctive door, the black-and-white path.

And then –

Yes. There it is.

68 Bury Avenue.

Isabella's home.

Emilia tears her eyes away from the screen to look back to the house – the mansion with the husband who may or may not be cheating; the wife who may or may not be paranoid. But when faced with this – the Confession Room, life or death – what's going on in that house, behind closed doors, is meaningless. Isabella's home, her family, what happens to her – that means something.

Besides – her client won't miss her for one morning.

Emilia puts the address into her navigation, then turns the key, the engine coming to life.

But as the car rolls away, the house now behind her, Emilia throws one final glance in her rear-view mirror. A woman, elegant in high heels and an oversized coat, a large scarf wrapped around her, blonde hair tucked in at the back, is approaching the door, and slips inside.

She slams on the brakes, her stomach sinking.

Shit. How did she not see her approaching? A car didn't pull up – did she walk?

She stares in her rear-view mirror, her heart pounding. She should wait for the woman to come out. She should make sure that she gets some evidence.

But Isabella . . .

The Confession Room is life or death. This isn't. Finding out who this woman is will have to wait.

She looks back again, at the now quiet house and gleaming front door, and accelerates away.

9th November, 10:30 a.m.

The house at the end of the terrace looks just like the one in her photographs on social media. The sage-coloured front door. The dying fern in its black pot to the side. This is Isabella's house. Emilia is sure of it.

Others might not notice certain details – the closed curtains; the redirected traffic around the road, 'no through road, residents only'; the car parked directly outside which she is quite certain is a detective's car. The police will be here, speaking to the family, trying to reassure them that their daughter, their sister, won't end up dead in the middle of a London park like the other girl. But what other outcome could they possibly be imagining right now? Human minds work tirelessly to recognize patterns in their surroundings, in the events that roll into their lives like a wave. And here, now, there is a clearly trodden path for them to follow: a girl was named on a forum as a victim of murder, the girl was missing, the girl was found dead, a single bullet to her forehead. It would take someone entirely inhuman to push their way through all of the repeating messages to find any other resolution to this story.

A rap of knuckles on the car door jolts Emilia's attention away from the house. A group of teenaged boys, walking with their bikes alongside them, have paused outside her window. The one closest, the one who knocked, is leaning forward, his eyebrow raised, a vape clutched between the fingers of his right hand. Emilia smiles, small and polite, and rolls down her window.

'Morning,' she says, keeping her voice as neutral as possible. 'Shouldn't you boys be at school?'

They laugh, some of them nervously, as they throw glances around their small group.

'Are you a copper too?' one of them says.

'Too?'

He jerks his head towards the house. 'There's police in there right now.'

'Are you connected to the family?'

'I asked my question first,' he scoffs.

She pauses for a second, weighing up the cost of the lie. 'I'm a detective . . . Now your turn.'

He nods slowly then glances down at the road, scuffing his shoe on the pavement. 'Isabella's my sister.'

A sudden rush of sadness hits Emilia as she reaches for the door handle and he steps back, his friends all adjusting their positions around him as she steps out of the car. Isabella is his sister. Will he ever see her again? Will his last memory of her be her name plastered all over the news, her body found abandoned in the middle of nowhere?

'I'm sorry – what's your name?'

'Jordan.'

'Jordan . . . I'm sorry this is happening to your family.'

'She going to be killed like that other girl?' one of the other boys asks.

'Nathan, man, shut up,' interrupts another.

Jordan lifts one hand to cover his mouth, his other hand twisting in the material of his loose jeans.

'The police are doing everything they can, I can promise you that . . . When did you last see her?'

'A few nights ago. She went out with her friends. Before she left her ex came round –'

'Gregory?'

'Yeah, Greg. He tried to come into the house but she wouldn't let him. I was up in my room, though, and I heard them fighting outside. He didn't want her to go to some club. Was shouting like mad. Then he left and she went out. But she never came home. And we haven't seen her since.'

'What were they fighting about?'

'Same old shit. He was jealous – didn't like her going anywhere without him.'

'Have you told the police this?'

'I'm telling you, aren't I?'

'Yes, but the officers inside?'

'Nah . . . not yet.'

'Okay, well make sure you do . . . One quick question: do you know if Gregory or your sister have a friend called Luca?'

'Like Luca Franco? The first guy?' He frowns. 'Not Isabella, nah. But Greg? I don't know . . . maybe.'

Her phone buzzes in her pocket.

'One second, Jordan, sorry.'

It's Ciaran.

The boys disperse and Jordan makes his way up the path to the house, nodding his head to Emilia, his hand raised.

'Hi Ciaran,' Emilia says into the phone, forcing nonchalance as she folds herself into the driver's seat and lowers her head, shielding her face from the window.

'What are you doing here, Emi?'

The story she had been conjuring disappears instantly. He has seen her. Where is he? In the house? In the front room, glancing through the sheer white curtains?

'I–I –'

'Emi, seriously, you need to go home before somebody else sees you. Henry won't be happy if he finds out you've found the family's house and spoken to one of the children.'

'I . . . I'm sorry,' she whispers.

He sighs. 'I know . . . '

'Ciaran, I –'

'Just go home, Emi.'

Emilia blinks slowly at her computer as she takes in the results from her Twitter search for Luca Franco. If he really is the prime suspect, maybe she can find something that will connect him to Gregory and Isabella. And there is post after post demanding that Luca be found, that there must be some connection between him and the new victims.

She swipes down and the feed refreshes and Emilia's eyes widen as she scans the most recent post.

Luca Franco's house: The Bellhouse, Totteridge Lane.

His address: they've somehow found an address. The police will already know it, they'll have already been there, searched, taken away anything that might point towards his location or his involvement. But now that it's public, what will others do?

Sighing, Emilia opens the video of Hayley and Luca. It's all over the internet now, just like Ciaran said. She presses play, her fingers tingling with anxiety as the footage begins to roll and their frightened voices tremor through the speakers.

There must be something in this video. Some small clue. Something to give an insight as to where they are.

She replays the video, over and over again, her mind switching off from the horror of the events, instead absorbing every detail.

But wait – what's that?

She pauses the video and leans in close to her screen, her eyes focused like a laser on the millisecond of handheld camera footage. For just a moment the camera wavers, the hand of whoever is filming unsteady, and a door becomes visible.

Emilia captures the image and drags it across to her second screen into her photography software – the one she uses for her investigations. She runs the image through several filters, brightening, maximizing, depixelating, all the while her heart pounding in her ears.

But then it all falls silent. Because there, still blurred but visible, is an open door. She narrows her eyes. Is that really . . . ?

Yes. Beyond the open door, a set of stairs, heading upwards.

It all makes sense: the lack of natural light, no windows, the grey, dull cement.

A basement. They were in a basement.

She frantically turns back to her other screen and copies Luca's address into the search engine. Property websites appear, photos showing a large country house hidden behind gates, in the centre of fields and woods.

She clicks on one after another, scrolling down to the details, searching for the floor plans. There must be something. And finally – there they are. The house spread out over three sprawling levels. The lowest of the three labelled: Basement.

She reaches for her phone and taps on Ciaran's name.

'Please answer,' she mutters. 'Please. Come on, Ciaran.'

'Hi,' he says, his voice strained. 'I don't really have time to chat. Everything okay?'

She sighs with relief. 'Hi! Ciaran – have you seen the address that's been posted online? The Franco address?'

'Emi, you can't be serious.'

'It has a basement. And I was looking at the footage and –'

'Emilia, listen to me.' She balks, not just at his tone but at the use of her full name. Her hands turn clammy. 'Just listen,' he continues. 'We've already been to that address. So just leave it.'

'But Ciaran, the basement –'

'Listen, we've had countless online sleuths investigating from behind their computer, telling us about this house. It isn't helping.' He sighs. 'Seriously, I have to go. I know you mean well, but please, just leave it.'

Emilia's head is pounding as a migraine begins to take hold. She should leave it, just like Ciaran asked.

But the address isn't that far away – about forty-five minutes without traffic. Luca is the main suspect. If she doesn't check it out, and Greg and Isabella turn up dead, how will she forgive herself if there was the smallest chance she could make a difference? And if it's nothing but a mistake, then she'll just leave.

Ciaran doesn't need to know.

No harm, no foul.

Emilia brings her car to a halt, lifting her visor to stare at the house across the lane. Twenty miles outside of London, the area is quiet, surrounded by fields and country lanes. The house is set back far from the road. A sign is staked into the grass by the fence: *No trespassing!*

Her phone vibrates and she glances at the screen.

Message from Violet Palermo.

Her client from this morning. Shit.

She taps on the message:

I was expecting an update today and have emailed several times. Where are you?

Emilia hesitates – she should call her now, offer up some anodyne excuse or tell her that she didn't see anything today. But she's here now. And she'll only be a few minutes. She pushes her phone into her pocket, then opens her door, heaving herself out of the car, her back clicking.

This is crazy, she thinks. If Ciaran could see her now . . . he would kill her. Stay out of it, he had told her. Go home. And she's done nothing but ignore him. But she's doing no harm. She's just going to take a look and then she'll leave.

She dashes across the road, slowing as she approaches the fence, keeping to the left side to peer up the drive that leads to the house.

'Who are you?'

Emilia spins around, her heart flying up into her mouth. A man is standing behind her, staring at her through sad, wrinkled eyes. He must be in his late seventies.

'I'm . . . I'm Sophie. I'm just looking for –'

'You're not the first person who has come here to gawp at our house.' He walks towards her quickly, his steps uneven, his mouth curling downwards with disdain. 'Since my grandson went missing, people have found our address. They search for his name, and this place comes up.'

'Your grandson?'

'Luca Franco. Named after me. Brilliant boy. And I wish everyone would leave us in peace. He's missing and everyone is talking about him as if he's a murderer! Instead of him being treated like a potential victim, there's a man hunt. You're all vultures!'

'I'm so sorry,' Emilia stammers, backing away. 'I wasn't –'

'Yes, you were, girl,' he shouts, his face turning red. 'Just like the others. So just get back in your car and go back to where you came from.'

'I'm sorry –'

'Just leave us alone!'

Emilia turns and dashes towards the road, her heart racing in her chest as she thunders to a stop, her feet skidding on the asphalt as a car races towards her, blaring its horn. It swerves into the other lane, the driver waving his hand out of the window, his mouth moving in outrage.

She crosses the road quickly, throwing herself back into the car. Her hands scramble with the key as she tries to force it into the ignition, her fingers failing to do what they are supposed to. Finally, the key turns, and she accelerates away. Her eyes dart up to the rear-view mirror, her tearful gaze reflected back at her. And beyond that, the man stands on the verge, watching as she drives into the distance, his head shaking.

And his words echo in her mind the whole drive home, her body flush with shame.

You're all vultures. Just leave us alone!

There is a link on the forum. Another one, just like before: one click and Emilia will be redirected to a video. A video of somebody being murdered.

Her finger is frozen on the mouse, her gaze fixed to the screen. She can't bear to look at her phone. After leaving the Franco house, she rushed home, resisting the urge to message Ciaran with another apology. She had gone too far. Not just once. Multiple times. But she knew that she needed to leave it. *I need to give him some space*, she thought. *Some breathing room.* So instead, she had tried to distract herself by taking Mimi for a walk, and when she returned she tried to read, but instead she has been scrolling for hours, watching, anticipating that something will happen at any moment. But new posts about the Confession Room slowed. Like being in the eye of the storm. Waiting. Now, however, there is a run of posts, constantly being replaced by new exclamations. A constant stream of shock and awe.

She clicks on the link. Her fingers are tingling, her palms slick with sweat. She curls them into fists, her nails digging into the centre of her palm as she waits for the page to load.

The title is there, just like before.

THE CONFESSION ROOM. GREGORY WEISS. ISABELLA SANTOS.

She presses play, her breath suspended.

The room appears again, the same view from above, but zoomed in on a person's face, cowering in the corner. Emilia's eyes widen.

It's Gregory.

He breathes in deeply, a loud gasp, his eyes filled with rage. 'Fuck this!'

'Greg, please just say something!' a woman's voice cries. *Isabella?*

'Why? So I can end up with a bullet in my head like that girl?'

'Please! We don't know what's going to happen! Just tell the truth!'

'What truth? What have you told them?'

'I haven't told anyone anything but it's clear from the boxes what they want you to confess –'

'Oh, I know what you tell people. You love telling people lies about me. Don't you? You tell them that those bruises are from me. Well fuck you, Isabella. If history is anything to go by, it'll be you with a bullet in your skull. And good riddance, you fucking bitch.'

The video turns black. Emilia's heart is thrumming, his venomous words echoing in her ears. And something that Isabella said is gnawing away . . . *The boxes.* What boxes?

The video crackles and the footage returns, just like before, the hand-held camera shaking, and Emilia gasps, her hand moving to cover her mouth.

Gregory's eyes are round and filled with fear, his face pale. The gun pressed to his forehead.

'Why?' he says, his voice breaking. 'Why are you doing this?'

There is crying coming from somewhere behind the camera. Wails coming in bursts before she stops suddenly. As if she is holding her breath.

And then —

A gunshot.

Isabella's frantic cries.

He is gone.

10th November, 7:30 a.m.

Birdsong ripples through the air as Emilia approaches the park.

She tugs on the lead, bringing Mimi to a stop on the edge of the pavement, and fixes her eyes on the blocked-off gate, her hands curling into anxious fists at her sides. What would Ciaran say if he knew that she'd come here again? And what could she possibly achieve by going inside? But just like so many others who have been gathering outside the gates, she is drawn to the darkness, her mind seeking answers.

Mimi pulls on her lead, desperate to be walked. Emilia turns away from the gate, glancing over her shoulder one final time at the police cars before following the road around until she reaches a public footpath that cuts behind the park and into the woods beyond.

She lets Mimi off the lead, smiling as she trots into the nearby trees, then pulls her coat tightly around herself, her arms gripping her elbows as the wind billows through the trees, dead leaves swirling around her feet.

Emilia moves further into the woods, every so often calling Mimi's name to make sure that she is following behind. But other than their footsteps and the rustling of leaves, it is completely quiet. The silence is eerie, the devastation of tragedy still lingering in the air.

Something snaps behind her and she spins around, her

eyes searching desperately, fists clenching at her sides. But there is nobody there.

'Mimi?'

Barks echo through the trees, a flash of her pink harness visible beyond the undergrowth.

She turns back around, shaking her head at the ground. She is alone.

But . . . that isn't true.

She squints, focusing on the distance. There is somebody walking towards her. Somebody stooped over, their hood lowered over their face.

They stagger forward suddenly and Emilia gasps as their hood falls away. It is a woman. Her lip broken. Her mouth wide open in a silent cry. Her hands bound in front of her.

Isabella?

'Isabella!' Emilia cries, sprinting forward, Mimi chasing behind her, as adrenalin and fear fuse together in an overwhelming mixture.

She reaches her and Isabella's arms flail forward, stumbling towards Emilia as she loses her footing. Emilia wraps her arms around Isabella's shoulders, bracing her legs against the frozen ground.

'Don't touch me,' Isabella screams. 'Let go of me! Don't touch me!'

Emilia releases her, holding her hands up in front of her.

They both freeze, Isabella's breaths coming out in desperate pants, her mouth hanging open in a silent cry. And then suddenly her chest is heaving, her hands clenched together, fingers grappling with the frozen leaves, her sobs hoarse and desperate. And there is something else there, something other than terror and trauma.

Relief.

She has been found. She is alive.

Emilia shuffles closer but Isabella flinches. Emilia holds her hands up again. 'I won't touch you, I promise,' she says quietly. 'But I just need to get my phone from my pocket. We need to call an ambulance and the police –'

Isabella's cries escalate, morphing into a flurry of words, unintelligible and blurred. But there is one Emilia can make out. She is saying a name.

'Greg! Greg!'

Emilia tries to look her in the eye but they are closed tightly, her entire face screwed shut. 'Gregory Weiss?' she asks.

Isabella's eyes fly open, the whites flooded with red. Maybe she has cried so hard her blood vessels have burst. Or maybe they did this to her. Just like her lip, bleeding and red-raw. She nods.

'His body is here,' she whispers. 'We need to go to him!'

Emilia's breath catches in the back of her throat. 'Here?'

Isabella looks backwards over her shoulder. She raises her hands together, and points to where she came from, where the path that cuts through the woods goes over the crest of a hill and disappears.

'He's over there?'

Isabella nods wildly, gulping down air, unable to breathe.

'Okay . . . I'll go and then I'll call the police, okay?'

She nods again.

Emilia stands but Isabella immediately cries out, her eyes wild and confused. 'No, wait, don't leave me!'

Emilia crouches down again, careful to meet Isabella's eye. 'Would you feel safer coming with me or staying here?'

Isabella blinks at her, her mouth crumpling with emotion. 'What's your name? Who are you?'

'My name is Emilia. Emilia Haines. I used to be a police officer. And I'm going to help you. Okay?'

She nods, faster and faster, her tears once again silent, streaming steadily down her pale cheeks.

'You'll come with me?'

She continues to nod, but holds up her hands towards Emilia, glancing at the binding around her wrists.

'Oh Jesus . . . I want to untie them but I think I need to leave them like this so the police can see. I don't want to touch the rope. Do you understand?'

'Yes,' she whimpers.

'You're safe now . . . Can I help you stand?'

'Yes.'

Emilia entwines her arm around Isabella's shoulders and lifts her slowly to her feet. She scans the woods, searching for Mimi, then realizes that she is still beside them, her tail sloped downwards, her eyes wide.

They begin to walk together in the direction Isabella had indicated, taking steady steps, Isabella's breathing loud and heavy. She begins to shiver, her teeth chattering, her lips so pale they are almost blue against her brown skin.

Emilia glances down – Isabella's feet are bare.

'Isabella, your feet . . .'

She stops, staring down, bewildered. As if she hadn't realized either. She glances up again but as she does, her eyes widen, round and glassy. Emilia follows her gaze to the bottom of the slight hill and her mouth drops open.

There, in the distance, lying across the path, is Gregory Weiss. His skin ashen. A cascade of dried blood showing the path where it pumped from his temple down his white shirt. The bullet hole.

And his hands bound, just like hers.

Isabella's scream rips through Emilia and the hairs on the back of her neck stand on end. She remembers that scream. The feeling as it burst out of her when she found Sophie. No matter how many times she turned away from her sister, the moment she glanced back, that scream would be tugged out of her involuntarily, as if her broken heart was trying to escape the confines of her body. As if it was searching for what it had lost, hoping that Sophie would answer its call.

Emilia spins Isabella around. 'Don't look at him,' she whispers. 'Don't do it.'

'I'm sorry!' Isabella cries through ragged breaths as she collapses against Emilia's shoulder.

'It isn't your fault. This isn't your fault –'

'Why did they choose me? Why!'

'Choose you –'

A loud gasp – somewhere over Emilia's shoulder – interrupts them, and she cranes her neck, her protective arms never leaving Isabella's shaking frame.

A woman is standing just a few feet behind them. Her eyes are fixed on Gregory's body, her face turning almost grey.

'Is that . . . Is that –'

'Yes,' Emilia whispers, trying not to panic Isabella. 'Call the police. Now.'

The woman finally looks at Emilia, as if she is just realizing that there are other people standing right there. She takes in Isabella. Her bloody clothes. Her bare feet.

'Call the police,' Emilia repeats. 'And we need an ambulance!'

The woman nods, her fingers fumbling frantically at her pocket for her phone.

Isabella lifts her head and stares at Emilia, her eyes wide and panicked, darting around from sky to ground as she gulps for air.

'I can't . . . I can't breathe!' she gasps, her fingers tangling themselves in Emilia's scarf.

'You can, I promise you,' Emilia says, forcing her voice to remain level. Controlled. This is like any other victim she interacted with as a detective. She must remain calm. 'If you can speak, you can breathe. Here – come with me.'

Emilia pulls her away from the woman, away from Gregory. She needs space. She needs to focus.

Questions. She needs to ask Isabella questions – concentrate her mind.

'Listen to me. Don't look at him. Don't listen to what that lady is doing. Listen to me. I'm going to ask you some questions, okay?'

She nods.

'Isabella . . . Do you mind if I turn the video on my phone on?'

'No,' she whimpers.

'Okay.' Emilia turns on the camera and holds it down by her side, aiming upwards to capture Isabella. 'How did you get here?'

She blinks rapidly, trying to process the question.

Her eyes glaze over, her mind forcing her inside, into the memory.

'In a van . . . we were in a van.'

'Okay, did you see the van? What did it look like?'

'No . . . I was wearing a hood. Like a black cotton bag, over my head.'

Emilia glances down at her phone, checking that Isabella is still visible on the screen. 'How long have you been here? Was it light when you were brought here?'

She shakes her head, her eyes suddenly focusing, a glint of anger in her eye. 'It was still dark.'

'And what happened?'

'They led us here and then just dumped us on the ground. Then they took off my hood –'

'They. A person? Or more than one person?'

'Two . . . two people.'

'The same people who took you to the Room?'

'Yes.'

Emilia's heart thunders. She was right. This isn't just one person. One killer. If Luca is involved, he isn't acting alone.

Sirens blare in the near distance. Police are coming.

'After they left, what did you do?'

She blinks rapidly, tears that have been suspended on her lower lashes finally falling down her cheeks in hot streaks.

'I waited,' she whispered.

'For how long?'

'I don't know. I just waited. It could have been hours. I just lay there, waiting for it to be over. Waiting for someone to find us. But once the sun came up, I realized that I could get out of my binds if I tried –'

'They tied you up? Your feet as well?'

'My ankles were tied together. But they were loosening and I managed to get out of them. I untied my feet and tried to run. And that's when you found me.'

She exhales loudly, as if she's been punched, winded, her expression a strange combination of horror and relief.

'Isabella, you don't have to answer this if you don't want to, but . . . what happened to you and Gregory inside that room? Why were you there?'

She shakes her head, her eyes screwing shut.

Emilia feels a pang of guilt – she's pushing too far. 'It's okay, you don't have to –'

'They made us both confess something,' Isabella whispers. 'We had to make a confession.'

Emilia frowns, lifting her hand to gently squeeze Isabella's shoulder. 'And then?'

She blinks and stares straight at Emilia, her eyes empty. As if she is no longer there, her body an empty shell.

'And then they chose which one of us deserved to die.'

The colour drains from his face, rapidly, like cold water swirling down a sink and disappearing completely.

I smile. I shouldn't — I know I shouldn't, but I can't help it. Everyone who has been brought to the Confession Room was brought for a reason. He shouldn't need a photograph in a box to understand. The answer is obvious. His shock is laughable.

If anyone deserves to be here — it is him.

He lifts the photo close to his face, his hands shaking violently, and after a few more moments of staring, his eyes wild, he screws them shut, as if he can't bear to look for a moment longer.

But that is the entire purpose of this place. To force you to stare down your actions and see a reflection of yourself. A reflection of who you are. There's no consequence-free confession here. No anonymous atonement. No turning away or averting your gaze.

Look.

Look at what you have done.

The Room

He holds her photo, his fingers trembling violently.

She shouldn't be here.

He shouldn't be here.

Why is he here?

A low whimper escapes his lips and he brings his hand to his mouth, curling it into a fist before biting firmly down on his knuckles.

He can't cry. He can't scream. He needs to stay calm. There will be a way out of this. There must be. There always is.

The photograph must mean something. And there are three more boxes.

His gaze darts to the box in the corner directly opposite him, then down to his foot, tethered to the wall. The chain will reach: the room is only narrow. He crosses the floor slowly, dragging his left leg behind him, his ankle throbbing from where he was tugged violently back towards the wall when he tried to escape.

Clutching the photo to his chest, he leans down and lifts the lid.

He frowns. The photograph in this box is not face down, and a very familiar face is staring up at him.

Mum?

He reaches quickly down into the box and grabs it, his fingers now slick with sweat.

In the photo, she is standing under the porch of their family home, her heavy brow low over her tired eyes.

Has someone been watching them? Watching the house?

Fear trickles down the back of his neck, like freezing drops of rain. They've been watched. Whoever has done this, whoever has been taking all of these people, they haven't been random attacks, snatching the first pair of people they come across . . . they've been planned.

His eyes dart around the room. A flash of white in the darkness of the box catches his attention. There's something else in there. A few pieces of paper, folded in half.

He pulls them out, unfolding them hurriedly, his rough movements creasing the crisp pages. But as his eyes scan the first page, it's as though the world has stopped, his heart slowing, the room itself freezing in this moment. His grip slackens and the photographs scatter to the floor.

How did they get this? How?

His letter . . . the one he wrote for somebody to find. The one he wrote after he lost his girlfriend and everything became . . . too much. The one he had deleted when he changed his mind.

They shouldn't have this . . . it's impossible.

He riffles through the pages – three sheets of his manic thoughts spilling out, recorded in perpetuity. They were meant to be gone forever.

He tries to look away but –

I'm sorry to whoever had to find me.

And Mum . . . I hope you can forgive me.

I'll see you on the other side.

11th November, 8 a.m.

The news is playing on an endless loop. It didn't take long for the media to discover that Isabella and Gregory had been found. One alive. One dead.

She looks down at her hands, focusing on her fingers as they turn one of her rings over and over, the metal gliding across the skin. This ring usually gets stuck – it's getting too small – but today her hands feel cold. She feels cold all over. Panic is still present, leaving her system slowly, like a dripping tap that will eventually come to a complete stop.

Holden looks even more tired on the screen – his eyes are small and watery, as if he hasn't slept. He's been Chief Inspector for so long, but this case – this case is different. It isn't just London watching. Not even just the country – since the second murder, the whole world seems to be watching the Confession Room, commenting on the investigation, critiquing every decision – and each moment that passes without any progress, each second of the clock ticking down to another confession, only intensifies their focus.

But the police haven't named Emilia. And the media haven't found out who she was. They simply said that a dog walker had stumbled upon Isabella.

As soon as the police arrived, she was manoeuvred out of the way. Isabella's eyes grew wide, searching for Emilia, her hands clenching into fists and then stretching open again, over and over. From the back of an empty police car, Emilia searched the faces of the officers who had arrived, scanning for a familiar gaze or feature, hunting for Ciaran's reassuring nod. But she didn't recognize any of them. One officer came over and asked if she was happy to go to the station to make a statement. She nodded yes, turning to glance at Isabella one last time. She was sitting in the back of an ambulance, her legs dangling off the side and not quite reaching the ground, like a little girl. But she didn't look up.

The interview room at the station felt so different to sitting on the other side of the desk. The witness side. Everything is reversed, the world flipped as if it has been dragged into an alternate dimension. A dark version of the world that Emilia was so accustomed to.

And it felt like that the last time. When she was brought to a very similar room after Sophie was killed. She sat on the wrong side of the desk and realized that she would never be able to look at an interview room in the same way. That her place of confidence and security – the place where she was always in control – could now only ever be the place where she recounted the murder of her sister.

And now this. Isabella's name will always be synonymous with that place, with what she experienced. She'll never be able to separate herself from the Confession Room. And by extension, neither will Emilia. She'll never be able to unsee Gregory's body lying there or rid herself of the experience of witnessing Isabella's panic and horror.

A familiar rhythm of knocks sounds from the front door.

Ciaran.

Her body jumps into action, her feet moving quickly as she rushes to the front door, yanking it open. He is standing there, his arms crossed, his face crumpled with worry.

He knows.

'Emilia –'

She steps quickly towards him, throwing herself into his arms. And suddenly, all of the emotion that has been trapped inside, bursts outwards. All the images that have been plaguing her mind explode through the surface: Gregory's lifeless face flashing violently, melting away, transforming into Sophie and her wide, staring eyes.

'Shh, you're okay,' Ciaran whispers, stroking her hair as tears seep into his jacket. 'I'm here.'

Eventually her cries subside and he curls one arm around her shoulders, holding her hand with the other as he leads her back into the house. They drop on to the sofa, him sitting in the corner, Emilia tucking her feet beneath her to curl up beside him. But he is still holding her hand. She stares down at his thumb as it moves back and forth along her knuckles, a frisson of energy humming between them. And there is something in his gaze. An emotion Emilia can't quite place.

'What were you doing in those woods, Emi?'

'I was just going for a walk –'

'No,' he says, shaking his head firmly. 'Don't give me that. Come on, I know you. Why did you go there? To those woods, so close to where Hayley's body was left. What were you thinking?'

She pauses, her brow furrowing at the tone of his voice. The tone matches that unfamiliar look in his eye. Anger.

Tingeing his usually gentle voice and kind eyes with darkness. He's furious.

'I . . . I wanted to see what was happening. I wanted to see if police were still there. I didn't think –'

'No, you didn't!' He releases her hand, her fingers suddenly empty as he shakes his head. He pushes himself to his feet and glares back at her.

'Wait!' she shouts, standing, her fists curling at her sides. 'Why are you angry at me?'

'Why am I angry? Are you serious?'

'Yes!'

'You let your obsession with this case take over and you put yourself in danger! How would you feel if you were still a detective? Remember how disruptive it is when the public suddenly decide that they know more than us?'

'I'm not just "the public",' Emilia snarls.

'No, you're not. But you're not in the police either. And we're finding this hard enough. We have no idea how these killers are planning what they're doing, how they're abducting people, when they bring them back.'

'Ciaran –'

'What if they'd been there? What if something had happened to you? And not even that, what if the press had named you? They would know who you are!'

'Even if I am putting myself in danger, it's my choice.'

She stares at him, breathless, her chest rising and falling. He doesn't understand. He'll never understand how much she wants to help yet how helpless she truly feels.

She sits back down on the sofa, but choosing the opposite corner, tucking her knees up to her chest, a barrier against any further attacks.

'Look, Emi, I'm sorry –'

'Don't, Ciaran, it's okay –'

'No, really. I shouldn't have shouted. I just . . . you know how much I care about you. And I'm scared that your desire to help is just going to put you in danger. I want you to be safe. What's happening is scary.'

She rests her chin on top of her knees and nods, smiling gently across at him. 'I know. And I'm sorry. I know I've put you in an awkward position.'

'I just want this to be over,' he mutters. 'And maybe we're one step closer . . . '

Her brow lowers. 'Has something else happened?'

'Luca Franco . . . '

'Has he been found? Has he been arrested?'

'He's been found . . . But he's dead.'

Emilia's breath hitches, a lump forming in the back of her throat. 'He's dead?'

'Somebody found him in some woods about forty miles from here.'

'That far away?'

He nods. 'He's with the coroner . . . they're trying to figure out what happened.'

'Well, how did he die?'

'Gunshot. To the head. But –'

'Suicide?'

'That's what they're trying to find out, yes. But you know how it is – with a gunshot to the temple, it isn't easy to tell. We might never know.'

'But what if . . . what if it wasn't him?' Emilia whispers. 'And Isabella said there were two people. So even if Luca was one of them, the murders could continue . . . If it

96

continues – when will they be satisfied? Serial killers don't just stop. They have to be caught.'

That is an absolute truth. For people like this – people who kill – the satisfaction never goes away. They'll have started with something far more subtle, something hidden and buried. And maybe they'll have spent some time trying to restrain themselves, trying to push away that feeling of wanting more. But like an animal, starving, they'll always feel disappointed. And with each kill, that feeling will need something further to be satiated. Something bigger. More wild. More likely to end in capture.

Ciaran doesn't engage with this line of thought. 'Hopefully it's all over now,' he says firmly. 'But if it isn't – if more confessions come – I need you to stay safe . . . I need you to say you understand.'

'I understand,' Emilia whispers.

Ciaran sighs, his face a confused mixture of relief and disbelief.

Emilia clears her throat. 'Has Isabella said anything in interview about who did it? Or the Room?'

'No . . . So far she's not answering any questions. She's just terrified.'

'What about when she was abducted? When she went missing . . . Any clues there?'

He puffs out his cheeks. 'No. Her family said they hadn't seen them for a few days. Greg had come to find her on a night out and insisted on her coming home with him. We don't know when in that period of time they were taken. And so far there's nothing we can trace on CCTV. No footage of them being taken. No cameras outside Greg's house.'

'How?' Emilia says. 'How are they doing this?'

Ciaran's phone rings, and they both jump as the low buzz of vibration rattles against the side table.

Ciaran picks it up. 'Shit, it's the Inspector.'

'Wild?' Emilia asks and he nods.

'This is Ciaran Jones,' he mumbles into the receiver, his voice low. He pauses, listening. His eyes veer towards Emilia and she sits up straight, frowning, as she catches her own name in Wild's muffled voice on the other end.

'Yes, that's fine,' Ciaran says. 'I'll . . . I'll speak to her and let you know . . . Within the next ten minutes, yep . . . Okay. Bye.'

He turns to face Emilia. 'Isabella Santos has said that she's ready to speak about what happened now. But . . .'

'What's the problem?'

'She wants to speak to you first.'

11th November, 10 a.m.

'Emilia, thank you for agreeing to come in. We really appreciate it.'

Detective Inspector Penelope Wild extends her hand outwards, a strained smile stretching across her face.

'You're welcome,' Emilia says, shaking her hand tightly. 'I really want to help if I can.'

Emilia swallows — it feels so strange being back in this environment, speaking to a senior officer leading on the biggest case plaguing the country. She glances across at Ciaran who smiles reassuringly — she is bolstered once more. She can help. She is here for a reason. 'Where's Isabella?' she asks.

'She's in the witness room. You can speak in there and that way we'll record and observe from the next room. If she does tell you anything important it will be captured . . . But really she just wants some reassurance. You're not a police officer any more, so you can't interview her. Just try to make her feel comfortable. This might make things tricky evidentially, but I'm at a loss of what else to do.'

'I'll make sure not to do anything that'll jeopardize any evidence. I promise.'

'Thank you, Emilia,' Wild says, coming to a stop, her face stern and serious. She gestures towards the door in front of them, which is slightly ajar. 'She's just in here.'

Ciaran reaches for Emilia, his fingers briefly touching

the inside of her wrist. Emilia shivers. He pulls away, glancing down at his shoes.

'I'll wait for you out here.'

'Okay.'

She steps through the door, nodding at both Wild and Ciaran before closing it behind her. She spins around and there, sitting in the furthest corner of the sofa, her head lifting at the sound of the door closing, is Isabella.

It wasn't so long ago that they were together in the woods, but Isabella somehow looks worse. While she has been cleaned up, her cut lip stitched, her clothes now clean, she looks even more exhausted, her skin grey, her eyes heavy with emotion. Before, there was horror and panic there, but now there is so much more. Sadness, anger, fear. Grief. How will she ever recover?

Emilia sits down in the armchair opposite her, her attention drawn to the camera suspended above Isabella's head, the red light indicating that its all-seeing eye is awake and watching.

'I looked for you when all the police arrived, but you were gone,' Isabella says.

'I know . . . I'm sorry, I just had to let them do their jobs. I got ushered away.'

Isabella sniffs. 'I wanted to thank you. I don't know what would have happened if you weren't there . . .' Her voice breaks and she squeezes her eyes shut, fresh tears replacing the ones she wiped away just minutes earlier.

'You don't need to thank me. I was just in the right place at the right time . . . How have you been feeling?'

Isabella swallows, lifting her hand to cover her mouth.

'I'm so tired. I just want this part to be over so I can go home and try to pretend that this never happened.'

'So why don't you want to talk to the police?'

'I want to,' she says, her voice cracking. 'I do want to, I'm just . . .'

'What are you afraid of?' Emilia leans forward. 'Of whoever did this?'

Isabella nods. 'What if they come and find me?' She hugs her knees tightly, her bottom lip trembling. 'I'm so scared.'

'I know you are. And I know how terrifying it is. When I was a detective, I did so many of these interviews and the victims were always, always afraid. But if it brings whoever did this to justice, it will be worth it. Don't you think? They need to be punished.'

'Yes,' she whispers, a lone tear spilling down her nose.

'I'm so sorry this happened to you.' Emilia reaches out slowly, and curls her fingers around Isabella's hand. 'I really am.'

'I just wish I could go back. Instead of being out with Greg on Sunday night, I could have been at home with my parents. Maybe it might have been different.'

Emilia's body stills, her pulse slowing loudly in her ears, as if time moved backwards, just for a second.

'Sunday night?' She frowns. 'You were taken to the Room on Sunday night?'

Isabella nods, her brows stitching together as she takes in Emilia's confusion. 'Yes . . . that's when they came for us.'

'But . . . but that's the night the confession was posted.' Her eyes widen, her cheeks turning hot. 'Are you sure?'

'I . . . I'm positive.'

'Can you remember a time?'

'Um ... I ... it must have been somewhere around midnight.'

Somewhere around midnight.

That's when the post went up on the forum.

Which means when the confession was made they were both still alive.

The confessions haven't been confessions at all.

They have been warnings.

11th November, 11 a.m.

Emilia's seatbelt clicks into place, her thoughts whirring, a spinning top turning ceaselessly. She glances over at Ciaran, his eyes wide as he stares out through the wind-screen.

'I just don't understand,' she mutters. 'How weren't they captured on CCTV or something in the hours leading up to the confession? We would have known that they were alive when the confession was posted!'

'Isabella went out with her friends the day before,' Ciaran says. 'And that's the last time she was captured on CCTV. After that she was with him, at his house. There was nothing.'

'And Hayley and Luca?'

'The same – the last they'd been seen by anyone was the day before when they went to lunch with friends. After that they weren't captured anywhere. They just disappeared. So when the confession was posted it looked like what it said it was – a confession.' Ciaran looks over at her. 'Something else happened while you were speaking to Isabella,' he says.

'What is it?' She glances down at her phone again. Still loading.

'The coroner . . . from the angle of the shot he's determined that Luca Franco did not commit suicide.'

'What?'

'He was shot by someone else. And not just that . . . He's been dead for some time. He died around the same time as Hayley. They were most likely killed together.'

Emilia's stomach lurches. She's always thought that Luca being the main suspect was too simple, too convenient. But she had been hoping – at least then, they would have known something. Without Luca in their sights, they are running blind. 'So it was never him?'

He nods. 'But now that we know that the confessions pre-date the murders, we can try to protect whoever is next.'

Whoever is next . . . When will the next confession come?

Emilia unlocks her phone, quickly typing *theconfessionroom.com* into her search bar.

It loads slowly, the signal lagging.

A shrill ring pierces the silence. Ciaran's phone.

And it's as if she knows it then, before he even answers the call – Emilia knows what is coming.

'Jones,' he says abruptly.

'We need you on alert,' a voice says as the phone connects to the car's loudspeaker. 'The next confession has just been posted.'

'Who are they, Rory?'

Emilia holds her breath, the world outside the car suddenly blurring, nothing else except the words that have just been uttered being of any consequence.

'Freddie and Joseph Henley,' Rory says. 'Brothers.'

Emilia glances back down at her phone, her eyes swimming with tears. The page has loaded. And it is there, the words set out in black and white. The next set of fodder announced for the masses.

Two more names. Brothers ensnared by the Confession Room.

Two potential victims who, at this very moment, are probably still alive.

'Brothers,' Emilia mutters, her heart racing. 'Why would they do this to brothers?'

She turns to look over at Ciaran but for a second it isn't him sitting there, his fingers white-knuckled on the steering wheel.

It is Sophie. Laughing. Throwing her head back, her long hair billowing towards the window as it's caught on the warm summer breeze. Her sister. Emilia thought she had lost her in the worst possible circumstances. But this . . . one of them chosen to live and the other to die? She wouldn't have survived this.

'I don't know,' Ciaran mutters, breaking her memory. 'We can't even try to understand their motives –'

His phone rings again, amplified by the car's speakers.

'Tell me you've got their address,' Ciaran says.

'Yes – 155 Mordon Avenue –'

'We're not far from there at all,' Emilia says. 'I had a client who lived just around the corner.'

'Response units are almost there,' the voice on the call says.

'I'm on my way,' Ciaran barks.

He ends the call and reaches forward to the switch in the centre console. Blue lights and sirens scream out and up into the sky. The engine roars beneath them.

He weaves on to the main road, past cars which are

pulling over at the sight of their approach, braking suddenly as a van moves into the lane directly in front. He pushes a button which sends the siren wailing louder.

'I'll never understand why people don't move out of the fucking way!' he shouts, clenching his jaw.

The van pulls over slowly, the driver sticking his hand out the window and raising it nonchalantly.

Ciaran manoeuvres past him and they drive on in silence, both focused on the road. The lines in the centre of the tarmac flash past and fall into a strange sort of rhythm with the lights and the siren. Emilia stares at them, listening intently to the rise and fall of sound bellowing from the car, pouring her focus into anything except those two souls. Brothers. Taken.

Line. Flash. Siren.

Line. Flash. Siren.

Line. Flash. Siren.

'We're here,' Ciaran says.

He swings quickly into the road on the right and she stares out of the window, catching the street sign as it flashes past.

Mordon Avenue.

The car flies down the road, and Emilia scans the houses as even numbers pass on the left, odd numbers on the right.

'There!' she cries, pointing, even though it is completely unnecessary – Ciaran is already pulling in, the tyres screeching as he brakes quickly.

'I know you're involved now, but you need to stay here,' he says, opening his door.

'Ciaran –'

'Just stay in the car.'

He slams the door and darts towards the house, his movements swift and precise. He pounds his fist on the front door and shouts their names, so loudly that she can hear it through the glass. A wailing sound rises from the near distance. The response units are coming. They'll be here any minute. But . . . where are Joseph and Freddie?

Ciaran moves over to the window on the left-hand side of the front door, cupping his hand to the glass to stare inside.

They aren't answering.

Emilia's stomach churns but she shakes her head, forcing her mind to conjure up scenarios other than the worst. Maybe they're at a friend's house . . . Or maybe they have partners and they're with them. Maybe they're with their parents. The police will be making contact with anyone connected to them, warning them, trying to ascertain their whereabouts, to bring them to safety. Just because they're not here, doesn't mean that it's too late.

She scans the front of the house, up to the top level. No windows are damaged, no glass smashed or panes forced open. And no lights are on. Maybe they're somewhere else . . . they must be somewhere –

But wait.

There.

Her breath catches at the back of her throat, a tightly knit ball of anxiety forming at the very top of her chest – the side gate is ajar. Just slightly. Such a slim gap that she didn't notice it at first glance.

She throws open the passenger door and runs.

'Emil!' Ciaran shouts.

His footsteps pound behind her, his voice still calling her name. But she ignores him. Sprinting down the narrow alley that cuts a path down the right-hand side of the house, she stumbles, her ankles thrashing through the tangle of nettles that are bursting through the ground, taking their territory. She rights herself then sharply turns left, her feet scrambling beneath her and –

She falters, that tight ball of anxiety forcing its way out of her chest and up into her throat, bursting out in a low cry.

The back door has been forced open.

Just like Sophie's.

The wooden frame is splintered, a large chunk of it missing from where something – a crowbar – has been jammed in, the door prised open.

A hand grabs her shoulder and she jumps, spinning around to come face-to-face with Ciaran.

'Oh no,' he whispers.

He moves forward quickly, blocking Emilia's view, his hands already reaching inside his jacket for latex gloves which he pulls on smoothly. He gently pushes on the fractured wood and the door swings inwards.

Sirens wail loudly and brakes screech. The response units have arrived.

Emilia rushes forward, her body seeming to move on its own, out of her control. She knows that she shouldn't look. She knows that whatever is inside will be too much, too close to what she witnessed when Sophie was killed, but . . . she has to. She has to know what's happened.

She pushes past Ciaran's outstretched arm and stares inside, wide-eyed. Her chest heaves up and down, panic spiralling through her, her muscles tightening, ready to flee.

A smashed bottle of beer on the floor. An open can of lager on the counter. A chair thrown on to its side.

And a feeling – thick and cloying – hanging in the air. *Fear.*

11th November, 6 p.m.

'In breaking news, two more people, twenty- and twenty-two-year-old brothers Joseph and Freddie Henley, have been named anonymously as victims of murder on the forum, the Confession Room.

'Early investigations indicate that they were snatched from their home where they live with their parents who were away visiting friends in Surrey.

'Joseph and Freddie are the third set of people to be named on the forum in this way. However, this is the first occasion where family members have been named together. As always, the police have urged the public to be vigilant at this time and to refrain from visiting the forum.

'We will now pass over to Detective Chief Inspector Henry Holden, who is live:

'"We are deeply disturbed at the naming of two more people on the forum, the Confession Room. The previous cases have both followed the same pattern and we are highly concerned for Joseph and Freddie. We are working around the clock to find them and bring the perpetrators of these serial crimes to justice.

'"We would strongly advise and recommend that at this time, people in the Greater London area should avoid going out on their own at night, and if possible, should follow a seven p.m. curfew except where night-time travel is absolutely necessary.'"

Emilia turns off the television, feeling nothing but emptiness. As if all the emotions she felt earlier – all the emotions she has ever felt – have been scraped out of her, piece by piece, until there is nothing left.

A curfew? This can't be real, surely? When was the last time a curfew was imposed because of a murderer? The Yorkshire Ripper? And look how well that turned out. There were protests in the streets, the unleashing of the rage of thousands of women who refused to be turned into prisoners because of the actions of one man.

But this isn't just women . . . The victims could be anyone. The Confession Room killers are not discriminating; they don't seem to be targeting anyone in particular. They are drawing out people – people in relationships, people who love each other – and forcing them to confess. And then they make their judgement.

What will the Henleys be made to confess? Their parents have been on the news, speaking to the reporters who gave them less than a few hours' peace: they have stood together, arm in arm, the prospect of loss glazed over the surface of their eyes.

Emilia heads over to her desk and reaches for her phone, clicking on her client's most recent message, hesitating just for a moment before she taps out a response.

Hi Violet. Many apologies for failing to communicate with you. Something has occurred in my personal life and

I will have to take some time off. I will
message again soon but understand if
you wish to find another detective.

She taps the arrow and listens as the message whooshes away. Usually, letting somebody down like this would swamp her with guilt, but it all seems so insignificant.

The Henleys' house was overrun with police within minutes. Officers moving across the crime scene, cordoning off the house, the road, speaking to neighbours. The parents arrived, the mother falling to her knees. 'We only left for two nights!' she wailed, as her husband held her, her face buried into his chest, his face fixed with bewilderment, unable to understand how this was happening to him, to his wife and his two children. And all Emilia could do was sit in the passenger seat of Ciaran's car and watch.

He has been messaging non-stop since she left the scene, escorted back to the house by a police officer at his insistence, but she keeps telling him that she is fine, that he just needs to focus on the case, that he shouldn't worry about her, even though she feels so rattled she can't eat and her stomach is constantly churning.

Emilia turns to her computer, staring at the forum which is open, as always. She wishes now that she had never heard of it – wishing that its very existence came as a shock. If only she could detach from it. Others will watch what's happening on the news and look on in horror, but after some minutes pass, they will forget it, moving on to focus on something else.

But her? She is consumed by it.

Every breath. Every step. Consumed.

The hashtag on Twitter is relentless, constantly refreshing, hundreds of comments every second. The police have asked countless times for people to stop discussing it on social media, to stop visiting the forum, but . . . how can hundreds of thousands of people be prevented from gorging on this as if it is entertainment? It's spreading, a wildfire that has no hope of being extinguished. And with each comment that is posted, each video that is shared, the reactions growing exponentially more visceral and outraged and emotional, they are feeding the beast. They are giving the killers what they want. There's a reason they have made all of this public, posting the videos online and confessing before it even happens. They are bolstered by the attention, basking in its glowing light, their violence fired up by the frenzy. In a case with so many questions, Emilia is sure of one thing: *we have made it worse.*

Her eyes narrow as a new hashtag is suggested at the top of her search screen.

#ConfessionRoomVigil

She clicks on it and then scrolls, scanning the posts, most of which are the same tweet shared over and over again — the hashtag suspended above an image:

#ConfessionRoomVigil

A VIGIL FOR THE VICTIMS OF THE
CONFESSION ROOM

AT 7 P.M. ON THE 12TH NOVEMBER THERE WILL
BE A CANDLELIT VIGIL IN HOLMER HILL PARK FOR
THE VICTIMS OF THE CONFESSION ROOM.

WE REFUSE TO KEEP TO A CURFEW OR LIVE IN
FEAR OF THESE MONSTERS WHO ARE SNATCHING
OUR LOVED ONES.

IF YOU FEEL TOO SCARED TO COME – REMEMBER:
WE ARE NOT SAFE AT HOME EITHER! THE HENLEYS
WERE TAKEN FROM INSIDE THEIR OWN HOUSE!

JOIN US – LIGHT A CANDLE – STAND UP TO THE EVIL
OF THE CONFESSION ROOM KILLERS.

SHOW HAYLEY JAMES, LUCA FRANCO, GREGORY
WEISS AND ANY OTHER VICTIM THAT THEY WILL
NOT BE FORGOTTEN.

SHOW ISABELLA SANTOS AND THE HENLEYS
THAT THEY ARE NOT ALONE.

DO NOT FEAR.

WE ARE SAFER TOGETHER.

The image has been shared 456,343 times. There are countless posts of people committing to attend, hundreds of people from all over the country – all over the world – insisting that people should refuse the curfew and take to the streets. And aren't they speaking the truth? Is Emilia in more danger here, alone in her flat, than out there?

A door slams on the laptop and her skin turns cold.

A new confession.

And before she even turns to the forum, she knows what it will be. Just like clockwork: the video. But which Henley will appear on the screen? Freddie? Or Joseph?

She clicks on the link and waits, her gaze blurring as the video loads, her mind attempting in some feeble way to transport itself to somewhere else, anywhere other than here. She knows what's going to be in this video . . . one of them dying while the other watches. So why does she feel such a compulsive urge to watch? Why does she have no doubt that all over the country – all over the world – there are people watching it at this very moment? Why do they need to see it? What is it that pushes us towards the darkest parts of humanity?

The video loads and her eyes instantly focus, her heart beating faster and faster, her breaths shallow.

THE CONFESSION ROOM. THE HENLEY BROTHERS.

Chills run down her arms. *The Henley Brothers . . .* When the confession was posted, they named them individually. It was the media, the public – social forums – that dubbed them 'the Henley Brothers'. Are they taunting everyone? Are they holding up a mirror to say: *look at what you are doing*?

The footage begins to play.

A face appears, the footage zoomed in, just like the previous two, the skin red-raw, the eyes dazed.

'Freddie, it's counting down!'

Freddie. It's Freddie. He blinks slowly, his eyes almost sleepy, as if he is just waking from a dream. There is no blind panic like in the previous videos, no angry outbursts.

'I don't know what they want me to say,' he whispers.

'Just say something, Fred! Do something!'

He stares blankly, the edge of his lip curling upwards.

'Don't act like you're scared for me, Joe. You're desperate for it to be me.'

'Please, Freddie! Just play by the rules!'

'What fucking rules? This isn't a game we can win. It's rigged. One of us is gonna die. And you hate my fucking guts, so just shut your mouth and let it be done.'

Joseph cries out and Freddie rolls his eyes, scoffing.

'I haven't done anything,' he mutters, setting his jaw. 'Nothing that I need to confess –'

'Well, there must be something, because they've chosen you! What about those forums you go on?'

'Oh fuck off, Joseph. What, because I go on forums and complain about my lot –'

'Complain about your lot?' Joseph shouts, suddenly fuelled by anger. 'They're Incel sites, it's full of men who hate women – violent, horrible men!'

'So now I deserve to die?'

'I never said that! Freddie, you need to do something – think of Mum and Dad –'

'Oh, I am,' Freddie says, glaring at him. 'You're the golden child and I'm the problem. If Mum and Dad could choose one of us to save, it would be you. So just fuck off and leave me alone.'

The screen turns black.

Emilia shoves the mouse forward and clicks the X in the top right-hand corner. The low buzz of white noise from the video disappears and she is back in her living room again, the confines of the forum evaporating around her. She exhales slowly, releasing the breath that she had been holding, unable to steady her hands which are trembling violently.

She can't watch any more. She can't play witness as the hand-held camera returns. She can't stare blankly as Joseph cries in the background. She can't simply wait for what everyone knows will come once the footage resumes:

Freddie's face, the video shaking.

The inevitable gunshot.

And then silence.

The park is awash with people: countless men and women standing shoulder to shoulder in wave after wave.

Ciaran begged Emilia not to come. The morning after she watched the video, he knocked at her door with that familiar rap of the knuckles. He had been calling endlessly, leaving message after message asking her to please answer the phone. He had called straightaway – less than five minutes after the Henley video had been posted. He knew. He understood how her mind would react to that image: siblings, one alive, one dead. And not just her mind, her body too. It immediately shut down – like a computer that is so overloaded, so overwhelmed with information that it simply freezes before switching off entirely. It's as though she has been thrust back in time, to when it first happened, to when she was unable to sleep, or move, or function at all. All she did was survive.

'Emi,' he said softly. 'Please open the door. I know you're in there.'

She rolled over, turning away from the front door, her nose to the cool leather of the sofa, and lifted her arm to cover her face as tears flooded down her cheeks. She squeezed her eyes shut. She didn't want him to see her like that. Not again.

'Emi, do you really think I don't already know what state you're in right now?' She held her breath. 'Do you think I don't know that you'll have spent all night staring up at the ceiling? Do you think I don't know that you'll have spent an hour in the shower this morning because you forced yourself out of bed but once you were there you just couldn't bear to get out again? I know that you won't have eaten anything today, you have a headache because you haven't had any water in fifteen hours, and your face is probably like a panda.'

Please just leave me alone —

'Freddie Henley's body has been found. And Joseph — he's alive . . . Please. Let me in.'

And she did. He came inside and held her on the sofa, stroking her hair, whispering over and over again that she was safe, that Sophie would be proud of her, that she had done so well — *don't let yourself be dragged back to that place, Emi.*

'I might go to the vigil,' she whispered. His eyes narrowed, a slow shake of his head indicating his silent disbelief.

'Please don't.'

And finally, after more cajoling on his part, practically begging her, she promised that she wouldn't.

But then — Isabella called.

The unknown number flashed up on the screen, and when Emilia answered a hushed voice whispered her name.

'Emilia?' she said. 'Is that Emilia Haines?'

'Isabella?'

'Hi . . . yes, it's me. Sorry for calling you like this —'

'It's absolutely fine. That's why I gave you my number. Is there something I can help you with?'

'I was wondering . . . no, never mind, it's so bloody stupid —'

'What is it?'

She paused, a gentle sigh fluttering through the speaker. 'Are you going to the vigil tonight?'

The question lingered in the air as Isabella explained that she wanted to go, she felt like she needed to be there – to witness it, if just for a few minutes – she had even discussed it with the therapist she was seeing, but her family didn't want to take her. They didn't think she should go, thought it was dangerous, for them and her brothers, as well as for her. Their family had already been hounded, members of the public finding their house and treating them like some sort of circus attraction. But they would let her go with Emilia – Isabella had told them that they could be discreet, and Emilia would keep her hidden.

'Please?' she whispered.

Just a few hours later, Isabella was at her door, her mum staring worriedly out from the driver's seat.

'I'm never going to be allowed to go anywhere,' Isabella sighed. 'It's like I'm a teenager again.'

'It will get better,' Emilia said, stepping out on to the front porch. 'You just need to give them time. Shall we go?'

And now, here they are, surrounded by the communal pulse of hundreds of people.

Emilia leads the way, Isabella following behind, her head lowered, a thick woolly hat and hood pulled low over her face. Frozen leaves crackle beneath their feet. Inhaling slowly, Emilia breathes in the fresh air tinged with the smell of smoke. Somebody's burning a bonfire.

People are leaning in close, passing a small flame from

one wick to another, nodding to each other as they pass on the flickering light.

But how long will it take for the police to arrive, to force people to disperse? There is a tense, rippling energy in the air around them. And at some point, at some unpredictable moment, it will erupt – Emilia is sure of it. That's how people react to scenarios like this one: they are already being attacked, targeted by some unknown evil, and now the people who should be solving it for them are seeking to hold them prisoner too. The only response will be rage.

They walk around the side of the crowd towards the front, where a woman is standing on the top step under a gazebo: the vigil organizer. She is clutching a microphone and scanning the crowd, which is becoming more dense every second as people keep on arriving. And there, on the steps in front of her, are large posters, the faces of ghosts staring back at the crowd.

Hayley James. Gregory Weiss. Freddie Henley. Luca Franco.

Each photograph shows a happy, smiling, young, vibrant person, their life snuffed out – and for what? For the deluded beliefs of some psychopath.

And more will follow.

A loud buzzing comes out of the speakers, followed by a screech of static.

'Sorry!' the woman at the front says, holding her hands up with an embarrassed grimace. 'Didn't mean to deafen you all.'

There's a smattering of nervous laughter among the otherwise silent crowd.

The woman looks out and some people in the front nod encouragingly, their faces sombre. She lets out a wavering breath and lifts the microphone close to her lips.

'Thank you all so much for being here,' she says, her words slightly muffled. 'I know how much it must have taken to leave your homes at a time like this, especially when you've been told not to. And you have no idea how much this means to so many people who have been affected like I have. My name is Gina Franco – Luca was my brother and Hayley was one of my best friends. And I lost them both. Hayley was the first known victim of the Confession Room. And we hoped more than anything that we would find Luca alive. We didn't know where he was or what they had done with him. But we knew without a doubt that he wasn't responsible for what had happened to Hayley. And we knew that he wasn't responsible for the other murders. Even when the police were treating him as the main suspect. We hoped that maybe he was out there, just too afraid to come home.'

She pauses, chewing on her bottom lip, as if she is trying to process what is happening. What has happened. Emilia remembers that look. She witnessed it every day in the mirror in those moments where it would suddenly hit her, and both her body and mind would have to take it all in, living through the trauma again and again.

'But that hope was useless. They took Luca away from us too. We don't know why they killed both Hayley and Luca. We have no idea why whoever is doing this has decided to act in this way. None of them – not Hayley or Luca, not Gregory, not Freddie – deserved to die for what they had done. No person can choose who lives or dies.

And that's what these bastards are doing. They're playing God.' Her brow lowers, fury flashing across her eyes. 'And what are the fucking police doing?'

Anger begins to ripple out from her, like a stone thrown into a pond. The crowd is less still, less silent. That feeling, the feeling that was hanging in the air when they arrived, is growing, thickening, a storm ready to break.

'They're not solving what's happening, they're not doing anything except blaming the wrong people, innocent victims, and telling us to stay in our homes and hope the big bad wolf doesn't blow them down. Well I say, fuck them! And fuck the wolf!'

Cheers erupt, the crowd moving together, shouting, booing, roaring with approval: a hive mind buoyed by anger and fear and resentment.

Emilia scans the outer edges of the park, searching for police, for signs that they are going to make a move, to shut it down. But they haven't entered. They are remaining in their cars, parked around the perimeter. Waiting.

Emilia looks back at Isabella, her face falling as she takes her in. Her hand is lifted up to cover her eyes and she is rocking back and forth, exhaling forcefully through pursed lips.

'Isabella?' Emilia whispers, leaning towards her.

Her body tenses. Just a minor movement, all her muscles clenching.

'Do you want to go?'

She nods quickly, her eyes glassy. 'I thought I would be okay but . . . this is too much.'

'It's okay . . . let's go.'

Emilia turns her back on the podium, steering them

through the ever expanding crowd, her shoulder knocking against people, not even stopping to throw a cursory apology over her shoulder. They need to get away from here.

They break away from the hordes of people, at last finding themselves in the outer reaches of the crowd, before emerging into the clear air of the road beyond the gate.

'I think we left at the right time,' Emilia says in a low voice as they climb into the car. 'It's going to turn at any moment. I can feel it.'

Isabella grimaces, her eyes flitting away from Emilia's as she pulls the door towards her, clinging to the handle.

They spend the entire journey back to Isabella's house in silence. Every so often Emilia glances over at her, but she is staring blankly out of the passenger window, her hands clasped tightly on her lap.

'Thanks for taking me,' she mutters finally as Emilia stops the car directly in front of her house.

'You're welcome,' Emilia responds with a smile.

Isabella sighs as she glances to the front door which has already opened at the sound of the engine – Melanie, Isabella's mum, waiting anxiously for her daughter.

'My life is never going to go back to normal, is it?' she says flatly.

'It will,' Emilia says. 'Eventually it will.'

'No,' she answers. 'For the rest of my life, I'm always going to be "that girl" . . . I'd give anything for them to have chosen someone else.'

'Why do you think they did choose you?'

'Because of what I confessed on the forum.' Isabella's face tinges with embarrassment. 'That's how they found me. That's how they found all of us.'

12th November, 9:35 p.m.

The drive back to her house feels long. Emilia measures the journey in the flashes of the streetlamps, the warm light blurring as it rushes past. She counts them, forcing herself to focus on something.

Count the streetlamps. It isn't much further.

Not much further.

Eighty. Eighty-one. Eighty-two.

She is safe. There's nothing to be afraid of.

One hundred and four. One hundred and five. One hundred and six.

This is her road. She is home.

One hundred and thirteen.

One hundred and thirteen streetlamps from Isabella's house to hers.

The door creaks open as she unlocks it and she is greeted by the sound of Mimi's barking.

'Hello, darling,' she whispers. 'What's all the fuss about, hey?'

Her claws click across the wood and Emilia lifts her up, breathing in her familiar puppy scent. 'Hello, gorgeous.'

She pulls her phone out of her pocket, pressing on the screen, but there is no response. It is black, a dark mirror reflecting her tired face back at her. 'Oh for fuck's sake,' she mutters, remembering that the charger which usually sits beside her desk is in her work bag, up in her bedroom.

She glances down at Mimi and her bulging, expectant eyes. 'Let me charge this and then I'll feed you, okay?' Mimi licks her lips, cocking her head to one side.

Emilia places her down on the floor and then runs quickly upstairs to her bedroom, plugging the phone in and then pressing on the power button. It lights up, turning on.

She goes back to the kitchen and pulls out the dog food from the cupboard under the sink, Mimi's eyes always on her as she waits excitedly, her wagging tail swiping against the tiles.

Emilia pours her food into the bowl and then retreats to her desk and sits down in the chair, smiling at the sight of Mimi skidding across the kitchen floor to reach her long-awaited feast.

She glances at her computer and her hand moves out of habit to nudge the mouse. The screens come to life – Twitter on one, the forum still open on the other.

Huh. #TheConfessionRoom is trending again. It must be because of the vigils.

Unless . . .

A loud burst of sound floats down from her bedroom, jaunty and bright. Someone is calling her. But she ignores it – what if another confession has been posted?

She pushes the mouse quickly over to the second screen and refreshes the page.

The ringing stops. But after just a couple of seconds, it begins again. Shrill and relentless.

The page loads. And there it is – a new confession – at the top of the thread in bold.

She skims the words quickly and pauses, her breath

catching at the back of her throat. She reads it again. And then again.

Anonymous 01

Murder. London. Ryan Kirkland. Emilia Haines.

He is still clutching the photographs, his hands clasped together around his knee which he has tucked up towards his chest, the other, chained leg splayed out beside him.

He spent some time pacing back and forth, as far as his tether would allow him, a steely look in his eye. As if he was trying to conjure up some way to free himself. But then the fear would return to his gaze, deepening to abject terror. And finally he sank to the floor.

How long should I keep him alone in here? How long should I torture him?

He knows that people face the Confession Room in pairs. That's always been the case. No exceptions. So why should he be any different? Why should he suffer less?

Because that's the true pain of this place.

Who will be the survivor? Who will be the victim?

And which would you prefer?

The Room

Ryan stares at the mirror from his position on the floor, his aching back arched against the rough concrete blocks. He's seen enough films, watched enough TV shows full of snarling detectives and elusive spies to consider that he might be staring at a two-way mirror. Is someone – whoever took him, whoever has been doing this – watching him right now? And when . . . when are they going to force him to confess?

He drags his eyes away from the mirror and looks up at the countdown, still frozen at 00:60. When will that begin ticking? The videos, the ones from the Confession Room, play on a loop in his mind: that first victim, did she and her boyfriend get a warning or did it simply start counting down? And what – or who – was making them speak?

He searches the room again, trying to take in every detail. There must be something. There must be some way to get out.

And there, on the far side of the room, are two things he's overlooked in his quiet hysteria, even as they sit there, plain as day.

Two more boxes.

He rushes to his feet but stops himself from galloping

across the room again at full pelt. The chain . . . will it let him go that far?

He limps carefully forward, each link unfolding and going taut against the next until finally, the entire manacle is stretched straight as steel wire. He leans forward, balancing on the chained leg, stretching his arms out in front of him. But his fingers don't even graze the box by the door. There's no chance of reaching it.

He retreats but doesn't slump back down to the floor. Instead he rests his forehead against the wall, flexing his knees, locking them into place and then relaxing them, again and again. He blinks slowly, and his gaze shifts along the floor from his feet to the opposite corner. And there, in a mirrored position to his own, is a metal hook, hammered into the wall. A place for another human to be kept prisoner.

And he doesn't have a fucking clue who that person will be.

He has heard of the Confession Room — of course he has. He's even been on the forum when other confessions have been posted. He watched as the one about the Henley brothers went live, a chill running through him thinking about where they might be, whether they could be saved. This time, they must have posted after he left for the pub. He had wondered why his mum kept on calling. He thought she was just being a pain in the arse. But she was trying to warn him.

Whoever this other person is, when will they bring them in?

What do they have to confess?

They must be bringing them in soon because nobody has faced this room alone. Nobody has been here without a partner.

No.

Not a partner. A competitor.

12th November, 9:45 p.m.

The phone is still ringing on repeat, but Emilia can't move. She is paralysed, her eyes locked on the screen. On her name.

This can't be real. They can't actually have chosen her.

She blinks rapidly and focuses on the screen again, silently praying that the words will morph and it'll become clear that she just imagined her name in the confession. Someone else's name is there in its place.

But it isn't. It's still her, there in black and white, just like all the others.

Emilia Haines.

Her eyes flit to the name sitting next to hers.

Ryan Kirkland. But she doesn't even know a Ryan. She doesn't know who this person is. All the other victims have been partners, family – this man is a stranger. Why have they paired them together?

She needs to get to her phone. She needs to call the police. But fear has locked her into place, the distance between her living room and her bedroom expanding.

Searching the furthest corners of the living room for shadows, she backs slowly towards the window. Holding her breath, she glances out on to the street.

Next door's cars are there – both parked on the road, even though they have space on their drive. *We don't want strangers parking here*, they always mutter. And the black-cab that belongs to two houses down is across the way. But . . . whose is that van?

There's a white van parked directly opposite the house. But she's never seen it before. In fact, she's never seen any vans park down this street. It isn't really used as a through road; it's quiet. Secluded.

The phone rings again.

She flies towards her bedroom, feet thundering against the floor, her mind imagining footsteps behind, like when she was little and Sophie would chase her up the stairs, laughing. But there is no humour bubbling away in her stomach, only fear. Fear in its truest, most visceral form. Her hand reaches out and snatches up the phone.

'Ciaran?'

'Oh, thank God,' he says, his voice breathless. 'Emi, you've been named in the latest confession. Police are in the park looking for you; you need to head to the main –'

'I-I'm not at the vigil –'

'Where are you?'

'I came home, I already left . . . I don't know what to do! Should I get out?'

'No, no – stay there!'

Rustling echoes through the speaker and his voice comes through in urgent muffled commands – he's on the radio. Direct to the command centre. His frantic voice spitting out her address.

'Police are on their way,' he says, his voice now clear again. 'I'm on my way too, I'm in my car right now. Just hide somewhere in your house and don't move –'

'Ciaran . . .' Her voice breaks. She presses her back to

the wall and slides down to the floor, eyes fixed on the open door. 'I'm scared.'

'I'll stay on the phone with you the whole time. They'll be there soon and you'll be safe. And we're trying to locate the other victim . . . who is he?'

'I don't know! I don't know him! Why have they put us together?'

'Maybe . . . maybe they've decided it's easier to pair people randomly –'

'Or maybe we're somehow connected,' she mutters. 'We just don't know it.'

'Emi, where are you in your house? Are you hiding?'

'I'm in my bedroom . . . But . . . should I hide downstairs instead? What if someone gets in the house and I can't escape?'

'Yes, go downstairs. Grab something heavy. Something you can protect yourself with. And then hide.'

She stands slowly, her skin prickling as the hairs stand up. 'Okay,' she whispers.

She presses the phone to her face, her grip trembling with the pressure, the screen hot against her cheek. She inches out of her room and down the stairs, taking each step one at a time, holding her breath as they creak beneath her.

As she reaches the bottom of the stairs, she runs quickly to the kitchen, her fingers curling around the handle of her largest knife. She holds it tightly, her fingers slick with sweat, slipping against the metal.

Her eyes dart towards the back door . . . If anyone was to come for her from the front, could she escape out the back? Even if she could somehow make it over her fence, she'd be escaping through a field – wide open. An easy target. She reaches out to test the latch and –

It's unlocked.

The back door has been unlocked this whole time.

'Emi . . . Emi? Talk to me, please!'

Ciaran's voice is echoing out of the phone, he is saying her name again and again, trying to get her to speak to him. But all she can focus on is the unlocked door. A horrifying chill runs up her spine as another sound leaks into the kitchen.

A long, low creak.

Somebody is inside the house.

A low growl rumbles out of Mimi, her hackles rising.

Emilia lifts the phone slowly to her ear, legs frozen in place, fingers tightening further around the knife.

'Ciaran,' she whispers. 'I think they're already in the house.'

'Get out of there, Emi! Get to the road, get to a neighbour –'

She flings open the back door, Mimi close to her heels, and throws herself down the first two steps, stumbling, but then –

She freezes.

There is somebody standing in the middle of the garden. Black coat. Woolly hat. Hood pulled low over their face. Standing in perfect stillness.

'Someone help me!' she screams into the night.

Turning quickly, she trips, her hands slamming into the rough stone step. She pushes herself up and staggers forward, scooping Mimi into her arms and running into the house, throwing the door shut behind her. It slams — the sound like a gunshot in the dark.

She turns the lock, fingers trembling, until it clicks loudly. Pulling frantically on the handle, she checks it again and again, as she stares out through the window into the darkness.

They are still standing there.

Watching.

Waiting.

She needs to get to the front door. She needs to get out of here. But how? There's still somebody in the house!

Another creak —

Hands grab her from behind. She tries to scream but her mouth is covered. It isn't skin pressing into her lips and nose but something else — material, sodden with foul-smelling chemicals. She tries to hold her breath, kicking out desperately, trying to lash out with her arms, but they are too strong. She tries to hold her breath but as panic takes over, her limbs thrashing uselessly — she gasps for air.

Her vision wavers, blurring the window, and the night, and the person beyond it, watching from just outside the glass.

Her eyes roll into the back of her head.

Please . . .

Help me . . .

Inside

'Hell is other people.'

Jean-Paul Sartre

She lies at my feet, her head lolling at an awkward angle, as if her neck is broken.

She was much more difficult than him. She fought hard. She ran.

But not hard enough. Not fast enough.

I cannot wait to see her face when she wakes up in that room. It's what I've been waiting for. To see the horror fill her eyes. The realization of what's to come.

She shifts slightly on the floor, her fingers flexing at her sides.

Her breathing is still deep, steady, but every so often she takes a juddering inhale, her eyes moving rapidly behind her eyelids.

Not much longer and she'll be awake.

It's time.

I stretch my arms out above my head, arching my back, which clicks loudly, the muscles in my shoulders screaming. But she shouldn't be too difficult.

I pull on the black jumpsuit that is hanging in the corner, tugging it up over my clothes, fastening the zip.

I stand, stepping over her shoulders until I am towering over her head, her neck still bent. I bend down, gripping firmly under her arms.

Pull.

Her body drags across the floor, her ankles thumping out a rhythm when she passes over the ridge as we move out of the room and into the corridor. Not much further.

I reach the door and let go of her arms. They drop to the floor.

Thump, thump.

I delve in my pocket and pull out the black material, thick and claustrophobic, only a small gap to see out of. The smell musty and cloying.

I drag the mask on over my head.

Close my eyes. Inhale deeply.

And unlock the door.

The Room

1 2th November

Ryan

His skin crawls at the sound of metal slowly dragging against metal.

Somebody is opening the door.

Ryan stands quickly and backs into the corner, nearly tripping over himself as his feet tangle in the chain. The door swings open, letting out a low rumble as it sweeps across the floor.

His eyes widen, his breath trapped in his chest as he forgets to breathe.

Two people, both masked, are holding a woman under the arms. Her head is rolling forward, her feet dragging behind her as they pull her into the room. She's unconscious.

'Hey!' Ryan shouts, in a brief rush of bravery. 'You can't do this!'

But they say nothing. They don't even look at him. Instead, they place her down on the floor, her back to the wall, next to the metal loop in the corner to his right. She slides sideways and they don't try to stop her from falling. Her head thuds on the concrete.

'What's going on?' he says, quieter this time. Maybe they can be appeased. Maybe. 'I don't even know her. This must be a mistake.'

The bigger of the two reaches into the bag they are carrying. They pull out a chain and hand it to the other person, who crouches down, looping the chain around her ankle and tying her to the wall. They pull on it several times. Nod at each other.

'Can you please tell me what's happening? You can't just leave us in here!'

They walk quickly towards the door.

'No, please. Please! Just tell me who she is! Who is she?'

They step out of the room and into the dimly lit corridor beyond.

Ryan rushes forward, even though he knows it is hopeless, that the chain will only allow him to reach halfway across the room. He lets out a scream from deep within him, a sound he has never made before – a trapped animal desperate to be freed.

'Let me out of here!'

The door slams shut.

He staggers backwards, collapsing on to the floor at the sound of them sliding the lock into place. His chest is heaving, his breathing ragged, cold sweat coursing down the back of his neck and on to his spine.

Is this it? Is waiting for what he knows is coming all that he can do? The whole country has seen it; they've all watched as three other sets of people have been through this: the timer, the confessions. The fear. And then . . . the choice. It will be him or her.

She is lying in the same position she was left in, her legs askew, one arm flopped partially over her face, the other at a twisted angle behind her. She has dark hair, olive skin. Pretty. Young . . . mid-thirties at the most.

But . . .

Who is she?

Emilia

2:48 a.m.

Her eyes open slowly and she blinks rapidly, shielding her face from the burning white light.

Where am I? What's happening?

The floor she is lying on is hard, grey concrete, but clean – the smell of chemicals rising up to fill her nose. Bleach.

She rolls on to her back and stares up at the ceiling. Strips of fluorescent lighting are stretched haphazardly above her, a gentle buzz emitting from them, the glare making her eyes water. She winces. Her head feels full – as if it is brimming with water sloshing from one side of her skull to the other.

I'm in the Confession Room.

'Oh my God, you're awake,' a voice says. 'I thought they might have killed you.'

She sits up quickly, backing away from the voice. Her vision swims. But another pain sears up through her leg and she gazes down at her right ankle through blurry eyes.

There, is a chain, heavy and tight, tying her to the wall. It has dug into her skin where she was lying on it, her weight pressing into the metal. Her flesh is red, the new layer below exposed and raw.

'I'm sorry, I . . . I didn't mean to scare you,' the voice

says again. 'I'm not here to hurt you. I . . . I'm tied here too. My name is Ryan.'

Ryan.

Ryan Kirkland.

She turns her head slowly, and waits for the room to fall still before taking in the man on the other side of the room. He is leaning against the wall, his cheek resting against the rough surface to look in her direction, his ankle bound just the same. He is slight with narrow shoulders, a lean frame. His hair is short, almost buzzed, and mousy brown. He is young, no more than thirty. Late twenties, she would guess. He looks like any normal guy. But . . . she's never seen him before.

'Ryan . . .' His name comes out in a strangled croak. She coughs hoarsely. 'H–how do we know each other? Do you know me?'

He tucks his knees up to his chest and hugs them tightly, gripping his elbows. 'I don't even know your name.'

She frowns. 'Didn't you see the confession?' Maybe he hasn't been following the news. Not everyone does. Some people prefer to be sheltered from the world and its darkness. 'Do you know where you are?'

He nods. 'This is the Confession Room . . . Right?'

'Yes.'

He shakes his head and stares up at the ceiling. 'I didn't see the post on the forum. After the Henleys, when the police figured out that they were naming people before they killed them, I thought maybe people would stand more of a chance. But last night . . . tonight – whatever the fucking time is – I decided to go out. I went to the pub with my mates and I . . . I missed it.'

'How long have you been in here?'

'I . . .' He shrugs. 'I'm not sure . . . an hour maybe?'

'How long have I been in here?'

'They brought you in about ten minutes ago. But I don't know how long they've had either of us. They might have kept us somewhere else . . .' His voice trails away and he stares at the floor. 'What's your name?' he asks after a few silent moments have passed.

'I'm Emilia.'

'Emilia . . . ?'

'Haines. Emilia Haines.'

He continues to stare, unblinking, but he pulls at the skin on his knuckles, his foot bouncing up and down on the floor in a fast, relentless rhythm, as if he is racking his brains, riffling through his memories for some kind of connection.

Finally, he looks her way.

'I've never seen you before.'

'How about my name?'

He meets her eye. 'Nope.'

She sighs, rocking her head backwards to rest against the wall. She's so tired. She's never felt this tired in her life. In all the years of working in the police, in the year of living through grief, actively mourning Sophie every day, she has never felt the weight of her body this way, pain burrowing all the way, deep inside. She allows her gaze to be dragged up to the ceiling across from them, to where the large digital timer is suspended, its glowing red digits paused at sixty seconds.

'The countdown,' she whispers.

'I guess,' he says, in a monotone.

'Sixty seconds to make a confession that could kill you.'

'Or save you.'

She glances across at him, and nods. Her lip trembles as the fear shudders through her.

One of us is going to die.

Blinking furiously, she wipes her sweaty palms on the fabric of her jeans. Ryan is showing no emotion – it's as if a switch has been pressed, and he is suddenly numb. He is still, not moving at all, except for his index finger which occasionally trails across the floor.

No . . . not on the floor. On some sheets of paper that have been set down next to him.

'What are those?'

He looks down, his eyes widening. 'The boxes. You haven't looked in your boxes!'

'What?'

'There –' he says, this time his turn to point. 'Next to you!'

How did she not notice that before? Her senses were so overrun with messages, stimuli pulling her in every direction, trying to make sense of why she is here and who she is here with, that she didn't even see the box set down in the corner beside her. And there's another one, further away, in the opposite corner.

Emilia reaches out and tugs the box towards her. Lifting the lid, she peers inside. Her heart drops. There is a face staring up at her from a photograph, the features so familiar she knows them by heart.

'Sophie,' she whispers.

'What is it?' Ryan asks.

She reaches inside, fingers trembling, and pulls out the

photograph of her sister, the paper shaking. It's a photo of her that Emilia has never seen before, taken from outside their house. She is looking over her shoulder, peering back inside, laughing at something. But this isn't some candid photograph, taken by a loved one. It is taken from far away, the view partially obscured by branches, as if the person who took it was hiding. It must have been taken by *him*.

'It . . . it's a photo of my sister. Sophie.'

She glances over at Ryan. He waits, his face expectant.

'She died last year . . . she was murdered by a stalker. It was in the news, you might have seen it.'

'I-I'm sorry –'

'But . . . what does this mean?' She clenches her jaw, fists curling as frustration builds inside her chest. 'What was in yours?'

He coughs, stretching out his legs in front of him. 'Um . . . the first one was my ex-girlfriend.' His eyes glaze over. 'And the other box was a letter . . .'

'You don't have to tell me if you don't want to –'

'No, it's okay, I . . . I wrote a suicide letter. But I changed my mind. And somehow, they've got it. I don't know how, I deleted it, never printed it out . . . Anyway –'

'I'm so sorry,' she says. 'People can get anything if they know how.'

'Did they catch him?'

'No, we never found him.'

He doesn't say anything and they retreat into silence.

'I should open the other one,' Emilia mutters, standing slowly, wincing as her ankle stings and a throbbing pain grips her temples. Hobbling across the room, the chain growing more rigid behind her, she stares only at the box. What could be inside it? Another photo of Sophie? An article from the investigation? Or something to do with Emilia's failure to save her?

What's inside that box?

The chain tightens completely and she jolts to a stop.

Lowering herself to the ground, her legs curl awkwardly beneath her. She stretches her arms outwards but it is just out of reach, the very tips of her fingers just touching the corner of the box. She growls with frustration.

'I can't fucking reach it!'

'Try using your legs,' Ryan says. 'Can you use the one that isn't chained?'

She leans back on the palms of her hands and manoeuvres her left leg, stretching it forward. Her foot knocks the box. She drags it along the floor and the box scuffs towards her. Slowly. Painfully.

Finally she grasps it.

'Good work,' Ryan says. 'What's in there?'

She pulls off the lid, fear and anticipation and dread curdling in her stomach –

It drops downwards, as if she is on a rollercoaster, the moment that you plummet down towards the ground.

Inside is another box. Still black, but not wooden with a lid.

This one is metal.

She squints down at it and frowns.

This one is locked.

Ryan

'Another box,' she whispers. 'But locked.'

'Why . . . Why would they do that? Why did I get two things and you only got one?'

She shrugs. She looks exhausted. Her face is pale, her cheeks sunken, mouth downturned.

She shakes the box from side to side but there is no sound. No movement. So it's something heavy, something that isn't shifting inside. It's secure.

'Could you force the lock?'

She scoffs, holding it out towards him, lifting the thick metal of the padlock. 'Could you?' she asks, her eyebrows raised. She clutches the box to her chest and then shuffles backwards, retreating to the wall by her chain.

'Are you okay?' he asks.

She meets his eye, a strange expression on her face. And Ryan knows what she's thinking. What kind of question is that at a time like this? In a place like this?

But what else is there to say?

'Am I okay . . .' she mutters. 'I . . . I just . . . I can't stop thinking about my parents. I can't stop thinking about what they'll be doing right now, what thoughts will be running through their minds. They already lost my sister, and now –'

She stops speaking suddenly, taking a deep breath as her voice breaks. She wants to cry, he can tell, but she squeezes her eyes shut, exhaling slowly through her nose.

'The truth is that nothing we do is going to make a difference. Nothing that's in these boxes is here to help us. It's here to taunt us. That photo of Sophie, the photo of your ex, and your letter — they put them here for one reason: to torture us. But we both know that when the time comes, they're going to make us confess. They want us to confess to what we posted on the forum. And then they'll choose. You did post on the Confession Room — right?'

Ryan nods then lifts his knees up to his chest again and rests his chin. 'What do they want you to confess?'

Emilia blinks slowly at him but doesn't speak. Maybe she won't tell him. If their confessions are going to be set against each other, she might not want him to know anything about it ahead of time. If they're going to choose between them, they can't be friends. They can't become attached. But that's what trauma does. Pain and suffering stitches souls together. It bonds people, in a way that nothing else will.

'I'm sorry,' he whispers. 'I know you might not want to tell me —'

'When my sister was killed,' she says in a rush, the words spilling out of her, 'I was on shift. I used to be a police officer. She called me. And I saw it but I didn't answer. I couldn't answer, you know, because I was at work. But then something came over the radio . . .' She sniffs, her voice breaking again. 'And I knew . . . even before I heard the address I knew it was her. And I was so

155

close. We raced the whole way, blue lights on. But . . . it was too late. He was gone, and she . . . she was gone too.' She lifts her fingers to cover her face, pressing the heels of her hands into her eyes. 'If I'd just fucking answered the phone, I would have been there. I would have made it in time. I would have scared him off and she'd still be here. And I . . . I . . .'

She stops speaking, her chest heaving up and down with the effort to control her emotion. What is she choosing not to say? He sighs. She'd loved her sister so much. And he had loved his girlfriend.

That's how they've got to this very moment.

Love led them here.

'So yes. That's the confession I posted,' she says, lowering her hands from her eyes, and blinking tearily over at Ryan. 'That's why they chose me . . .'

She rests her chin on top of her knees and sighs heavily, exhausted, as though recounting that story has taken everything from her.

'Why are you here?' she whispers, breaking the silence.

Ryan stares at her, his chin trembling as emotion floods through him, the current growing stronger and stronger.

'So basically, I . . . I had a girlfriend and it . . . it ended. And I wasn't kind. I did hurtful things. I just hated myself because she couldn't love me.'

She frowns, nodding, as though she is waiting for him to continue. But he says nothing. He simply stares into the empty space before him, lost in a memory.

'But . . . how does that end up with you being here?' she asks, her tone incredulous. 'I read some terrible stuff on that forum. You don't deserve to be here. Why choose you over anyone else?'

He sighs, his shoulders lifting. 'I honestly don't know. But the same could be said for you. It wasn't your fault that you didn't answer your sister's calls. It wasn't your fault.'

'What was your girlfriend's name?' Emilia whispers, quickly wiping the tears away.

Ryan glances down at the photograph which is discarded face-down next to him. He retrieves it, taking in her beautiful face, then clutches it to his chest.

'Fi-Fiona. I . . . I really loved her.'

She offers him a small, sad smile. 'Well, if it's any comfort, if it's my confession against yours, I think mine wins. Or loses, I guess. Depending on how you look at it.' Her smile disappears as quickly as it arrived, replaced by a melancholy frown.

They descend once again into silence, a silence which is already oddly comfortable. Even with the palpable fear in the atmosphere, they are not strangers any more.

Ryan glances back at her. She has drawn her ankle up and is tugging at the chain. She grits her teeth, he can hear them grinding against each other from across the room, and snarls as she tries to force the chain over the heel of her foot.

'I've tried that,' he calls out. 'You can't get it off.'

She throws a glance at him before she is able to lose the anger in her eyes.

'I'm sorry, but it's true,' he continues. 'And even if you managed to get that chain off – what do you expect to happen? The door is locked. It's bolted from the outside, I heard it when they dragged you in here. We have no idea where we are, so even if you got through the door, your chances of escaping are next to zero. We know they have weapons. And . . . we're being watched.' He gestures up to the camera. 'You get that chain off, all that's going to happen is they're going to come barrelling straight into this room and stop you.'

She lets go of the chain, her furious fingers falling still, her hands dropping down to her sides, her knuckles knocking against the floor. She hangs her head, her hair falling forward and shrouding her face.

'I . . . I can't die in here,' she whispers. 'I can't —'

'I know. I'm scared too.'

She lifts her chin to look at him, her face crumpled with emotion. 'I wasn't thinking about me being scared. I was thinking about . . . about my parents.'

'Oh.'

She rubs at the tip of her nose which has turned red. 'They won't survive this. I know they won't. Not another daughter. Not like this.' She breathes in, a jagged, rasping inhale.

'I'm sorry, Emilia. I . . .'

He falls quiet. He doesn't know what to say.

He shuffles sideways, his chain clanking on the floor as he drags it beside him. He reaches the centre of the wall, as far as his chain will allow him to go, and stretches his hand out to where hers is resting on the floor, and covers her fingers with his own. She flinches but doesn't move away.

'I'm sorry for everything,' he whispers. *Breathe*. 'I'm sorry for what happened to your sister. I'm sorry this is happening to you.'

He waits for a response. A nod, a word. Anything.

She clasps his hand in hers, their fingers interlacing.

There it is – shared trauma. The unequivocal bond.

'I'm sorry for you too.'

All he can do is nod. There's nothing else he can say.

'How about you?' she asks. 'Are you close with your parents?'

Ryan clears his throat. 'Um, it's just me and my mum. My dad, uh, left when I was little. And I've been living at home for a while and it hasn't been easy. Living with your mum as a grown man, it's . . . it's tough.'

'That's hard, I get it.'

'To be honest, I . . .' He pauses, surprised at his urge to be open. But what if she's the last person he ever speaks to? What if this is one of the last conversations he has? 'To be honest, I've been an absolute arsehole. To her.'

'Really?'

'Yeah, I just . . . it's fucking difficult because she wants to treat me as if I'm still a child, still her little boy, but I'm not. You grow up, you grow away from your parents, and they will only ever really know the person that you were before you left them. Right?' He turns his head to look at her, and she is nodding but her face is blank. 'Just me?'

She shrugs. 'Just you, sorry. My parents know me. At least, they did until Sophie died. But I think a lot of people must feel that way. And I'm sure your mum would understand. You could talk to her.'

He sighs. 'If I get out of here maybe I will.'

They both freeze, their eyes locked together, their hands still holding on, as reality hits once again. Will they both be killed? Or will one of them survive?

A loud, long tone blares out and the speaker crackles into life.

'Welcome to the Confession Room,' a distorted voice says.

Emilia gasps, and her fingers fly up to her face.

'You both made confessions on the forum. Confessions that you intended to always keep anonymous. But you don't deserve to keep your secrets.'

'Please!' Emilia cries, standing to her feet. 'We don't deserve this!'

'It is time,' the voice continues. 'The countdown on the screen above you is how long you have. You will each have your chance. And you must speak. If you attempt to remain silent, you will die.'

'Ryan Kirkland.'

He freezes. The sound of that voice speaking his name turns his stomach. He can't move, he can't stand like Emilia – it's as though he's sinking, their words pushing him down, down, down.

'You are first.'

'You have sixty seconds.'

'Please!' he cries out desperately.

There is a pause, the only sound in the room the crackling of the speaker and their fast, helpless breaths. Then that loud, long tone sounds again and they both gasp in horror as the numbers, which until now have been ominously frozen, begin to fall.

'Make your confession.'

Emilia

3:15 a.m.

00:59

The numbers tick down.

00:58

'Ryan,' Emilia whispers, her throat tight, her eyes stinging.

I can't do this. I'm not ready.

And he isn't ready either. He is just staring straight up at the countdown, jaw slack, watching the seconds as they disappear.

00:57

'Ryan. Say something.'

She reaches out to him. The chain pulls at her ankle but she manages to grip his shoulder.

'Ryan!' she shouts, shaking him roughly. 'Speak! You need to confess –'

'Emilia, I don't know what they want from me. I don't know why I'm here!'

'You can't stay quiet, you heard what they said! You're running out of time!'

She glances at the countdown –

00:35

'You should want me to stay quiet,' he shouts. 'If I stay quiet, they'll kill me and you'll live.'

161

Emotion swells over her in a wave, high above her head. She's lived all this time feeling as though her sister died when she should have lived. She can't have another person's life on her conscience. Not like this. Not even a stranger. It has to be their choice. Their choice — not because of her.

'We have no idea if these rules mean anything!' she cries. 'They could come in here and blast both our brains out but you're not giving yourself even the smallest chance! And I won't be able to live with myself if I survive by default. Please, just say something.'

00:12

He drops his head, his shoulders curling forward.

'You've only got ten seconds!'

Please —

00:10

'When my girlfriend broke up with me, I . . . I spiralled. And for the first time ever, I thought about hurting her. Only for a moment. I didn't mean it. And I'm sorry.'

00:01

He lets out a juddering breath.

He's done it.

00:00

The numbers climb rapidly back up, stopping again at sixty seconds.

Now it's Emilia's turn.

And then they will decide.

She braces herself, both of them staring upwards at the countdown, their heavy, panting breaths puncturing the silence.

The speaker crackles.

'Emilia Haines. You have sixty seconds. Make your confession.'

00:59

Emilia swallows, her mouth suddenly dry, her throat hoarse and tight.

00:51

'My sister was killed just over a year ago,' she stammers, licking her lips. 'I was at work and ignored her phone calls – if I'd answered maybe she would have survived. I've always blamed myself. I've always believed that it's my fault she's dead.'

She blinks up at the camera, waiting for the countdown to freeze. But it continues to drop.

What do they want from her? Do they want her to say it all? Even the part that she didn't mean about wanting the killer dead? Or maybe they always let it run down to zero, their torture extending until the very last moment.

00:39

'The man who hasn't been found. The police haven't been able to find him and he got away with what he did. I . . . sometimes – when I'm at my angriest, at my saddest . . . I wish that he was dead.'

00:22

She watches desperately as the seconds carry on falling away, time ticking relentlessly onward.

00:09

'I can't say anything else! What more do you want from me?'

00:03

00:02

00:01

She gasps, her heart hammering against her ribcage.

00:00

Emilia's head drops forward, her shoulders shaking.

'What happens now?' Ryan cries out. 'How do they choose?'

'Ryan, look at me,' she says, keeping her voice calm but his cries continue. 'Look at me!'

He freezes, his eyes round and childlike, searching hers for reassurance.

'Stay strong,' she whispers. 'Don't let yourself spiral.'

He nods quickly then closes his eyes, his shoulders rising and falling as he tries to regain control of his panicked breaths.

Emilia tears her eyes away from him and stares up at the camera, bracing herself for the crackle of the speaker and the sound of one of their names.

But instead, another noise breaks through.

Metal on metal.

The lock on the door sliding away.

Ryan

3:16 a.m.

The door swings open and they both back away, retreating to the wall.

The room suddenly feels different – the undercurrent of fear transforming into full-blown terror. The two people who dragged Emilia into the room are standing in the doorway, their masked faces peering in at them eerily.

'Please let us go,' Emilia says, her voice strangely steady, her eyes wide and pleading. 'We both have families who need us. You can just let us go.' She is fawning, doing everything she can to pander to their emotions.

But they say nothing. Instead, they simply step into the room and walk towards Emilia.

'Emilia,' a woman's voice says, standing in front of her. 'It's time for you to open your second box.'

Her second box. The box they couldn't open.

The other person walks over and pulls a key out of their pocket. They hand it to Emilia.

'Your fate lies in this box,' they say, their voice a low rumble. A man.

She hesitates just for a moment, meeting his gaze defiantly, before pushing the key into the lock with shaking hands.

It clicks.

Ryan strains his neck, trying to see inside. But he can't. All he can see is Emilia's face, her eyes widening, her face growing pale with terror. She whimpers, her attempt at bravery crumbling as her knees collapse beneath her and she cowers away from them.

'No, please! I don't want to die,' she cries. 'I'm not ready! I don't want to die!'

The woman stands, the box still in her hands, and suddenly he can see what was inside, in this room with them all along.

A gun.

Black matt metal. Deadly.

Emilia is the one who is going to die. Did they know they'd choose her all along? The man and woman swap places: she backs away to stand above Emilia, and he crouches down. She kicks out, terrified, but he ignores her as he reaches forward and releases her from her chain. He hoists her to her feet. She tries to collapse to the ground, making herself a dead weight, but he drags her up, her legs kicking out helplessly beneath her.

'No! Fucking let me go,' she screams, her voice now fuelled with anger. 'Let me go!'

He holds on to her, his muscular arms wrapped around her from behind, preventing her from hitting out. Ryan stares, unable to do anything as she kicks and cries, her movements growing slower and slower until her limbs finally go slack with exhaustion.

The woman pulls the gun out of its case, the black metal glinting in the fluorescent light.

Emilia whimpers.

The man releases her and she gasps, her body shocked by the sudden absence of restraints.

What . . . what's happening?

'Emilia,' the woman whispers.

Her voice sends a cold rush of fear up Ryan's spine – her voice has changed. No longer harsh, and full of menace. It is now soft. Kind.

'Emilia, you don't need to worry.' She lifts Emilia's hands out in front of her and places the gun in her grasp.

No. No no no no no.

The man strides towards Ryan and reaches for his chain, tugging him violently back towards the wall. Not loosening his binds – tightening them. The lock clicks into place. His leg is now fixed to the steel loop, only a length of an inch or so between him and the wall.

He and Emilia lock eyes, their mouths open in horror, until she breaks away to gawp at the gun held tightly in her hands.

'You're not here to die, Emilia,' the woman says. 'You're here to live. You're here for a very specific reason.'

The man steps towards her. 'You're here to kill him.'

Emilia

Emilia grips the gun, her fingers slick with sweat.

The man's face is inches away, his eyes wide and insistent. She breaks away from his gaze to look at Ryan. He is trapped, cornered, pulled against the wall.

'Don't look at him, Emilia,' the woman says. 'Look at us.'

'What the hell is going on?' Emilia mutters. Her voice sounds strange, as though it isn't her own. It's as if she's floating out of her body, watching the perverse scene as it unfolds. The two of them gathered around her, Ryan cowering in the corner, her – gripping the gun.

'You haven't been brought here to be a victim, Emilia,' the man says. 'It was never intended for you to be a victim. You were never in danger. You were brought here for one purpose, and one purpose only. To kill Ryan Kirkland.'

'I don't understand.'

'That's how the Confession Room works,' the woman says simply. 'Two people are named. One is meant to be a victim, the other is meant to be a killer. There *is* no choice.'

Everyone thought there were two potential victims, that they were deciding who should die but . . . it's been predetermined all along. They've always known who would live and who would die. But what happened with Luca and Hayley?

Her eyes flitter back to Ryan, his face full of despair. He shakes his head.

She can't do this. They can't make her do this –

She lifts the gun quickly, aiming it directly at the man's forehead.

'Emilia, don't be stupid,' the woman says calmly. Emilia glances sideways at her – she has pulled a gun out from somewhere. Something hard presses into her stomach. The man has a gun as well, and it is pushing into her abdomen.

'Lower it,' he commands. 'Now.'

Her arm shakes, hand trembling. She can't –

'Your weapon only has one bullet,' the woman says. 'Ours have full barrels. If you shoot one of us, you'll both be dead.'

A cry bursts out of Emilia and she drops her arm.

The man sighs, as if a gun being aimed at his face was just a mild inconvenience.

'Soon your countdown will begin –'

'My countdown?' Emilia interrupts, her face stinging with tears which have begun to fall in hot streaks. 'I've already confessed!'

'No ... this countdown isn't for confession. This countdown is for justice. The timer will begin and you will have sixty seconds to kill Ryan.'

'I'm not a murderer.'

'Neither were the others when they walked in here,' the woman says, one side of her mouth curling upwards in an eerie smile. 'But they are now.'

'I can't kill a person!' Emilia shouts. 'I don't want to do this –'

'This is exactly what you wanted.'

'What are you talking about? No, it isn't!'

'Hayley James posted on the forum that she was cheating on her boyfriend, Luca Franco,' the woman says. 'She complained that he had changed ever since he had become consumed with online discourse around women knowing their place and serving their partners, and that they owed them. She said that sometimes she felt so angry she could kill him.'

'But –'

'And Isabella Santos confessed about her ex-partner. He was abusive. Controlling. She wanted him out of her life. And Joseph Henley? His brother was an incel – a young boy slowly being radicalized in a way that he couldn't understand. His best friend was becoming someone else, a horrible person – resentful and bitter. He said that he felt guilty that sometimes he wished Freddie was just gone.' She shrugs. 'You all asked for this.'

'That's ridiculous!' Emilia cries. 'It's a turn of phrase, it's the way people speak! None of us actually wanted this!'

'We disagree,' the man says gruffly.

'This is madness! I'm not a killer. I can't just kill a stranger –'

The man cocks his head sideways then steps out of her sightline, allowing her to stare straight at Ryan. 'He isn't a stranger.'

'Y-yes, he is.'

'He might be a stranger to you. But you certainly aren't a stranger to him.'

She tears her eyes away from the man and stares at

Ryan, her eyebrows raised. He shakes his head, his eyes pleading.

'I swear, Emilia,' he cries. 'I don't know what they're talking about.'

They're lying. They're saying anything they can to make her do their bidding. To turn her into a murderer while their hands remain clean.

'He doesn't know me,' she says, trying to keep her voice firm. 'He told me he doesn't know me.'

'Ryan,' the woman says, spinning away from Emilia to face him. He shrinks back further into his corner. 'Be truthful. Do you know this woman?'

'No!'

'Yes, you do. You knew who she was the moment she told you her name.'

'No! I didn't! I don't –'

'He's lying, Emilia,' the man says. 'He knows you. And you know him. You just didn't know his name. And you did ask for this – in your confession: *if I knew who he was, I'd kill him.*'

Emilia stops breathing, every muscle freezing.

'This is the man who killed your sister.'

Ryan

'What?' Ryan shouts, panic thundering through his heart.

Emilia has fallen completely still, her arm – the one holding the gun – falling down to her side.

'What are you talking about?' she whispers, her focus passing back and forth between the man and the woman.

'Emilia – they're lying!' Ryan cries.

The woman walks slowly towards Ryan, her stare dark and cold. He flinches as she reaches him. But she doesn't touch him. Instead, she bends down, reaching for the pages of his letter which are scattered on the floor by his feet. He watches, his jaw slack, nausea plummeting through him, as she scoops them up calmly, placing one on top of the other in a neat pile, then stands, and walks back towards Emilia.

'We first came across Usurper95 in the dark web. Great username, right? We saw him on a forum. Not a very nice forum. The kind of forum where men who are sick in the head all gather together and convince themselves that they are the sane ones. And that women – women who reject them – are the devil. And deserve to be punished. It's the same forum that Luca Franco used to visit.'

'I've never been on one of those forums!' Ryan shouts. 'You've mistaken me for someone else –'

'Are you really going to say that, given what I'm holding in my hands?' She holds up the first page of his letter.

'When we first set up the Confession Room we used to linger in these kinds of places – the dark depths of the internet,' the man says. 'We used to have fun finding out who these anonymous posters actually were. In real life. And they were always like Ryan – sad, lonely little men, sitting in their childhood bedroom or alone in a flat, wondering why nobody wanted to love them. Well, Usurper95 used to talk about a woman in the forums. He used to say that there was this woman who he liked to follow home. That he was obsessed with her and he was sure that this was the woman who would finally love him.'

'That wasn't me! I don't go on these forums. I'm not a fucking psychopath. You're the ones getting a thrill from being there!'

The man's gaze darts to the woman, glaring at her, his head shaking. But she isn't even looking his way. Even through the mask, Ryan can see her eyes watering, the sudden emotion shining out towards them in a blazing light.

'Our daughter was murdered by one of these kinds of men. She was just a child –'

'It isn't any of your business,' the man says, his tone level and cold. 'It just matters that we use those places to find bad people. And we found Ryan. Months after his various rants on the forum, came the post on the Confession Room. Same username. Of all the usernames that could come up, it was the same one. Usurper95. And the voice, the way it constructed sentences, the words it used – it sounded the same. All about a woman who he had pinned all his hopes on and had thought about hurting. But the confession scared us. What had brought him to post on the Confession Room? What had changed? Had he actually hurt her? So we did what we do – we found out who it was. And it was the man in this room. Ryan Kirkland.'

'Are we wrong?' the woman whispers.

Ryan shakes his head, his breath trapped in his throat. 'I made that confession but I didn't hurt anyone, and I didn't hurt Emilia's sister!'

'We needed to find out who the woman was. So . . . we hacked his computer,' the man continues, staring him dead in the face, his expression unwavering. 'You spend a lot of time on your computer, Ryan, but you don't seem to know all that much about how to properly delete your files. And . . . we found this.' He points towards the woman. She holds up the letter towards Ryan with a raised eyebrow. A taunt.

'Your letter,' she says. 'A letter that you wrote when you were planning on killing yourself. This letter was written just days after Emilia's sister Sophie was murdered.'

'I . . . uh, I –'

'What's your excuse now?'

Ryan blinks slowly, his eyes stinging with fear-fuelled tears. 'I don't know how you linked me to any of this, but you've got it wrong. It wasn't me. That timing . . . it's just coincidence.'

'Well, let's read the part of this letter that sparked our interest, shall we?' She clears her throat. 'Let's see . . . where is it? Ah, here . . . *I'm sorry for what happened to Fiona.*

I wish she could have loved me but she chose not to. Who's Fiona, Ryan?'

'Fiona is my ex-girlfriend. And I ... it isn't how it sounds. And she's got nothing to do with Emilia's sister.'

'My sister's name is Sophie,' Emilia whispers.

The man laughs, a horrifying cackle from deep inside his chest. 'Ryan, you are the worst of humankind. Even when faced with death, even knowing that we have concrete evidence, you still can't admit what you've done. If telling the truth now could save you, would you even do it?' He holds up his gun. 'Who is Fiona? Be honest. Emilia deserves the truth.'

Ryan blinks rapidly, his gaze veering from the sneering man to Emilia.

'I swear ... it wasn't me. No matter what they say, you have to believe me. Please –' He blinks across the room at Emilia, and tears spill from his eyes and down his face. He licks them away as they pool near his mouth. 'Fiona is my ex-girlfriend.'

The man shakes his head, rolling his eyes. 'Right,' he says. 'Enough lies. You want us to give her definitive proof? Fine.'

He turns to the woman and nods – a small but definite gesture. Her mouth turns upwards in a smirk, her eyes shining with an immediate understanding.

Emilia

The woman takes a few small steps towards Ryan and crouches down.

Emilia frowns. This can't be real. She stares at his face, her body shaking. Is this really the person who killed Sophie? Is this the man who upturned her entire world?

The woman stands, spinning around to face Emilia with a strange expression on her face. Happiness? Excitement? No . . . It's anticipation. She walks towards her, her arm extended, something held out between her fingers.

'Take it,' the woman whispers as she reaches her. 'There are hundreds just like it on his computer.'

Emilia reaches forward and takes it, but her stomach sinks before her mind is even able to process what is happening. As though her body knows, warning her of what is to come.

Because in her hand, grasped in her shaking fingers, is the photo of Sophie.

The same as the one that was in her first box. The photo she had never seen before. She turns to look back at her corner, to where the chain is discarded and the box is sitting there innocuously.

Her chest grows hot, fingers tingling as rage stirs, rasping in her lungs.

The photo that was inside her box is still lying there. And it's printed on paper – a copy of an original. The original which is now in her hands. Pocked with marks. Just like the photo Ryan was holding earlier.

It's the same one, the very same.

He had said that it was a photo of his girlfriend. She had imagined a picture of both of them, or of her smiling, laughing. Happy. The features of the girl blurred in her imagination. But all along, he was consumed by a photograph of Sophie. A photograph she didn't know was being taken. Her little sister, Sophie.

Her name is Fiona.

Fiona. Fi. Sophie.

Rage burns inside her, a blazing fire consuming all the oxygen in the room, and her hand, the one gripping the gun, shakes violently. How many signs had she ignored or missed because of where they were and what they were going through? Why had she trusted him?

Emilia lifts her chin. She raises her arm and aims the gun to his head.

Ryan

3:27 a.m.

Her eyes are wild and burning with fury. She has seen the photograph. She knows that he lied about not knowing who she was. She knows that he lied about Fiona. He lied to her face from the moment he met her, only revealing enough of the truth to keep her at a safe distance.

'You lied to me,' Emilia shouts, her voice cracking.

'But I –'

'You have hundreds of photos of her? You took this photo of her! She was talking about someone following her for months, and it was you all along! You sick fuck!'

'But I never hurt her! Never! I just used to watch her –'

'She was scared of you! And when she called the police, she said that there was a man in her house trying to hurt her!'

'That wasn't me!' Ryan cries, desperation seeping out of him. 'I swear! I'm sorry – I know it was wrong to lie, and I know it was wrong of me to hide knowing who you were, who your sister was, but I knew that if I told the truth, you would think it was me. And it wasn't, it wasn't!'

'What kind of sick person makes up a whole story around a stranger? You said she was your ex-girlfriend! You didn't know her! You even gave her a fake name – Fiona!'

'I know it sounds mad – it is mad – but in my head, she was mine! Until she was in the news, I thought that *was* her name. I never spoke to her, never approached her to find out who she actually was. One day, I heard a voice coming out of the house, shouting goodbye to her. They shouted, "Bye, Fi!", and I thought Fi was short for Fiona, that's all. So that's what I called her.'

Emilia's face crumples, the gun dropping down to her side. 'Fi . . . short for Sophie. I hardly ever called her that any more. It was from when . . . when we were kids.'

She begins to cry, hanging her head, her shoulders stooped and heavy.

'Emilia,' Ryan whispers. 'I'm so sorry. And I know it might be impossible to believe –'

'Don't listen to him, Emilia,' the woman snarls. 'Think of how much he's lied to you already –'

'Listen to me, please!'

'Enough!' shouts the man, his voice immediately dulled by the close ceiling and walls. 'Enough.' He walks quickly towards the door and leaves the room, disappearing into the darkness of whatever lies beyond.

Emilia

3:29 a.m.

Emilia can't breathe. She can't process anything. All that is registering is the horror in Ryan's eyes. The fury pulsating through her. And the gun in her hand.

After all this time, after everything that has happened, *this* is the man who killed her sister. There's no denying it, no believing his lies. Her fingers grip the barrel, her knuckles flashing white. She always wondered how she would react if she ever came face-to-face with him, but now that she is here, she is unable to feel anything. All her emotions are mutating into each other, rage transforming into hopelessness, then into sadness, anger, pity.

The man comes back through the door and Emilia inhales sharply at the sight of what's in his other hand. A camcorder. The videos of the other victims, the shaky hand-held footage, rushes through her mind. Their terrified voices, the gun emerging in front of the camera. The other person's desperate pleas. They weren't begging for the other person to be saved. They were begging not to have to kill someone.

'Why are you doing this?' she cries. 'Why didn't you just give the evidence you have against him to the police? He could have been in prison! My family and I could have had justice!'

The woman's eyes come alive with anger. 'You should know more than anyone why we do this, Emilia,' she shouts. 'The monster who took our daughter did it without thinking twice. Just like your Sophie. And the police did nothing. They did nothing!'

'They must have done something –'

'They arrested that boy, sure, but then they let him go. They set him free! Not enough evidence. And we were meant to simply get on with our lives? No. No! It should have been us who killed him –'

'Quiet –' the man mutters, glaring at her sideways.

'He shouldn't have been able to do it himself!'

'Quiet!'

The man's shout bounces around the room, his booming voice silencing them all, the only sound the low buzz of the countdown above them, and their frantic breathlessness.

'Right – the next part has some rules too,' he continues. 'Three, to be precise.' He snaps his fingers in front of Emilia's face and she jumps. 'Are you listening?'

'Rules,' she repeats, nodding.

'Number one: you have sixty seconds. If you use a bullet and it doesn't work, we'll reload the gun for you. One bullet at a time. Don't think that aiming elsewhere or trying to kill one of us instead will get you anywhere.'

The woman laughs through closed lips. 'Hayley James tried that. Didn't work out too well for her.'

'Was it you who killed Hayley?' Emilia whispers.

'She couldn't bring herself to do it. She couldn't kill Luca, even after everything he had become. She aimed up at the ceiling. And after we reloaded the gun, she just kept saying "no, no, no" the man says, mockingly. 'So after the timer ran out, we had to follow through. She had been told the rules.'

'Luca was found dead – that was you. Wasn't it?'

'He tried to attack us,' the man says bluntly. 'That brings us to rule number two. If you do not kill Ryan by the time the sixty seconds is up, we'll kill you instead. Set him free. If Luca had stayed calm, we would have let him go. But he tried to hurt us.'

'You'll let Ryan go?'

'Yup,' he says casually.

Emilia coughs, her mind racing.

'Why was Luca hidden? Everyone else has been left in plain sight, but you hid him –'

'Hayley was the one who deserved to be found. She didn't follow through, so she couldn't be trusted to live. But she deserved to be found. Luca didn't. It was sheer luck that someone discovered him.'

Emilia's throat stings. 'Why did you release Hayley's confession and not his?' she growls. 'After killing her, you had to humiliate her as well?'

The man laughs maniacally. 'You saw yourself how helpful it was for Luca to be missing, Emilia. Almost everyone believed that it was him who had murdered Hayley. And even after the confessions continued, people still believed it was him. Even the police. There are rules for you – there aren't rules for us. And as long as you follow our rules, you have nothing to worry about. And I think you will. Most humans have a very strong sense of self-preservation when it comes down to it.'

Emilia's head is pounding, her temples held in a vice.

She drops her chin forward, her neck rolling. If she just passed out now, would they kill her?

'And rule number three. If you say anything once we're filming during the countdown to try to make people aware of what's going on here – we will kill you. And it wouldn't help you. We'd just edit it out. Got it?'

She heaves, but all that comes out is bile, splashing messily on to the concrete at her feet. She presses her hand to her mouth, fingers splayed. 'Please don't do this,' she whimpers.

'You'll feel better for it, Emilia,' the woman says, as she grips her shoulders and ushers her closer to Ryan. She tries to resist but the woman presses the barrel of the gun into her spine. 'And do it quickly. Waiting for the last ten seconds won't make it any easier.' She steps forward, her body pressed against Emilia's back, her mouth close to her ear. 'Do it for your sister.'

The loud tone blares out and Emilia gasps, craning over her shoulder.

The countdown.

The numbers.

She wheels back around and Ryan is staring at her, pleading silently. He is so close to her now – just feet away. If she was to stretch up her arm, the gun would be within inches of his face. And the man is standing just off to his side, the camera pointed like an arrow at a target.

She can't do this. She'll have to live with it forever. The knowledge that someone is no longer here because of her.

00:41

She needs to say something.

But she can't. They'll kill her.

But if she refuses to shoot, they'll kill her anyway.

'This is wrong,' she cries.

The gun presses against her and she lets out a startled cry. It's no longer at the base of her spine. It's aiming at the back of her head.

00:21

She can't do this. She closes her eyes, tears continuing to fall down her face and on to the floor. If she kills him – will she have a life worth living?

Ryan

00:20

'Please,' he whispers. 'Don't do this.'

His words leave him in a breathless sigh, his tears heavy on his cheeks, fear freezing him to the spot. But something else begins to stir inside him.

Hope.

She is hesitating. Her hand is shaking as it grips the gun, her eyes dancing from him to the man and then around the room before flying back to him. She hasn't simply pulled the trigger. Which means she is thinking, no longer acting on blind anger-fuelled adrenalin.

She isn't going to do it.

And the clock is running down.

00:10

'Why?' she cries.

Ryan's whole body is pounding, his pulse vibrating through him. This feeling – this feeling is like nothing else. So close to death and yet so far. Because . . . she won't do it. Emilia won't do it. In just the short time he has known her, he has seen who she truly is. And she isn't a killer.

So when the time runs out – she'll die, and he'll be set free. He'll be the survivor. And nobody will ever know his connection to Sophie. Nobody will ever know.

'I swear it isn't true,' he says again.

Keep talking. Keep her frantically wondering. Wind down the clock. Be the survivor.

'I would never do something like that. I swear on my life!'

00:05

He meets her eye, and frowns. There's something there – something has shifted in her face. A look in her eye that wasn't there before.

Resolve.

She knows.

00:02

She has finally realized the truth.

But it wasn't his fault! It was her fault. Fiona. Sophie.

00:01

If she had just agreed to love him, she could have lived.

Emilia

The sound of the gun erupts.

Ryan's body is flung into the wall, his knees instantly buckling beneath him.

Emilia stares down at him, the world slow and blurry.

All that's left of him is a crumpled sack of bones and skin. Everything he was – son, friend – obsessed, deranged maniac – gone forever.

Because of her.

A man is gone because of her.

Her ears ring loudly and the room spins, the world suddenly off-kilter. Nothing will ever be the same again.

She drops to her knees but she can't tear her eyes away from him. Is this really the man who killed Sophie? What if she's killed an innocent person?

But he had a photograph of Sophie. A photo that he told Emilia was of his ex-girlfriend Fiona. He was her stalker – the person Sophie had been scared of all along. What other possible conclusion is there?

But even if he is her killer . . . did he deserve this?

Is *this* justice?

'Emilia?'

Her body jolts at the sound of her name. The man and the woman are both now standing above her, their faces shielded by their masks.

'Emilia,' the man repeats, clasping his hands in front of him, his gun no longer visible. She's no longer a threat. 'What happens next is very simple. As long as you do exactly what we say, you can go back to living your normal life without any consequences. And you get to fall asleep every night with the satisfaction that you rid the world of someone like Ryan Kirkland.'

'I won't be able to sleep at all,' she whispers. 'How will I live with myself?'

'If you hadn't done it, you would be dead now instead of him,' the woman mutters. 'Is that really what you believe is right? Do you truly think that his life was worth more than yours?'

Emilia lowers her head, her eyes drawn back to Ryan's body. Blood is spilling from the hole in his head, coating the floor, pooling around her fingers. She pulls her hands away and wipes them frantically on her jeans. But they are stained now. Always.

The man holds up a piece of thick black material. 'We are going to place this hood over your head and take you into another room while we clean up,' he says, his face full of disdain at the interruption. 'After we've cleaned up, we will take you and Ryan's body to a location where eventually you will be found, just like the others.'

Ryan's eyes are still open: wide and bright blue. But empty, now. All of the emotion, the hope, fear, the horror, the life – gone.

'Emilia!' The man claps his hands in front of her face and she startles, a lost animal, bewildered and alone. 'What I'm about to say is very important. You need to focus. When you are found, no matter who you speak to – the police, your parents, a fucking stranger in the street – you need to say the same thing. You do not remember anything about this place except it's a concrete room with a countdown. You both had to confess and then we chose who should die. These lies don't just protect us; they protect you. And we will be watching you. So if you try to reveal anything about either of us, or this place and what really happens here, we can really hurt you. So stay quiet, be the survivor. Get on with your life. And live with the satisfaction that you killed the man who murdered your sister and nobody ever needs to know it was you.'

Emilia closes her eyes, trying to shut them out, to shut out the room and the glare of the lights, and the metallic smell of blood that is permeating the air.

'And if we call on you, Emilia – and we will call on you – you will do as we ask. Understood?'

'I'm not doing anything for you,' she spits.

'The others have,' the woman whispers. 'How do you think we got into your house?'

Emilia's eyes fly open and she blinks up at them, not understanding. But then a voice echoes in her ears, innocent and sad.

'*Can I just quickly use your toilet?*'

That's what Isabella asked her, just after her mum had dropped her off for the vigil. Emilia had thought nothing of it. She didn't even watch to see where Isabella went. But when Emilia came home from the park that night, the back door was unlocked.

She helped them.

'Isabella didn't want to help us,' he says, reading her reaction. 'But she did, in the end. Like I said: when it comes down to it, humans have a strong sense of self-preservation. And a strong need to protect their loved ones.'

Emilia sucks in air through gritted teeth. 'What did you say?'

'You heard me correctly. Killing you isn't the worst we can do. We know who is most important to you. And we know where they live.'

'I don't believe you –'

'David and Marie Haines live at 153 Garrett Wood Road. Both retired, carrying out the same routine, day in, day out. It wouldn't be difficult.'

Emilia hangs her head, the weight of defeat, all too much.

'If you don't do exactly as we say, you know what will happen. And that will be on your conscience too.'

'Do you understand everything we have said?' the woman asks.

Emilia stares at the floor, her body numb against the concrete.

'Yes,' she whispers.

'And you'll do exactly as we said?'

Her vision blurs, the room glazing over.

I have no choice.

'Yes.'

He lunges towards her and she freezes. The hood rustles in his hands, the material rough against her skin, his breath hot against her face until finally –

The room disappears and she is alone in the dark.

They're letting her go. Setting her free.

Something wet and warm soaks her fingers again – Ryan's blood.

She will never escape this place.

After

'Guilt upon the conscience, like rust upon iron, both defiles and consumes it, gnawing and creeping into it, as that does which at last eats out the very heart and substance of the metal.'

Robert South

13th November, 5:40 a.m.

The door clicks and the hood is gone. Emilia blinks rapidly, the low light of the warm streetlamp seeming bright after the pure black of the inside of the hood. The man, his face shielded with a scarf and beanie, is standing at the open doors of the van, staring down at her.

She digs her heels into the floor of the van and shuffles backwards, away from him. But she knocks into Ryan's body, and she can't suppress the cry that finds its way out through her tightly pressed together lips. She tried to stay away from him during the journey, desperately avoided looking his way, not wanting to acknowledge that the man who had been in that room with her was now dead beside her. But they hadn't secured him to anything. She had shrieked when he slid towards her, his bare arms coming to rest against her bound hands. His skin already cold.

'Emilia,' the man says, his voice low. 'Do you know where you are?'

He steps to one side, allowing her a clear view out on to the road. She scans the street, taking in the details: the uniformly spaced speed bumps, the streetlamps, the detached houses set far back from the road. It is familiar. She knows this road. Squinting into the distance, her eyes widen as it finally clicks into place. There, on the main road, perpendicular to this one, is a police station. Not her old station, but a neighbouring one. They are leaving her not even two hundred metres away from a police station. And he is standing here, in unassailable quiet confidence, certain that they won't be caught. Not now. Not today.

'Yes,' she whispers.

He reaches inside his heavy coat and pulls out a pocket knife, the blade glinting in the stream of light from the glowing lamp to his side.

He reaches towards her and she flinches. His eyes glint. 'I'm not going to hurt you, Emilia.' He tugs on her legs, pulling her roughly towards him, her head knocking against the side of the van. 'I'm letting you go, remember?'

She resists the urge to kick him square in the chest, biting down on her back teeth. He smirks. 'I know what you want to do –'

'Quit playing with her,' the woman snaps from the front. 'It's time to get out of here.'

His nose scrunches with annoyance but he doesn't respond. Instead, he presses the blade of the knife against the rope that is binding Emilia's ankles together, and slices it away.

'Get out then,' he snarls.

Emilia glances sideways, unable to prevent herself from looking at Ryan's lifeless body one last time. Nausea curdles in her stomach.

'Don't look at him. Just get out.'

She slides forward, shuffling her feet in front of her until she reaches the open edge of the van, and drops down to the ground, her bare feet flinching from the frigid tarmac.

Her eyes dart around the road, up at the streetlamps, searching for cameras. The houses are set too far back from the road to capture anything if they have security, but —

'There's one camera — just up there,' the man says, pointing upwards to a post at the far end of the road. 'It doesn't work. Now: go.' He points down the road, towards the police station.

Emilia starts to walk. One step after another. Just focus on each foot: left, right, left, right. But she winces at the sound of something heavy being pulled across the van: Ryan's body. There is a loud thud. And she knows she shouldn't glance back — just keep walking — but she does, and there he is: Ryan, discarded on the pavement, only a short distance from somebody's front door. Just two hundred metres from the police station. His face covered in blood. His eyes still open.

Emilia's mouth trembles and she snaps her head to face forward.

The van's ignition growls.

And she can no longer hold herself back, no longer restrain her limbs which have been screaming at her to do one thing, and one thing alone:

Run.

Her feet fly beneath her, her footsteps slapping against the road. Tears sting her eyes and she lets out a sob, her cries growing with each passing streetlamp, the light blurring as it flashes above her. Her entire body is aching, wailing out with exhaustion. But she needs to keep going. She is so close now. The station is growing closer, like a brightly-shining beacon, guiding her back to safety.

And justice.

She could tell them everything.

She turns her head to look over her shoulder, her legs still pushing forward.

The van is creeping away, not revving or doing anything that might awaken a curious neighbour, or late-night observer.

Run, Emilia. Run faster.

Her muscles burning, her sobbing breaths taking exponentially more effort, she forces her feet to move faster. The rough road tears into her skin, but it doesn't matter. She'll be there before they can get away. She can alert the police before they have managed to get too far.

She reaches the gate to the station and ploughs into it, the metal slamming into her waist. Pushing it open, she looks over her shoulder again.

These lies don't just protect us; they protect you.

No – she mustn't listen to them. They need to be caught.

She reaches the covered porch and its opaque glass – just an arm's reach away from the door.

David and Marie Haines live at 153 Garrett Wood Road . . . It wouldn't be difficult.

She collapses to her knees, exhaustion finally too powerful to resist. Her body rocks sideways, her head slamming into the paving. She squints up at the glowing blue light of the station, her lip trembling in a mixture of cold and fear and shame.

Because she won't say a word.

13th November, 1 p.m.

Bleep. Bleep.

Emilia's eyes fly open to the sound of machines.

Where is she? What's happening?

Her arms flail outwards and she winces at a sharp pain in the crook of her elbow.

Is she back there? Did they change their minds?

Is she back in the Confession Room?

The ceiling spins and she squints upwards into the low light. She presses her fingers into what's beneath her, supporting her, and they disappear into fabric. Not concrete. Both soft and stiff, as if it's been bleached over and over again. Sheets.

Yes ... she remembers now. She's in hospital. The bleeping is the machine they're using to monitor her heart because it wouldn't stop racing. The sting in her arm is the drip they inserted to force fluids into her system.

I'm safe.

For now.

Soon enough they will call on her.

They.

No names, but their masked faces are now etched into her memory, like a scar that will never fade. She will never forget the look in their eyes, their self-righteous scorn, their absolute certainty that they were in the right. That what they were doing was somehow a force for good.

That it would bring her some kind of strange satisfaction. Closure . . . Justice.

Ryan's face appears suddenly, his eyes open like saucers brimming over with fear. Her stomach turns, guilt rushing up to sting the back of her throat. Guilt that she took his life. Guilt that in some small way, it does feel like justice.

'Emilia?'

A gentle voice comes from the door, which has been left ajar. She turns her head towards the voice and blinks slowly at the nurse peering in at her, a pitying smile on her lips.

'How are you feeling?'

'I'm . . . I'm okay.'

'Someone came to see you while you were sleeping. Ciaran Jones – he didn't want to wake you . . .'

'Ciaran was here?'

'Yes, sweetheart. He was so worried. I told him that you were okay, you just needed rest.'

Emilia nods slowly, blinking away tears. 'Thank you.'

'On another note – the police are here to speak to you . . . Shall I send them away? I wouldn't want to overwhelm you, especially after seeing your parents –'

'No, I . . . I'll speak to them now.'

'You sure?'

She nods.

The nurse turns swiftly away, disappearing behind the curtain. The door clicks shut.

Emilia bites down on her lip as panic fills her lungs.

She had hoped that this moment would come after more of a respite, but they are already here. They will have their questions. And she will have to lie. It had been bad enough lying to her parents – avoiding their careful questions and diverting the conversation to ask about Mimi and if she was okay. But this will be worse.

The door opens again, the air rushing outwards, and Detective Inspector Wild appears with another officer. What is Wild doing here? An Inspector conducting a first interview is unheard of. She must be desperate, acutely aware of all of the eyes on her, watching the murders go unsolved.

'Hello, Emilia,' Wild says, nodding her head. 'This is my colleague DS Brennan.' Brennan smiles politely, lifting his hand in an awkward half-wave. 'I know that it's very soon after you were found, but as you know, it's best if we speak to you as soon as possible. As long as you're comfortable to, of course.'

'Sure,' she mutters. Pushing herself up the hospital bed, the lumpy pillows crumple over each other uncomfortably behind her back.

'Okay . . . Can you tell us about when you were taken? We have the recording of the phone call between you and Ciaran Jones, but we'd love to hear your side.'

She clears her throat, taking a deep breath, then tells the full story, every detail of the abduction, preparing herself for the inevitable deception which is already beginning to tighten in her chest, her ribs squeezing her insides.

The image of the figure standing in her garden, staring straight at her, sends her pulse racing, her hands clammy as they grip the sheets. Was it the man or the woman? It must have been her – the person who grabbed her in the kitchen was too large, too strong.

'The next thing I knew, I was waking up in that room.'

'What happened when you woke up?'

'Ryan was there —'

'Did you recognize him?'

'No . . . I didn't know him.'

'Did he know you?'

Her stomach turns. 'No. He didn't know me . . . He told me he'd been there about an hour. We talked for a bit, trying to figure out if there was any connection between us. And then . . . I don't remember.'

Wild frowns, her brow falling low over her eyes. 'You don't remember?'

'It all happened so quickly. We confessed. They chose Ryan.' She closes her eyes again, unable to look at them. 'And they killed him.'

'Did you see their faces?'

Their features, exposed through the slits in the material, instantly appear in her mind. His blue eyes. Her cruel, downturned mouth.

'No. They were wearing masks.'

'We've all seen Ryan's confession in the video. He said that he was sorry for hurting his ex-girlfriend. Do you remember that?'

'Yes,' she whispers.

'We've been trying to ascertain whether the people who are taken to the Room are all people who have confessed something on the forum. Did you?'

She picks at the loose skin around her thumb. Isabella didn't give the police this piece of information . . . so why did she tell her at the vigil?

'This isn't an inquisition, Emilia,' Brennan says softly. 'You don't have to tell us what it was if you did. Just say yes or no so we can confirm.'

She meets his gaze. Nods.

They look across at each other, eyebrows raised, a small, inconspicuous nod – a piece of the puzzle slotting into place. Victims are being plucked from the forum itself. It isn't just a place for confession. It is a place for selection.

'After they shot Ryan, what did they do with you?' Wild asks.

'They placed a hood over my head and put me in the back of the van.'

'Can you remember anything about that journey?'

'No,' she lies.

'Any detail you can muster could really help us pinpoint where this room is –'

'I'm so sorry . . . I wish I could, but I don't remember.'

'Nothing? How long did it take? Did you –'

'With all due respect, Inspector Wild, have you pressured all the victims like this?' she snaps, her voice trembling. 'Or just me?'

Brennan goes to speak, but Wild holds her hand out, quieting him. 'Emilia, we really don't mean to pressure you. And I sincerely apologize if it's coming across that way, but I had just hoped that you might remember more details of the journey than the other survivors because you're a detective.'

'When you've been this close to death –' Emilia raises her fingers a centimetre apart, her face flushing, '– and have seen a man murdered just feet away from you, trust me when I say that your detective skills don't really kick in. The only instinct that kicks in is the one we all have – do anything you can to survive.'

'I understand,' Wild says. 'Please accept our apologies.'

Emilia pulls her knees up, hugging them close to her chest. 'I'm sorry, but I'm really tired. I need to rest.'

'Of course, we'll leave you to the hospital staff,' Wild says.

They both stand, the air thick with tension. 'Thank you, Ms Haines,' Brennan says in a low voice.

She nods and they turn away, striding quickly towards the door. But Wild pauses.

'If you remember anything about that journey – anything at all – it would be incredibly helpful.'

'I understand . . . thank you.'

The door closes behind them and she stares up at the ceiling, unable to breathe. Unable to move on from the past few minutes, from their demanding gazes and their questions. And all the answers she wasn't able to give.

14th November, 9 a.m.

The door opens, the familiar rooms waiting beyond. But Emilia can't move. She is stuck at the threshold, staring into her house which now feels like a place of danger instead of safety. This isn't her home any more. It is just the place where she was taken; where the back door was unlocked, and the Confession Room seeped in. How is she meant to just return to normal life? How is it that she can simply be discharged from the hospital, with the police telling her that the victim liaison will be in touch very soon? What is she supposed to do now?

'Are you okay, love?' Her mum grips her shoulder, frowning with concern.

Emilia nods quickly, desperately wanting to shrug her away. *Don't touch me*, she wants to cry. They want to help her, she knows that. But she just wants to be alone. She can't stand the feeling of guilt that is carving away at her from the inside out. She killed a man. A person who was out in the world, living his life just a couple of days ago, is now gone. So being alone would be easier. And she isn't scared . . . not for herself, not any more. After all, what can they do? Choose her again? As long as she keeps her mouth shut, her family won't come to any harm.

She stares down at her feet, takes a sharp breath and steps through the door. Exhaling slowly, she glances around.

There's nothing to be afraid of, as long as she sticks to their rules. She repeats this over and over in her mind as she shuffles towards the living room, wincing at the pain that is thrumming through her entire body, her bones aching.

She turns on to her side, her tired eyes gazing at her parents as they move about the kitchen, trying to busy themselves with something, anything. Her dad is making her a sandwich, focusing intently on spreading butter evenly across the bread, as if perfecting that will make all of her horror disappear. And her mum is staring down at the mug on the counter, her eyes empty as she stirs slowly, the steam rising up towards her face.

They place the sandwich and tea on the table in front of her, both watching as she sits up slowly.

'Thank you,' she whispers.

They sit down awkwardly either side of her, silence consuming the three of them. Emilia chokes down each mouthful – anything to keep them happy. Anything to prevent them asking any questions. With just a couple of mouthfuls left, she puts the plate down on the coffee table, the china ringing on the wood, the only sound in the whole house.

'Thank you,' she says again, smiling gratefully at both of them in turn even though she is having to make every effort not to be sick.

'Whatever you need,' her dad says. 'Anything. Anything at all.'

Emilia nods. 'Well . . . I think what I really need is to rest.'

'Of course,' her mum says. Her comfort phrase. 'You go and rest and we'll wait here.'

'I . . . I really did mean it when I said I'm fine on my own.'

'Emi darling, we wanted you to stay with us and we understand you don't want that, but we really aren't comfortable leaving you completely on your own –'

'I know you aren't. But there's no point in you being here. I'm going to go into my room and sleep for the next two days. I'm not in any danger –'

'How can you say that?' her mum cries. 'After what they did to you!'

'They let me go,' Emilia says simply. 'And nothing has happened to Isabella or Joseph. I'm safer than most other people now. I've already survived it. And Ciaran will be here really soon, he's coming this morning –'

'Emilia –'

'Dad, please.' She meets his gaze, firmly. Pleadingly. 'I know it must be difficult for you to understand, but I . . . I really just want to be alone.'

He sighs and stands. 'Okay –'

'David!' Her mum follows him, wringing her hands. 'We can't just leave her –'

'If it's what she wants, we will, Marie.' He cups her chin gently, his finger stroking her jaw. 'We can check on her all the time. Okay?'

Marie swallows, her eyes filling with tears. 'You call us the second you wake up, Emilia. Understand?'

'I understand, Mum. And you're sure you're okay to keep Mimi for a while? I just don't think I can take care of her at the moment –'

'Of course, love,' her mum says. 'Don't even think on it. We love having her. Now, come here.'

Emilia slowly rises to her feet and allows herself to be pulled into her mother's arms. 'I love you,' she whispers.

'We love you so much, Emi,' her dad says, pressing a kiss to the side of her head.

'Call us,' her mum says. 'We're just around the corner. Okay?'

'I'm going straight to sleep and when I wake up, I'll call you. I promise.'

The door clicks shut.

But Emilia does not act as promised. She does not go to her bedroom and collapse on to the bed. She does not drink her calming tea and lie down on the sofa, allowing her sleep-deprived eyes to finally give in and close. All that she will see if she closes her eyes is Ryan's face, that final moment when the realization that she was going to pull the trigger hit him.

Instead, she heads straight for her computer. Straight for the Confession Room.

She types her name into the search engine. If she had searched her name before, it only would have brought up her sister. But now those results have disappeared, replaced instead by countless articles tying her to the Confession Room forever.

THE NEXT SURVIVOR FOUND – BUT WHEN WILL THE CONFESSIONS END?

THE THIRD VICTIM OF THE CONFESSION ROOM FOUND – BUT NO PROGRESS MADE TO CAPTURE THE PERPETRATORS

EMILIA HAINES FOUND ALIVE, AND RYAN KIRKLAND: ANOTHER INNOCENT VICTIM OF THE CONFESSION ROOM

Emilia clicks on the last one, her eyes drawn to the word innocent. If only the world knew what he had done.

She scrolls down, wincing at the sight of their photos: both of them smiling at the camera, the pictures chosen by the media to show them at their happiest.

> Hundreds of flowers have been placed outside Ryan Kirkland's home where he lived with his mother, Pippa Kirkland.
>
> 'My son didn't deserve this,' said Pippa, clutching a photograph of Ryan. 'He was a good man who was just trying to live his life. He had so many friends and people who loved him. And they've taken him away. Whoever did this has to be caught. They need to pay.'

Emilia forces her eyes closed as guilt shudders through her. But along with the guilt there is a low hum of rage. Nobody knows what he is. Nobody knows what he's done. She can't even tell her parents. And no one will ever know. He has died a victim and the truth has died with him.

She clicks away from the article and slowly types out the address, tears blurring her vision as the forum loads.

Her phone rings and Jenny's name flashes across the screen. But Emilia ignores it, her eyes dancing instead over the page, taking in all the confessions, all the possible victims. And possible killers.

Who will be chosen next?

14th November, 11 a.m.

A rhythmic thud sounds from the door and Emilia gasps, her eyes flying away from the computer.

She tiptoes towards the closed curtains, peering out from behind a gap to try to see towards the front door. She hadn't been home an hour before the media arrived. They gathered on the pavement beyond her gate, staring up at the house, waiting for her to emerge. Emilia called the victim liaison officer but she said there's nothing they can do. Just ignore them.

'Emi, it's me,' a voice says.

She takes a calming breath, shaking out her trembling hands. There's nothing to be afraid of.

It's Ciaran.

She strides quickly towards the door, emotion already threatening to overwhelm her. She thought she would never see him again.

She opens it slightly and the journalists and photographers surge forward, trying to catch her attention, but he slips through the gap and then turns to push the door closed. As he wheels around his eyes instantly lock with hers. His face crumples with emotion.

He rushes towards her, his hands curling around her head and into her hair. She wraps her arms around him, her fingers pulling on the fabric of his thick jumper, tears soaking into the wool.

She pauses – his shoulders are rising and falling spasmodically.

'Ciaran . . . Ciaran, I'm okay.'

'Okay?' he whispers, his breath hot against her neck. 'How could you be okay? They took you, Emi. They took you, and I –'

'I know . . . but I promise. Everything's going to be okay. I'm here. I'm not injured. They . . .' She bites down hard on the inside of her cheek, internally bracing against the words she is about to whisper. 'They let me go.'

'I was so scared. I thought that I'd never be able to tell you . . .'

His voice trails away as he gulps down tears.

'Tell me what?' she whispers, moving away from his chest to stare at his face. He lifts his eyes to meet hers.

'I-I fucking love you.'

They stare at each other, the space between them completely and utterly still.

'You what?'

'I'm still in love with you, Emi. It's never gone away . . . I'm not sure it ever will.'

Silence fills the room, the air between them thick with anticipation.

They pause, their eyes meeting, filled with questions. Then he is kissing her frantically, and she breathes him in, her entire body tingling with emotion. Stumbling backwards, she reaches out her hand to feel for the wall, their lips never parting. Breathlessly, she breaks away from him and they race up the stairs, tumbling into her bedroom.

For a moment they pause, staring at each other's faces. He traces her mouth with his finger, and she is struck by the inevitability of this moment. This was always meant to happen. She was always meant to come back to him.

'I love you, Emi,' he whispers.

'I love you too.'

He kisses her again, and that brief moment of calm dissipates as their hands peel off each other's clothes. They gasp together, and she digs her nails into his back as he moves above her. She closes her eyes, blocking out the world, blocking out the guilt and horror at what she has done, blocking out everything that has happened or will happen. Right now, there is just him, his ragged breaths, his mouth on her neck, his lips whispering her name.

Right now nobody else exists.

They face each other in bed, their faces just a breath apart in the dark.

'Don't leave me again,' Ciaran whispers. 'I missed you so much.'

Emilia's chest tightens, her heart filling and breaking at the same time. There is so much that she wants to tell him. And so much she has to keep secret.

'Are you on shift tonight?' she whispers.

'No . . . I've just finished fourteen hours. I'm meant to be off for three days now, but if another confession comes I'll have to go in.'

She inches forward, her fingers digging into his back as she tries to be as close to him as she can, as though she will be able to disappear inside him. They settle into a comforting silence, his chest rising and falling with hers.

He lifts his head from her shoulder, his hands moving

to cup her face, his long fingers covering the span from her chin and up into her hairline. 'Do you want to talk about what happened?'

She sighs shakily. 'Ciaran, I . . . I just told the police everything I remember, and I want to talk to you about it, but not now.'

'Of course . . . I just . . . When they let you go . . . that journey back to the police station – what can you remember?'

Her expression shifts, and she feels her skin turn cold, even under the warm comfort of his touch. Has he spoken to Wild and Brennan? Did they tell him that she was reluctant to talk about what happened after they took her away from the Room?

'I don't remember anything.'

'There must be some detail –'

'Ciaran, I just told you I don't want to talk about any of this right now.' She reaches for his hand on her face, covering his fingers with her own. 'I just need you to be here with me.'

He pauses, his eyes searching her face. 'Of course. I'm here.' He pulls her towards him, his hand cupping the nape of her neck, under her hair, and leans his head against hers.

She closes her eyes, listening to the sound of his slow breathing, her runaway heartbeat calming as it regulates in rhythm with his.

'Is there really nothing you can remember?'

She freezes, the brief sense of calm dissipating instantly as anxiety and panic flood in.

'Ciaran, I need you to stop.'

'Emi, please —'

'No!' She pushes him away, shrinking away from his arms. 'All I needed from you right now, in this moment, is your friendship. Your love. Your support. Why can't you give me that? You know what I've been through!'

'Yes,' he says, pushing himself off the bed to stare down at her. 'Yes, I do know what you've been through. I was so desperate to catch these people before, you know I was. And now? Now that they took you and made you live through this, after everything you've already had to survive? I will catch whoever is doing this if it's the last thing I fucking do, and I'm sorry that I need to ask you, but I have to!'

'And I've told you, I don't remember!'

'Emi, you're the best detective I know. And I've seen you under pressure. I've seen you in dangerous situations. You don't freeze, you don't crumble . . . you switch on, everything heightened. More intelligent, more alert. When memory fails, use logic, that's what we've always said. You would remember something! Or you'd be able to piece it together! You've always been so good at that – the best!'

'Well, I don't remember. And I can't.' She looks up at him, her heart breaking as he stares at her aghast. 'I'm sorry. And I wish there was something more I could give you . . . But there isn't.'

He crouches down, his knees creaking as he lowers himself, his face now below hers. He reaches out, his thumb brushing across her bottom lip. 'Emi – what aren't you telling me?'

Her skin turns cold. He knows. He knows there's something wrong.

'Nothing,' she mutters. 'Can you . . . Can you get me some water, please?'

He stands, sniffing, his nose scrunching up in the way she has always loved. She tells Ciaran everything. She always has. But this? She can't tell him this.

He retreats, walking backwards, pausing at the door to raise one hand to point at his eye, then down to hover above his heart, then to point directly at her. Their old signal: *I love you.* He nods and turns away. His steps thud as he trots down the stairs.

She exhales, the tears that she has been suppressing streaming down her face in hot, angry streaks. But she isn't angry with Ciaran for pushing her when she begged him not to. She doesn't blame him. She would have done the same if their roles were reversed. And she can't blame the police. Not even Wild and her forceful questions. She blames herself. For everything she is not saying. For every bit of information and evidence that she is not giving them.

Ciaran reappears at the door, his brow lowering with concern as he takes in her tear-stained face.

'Are you okay? I'm so sorry I –'

'I'm just tired.'

'You go to sleep then,' he says, placing her water down beside her and climbing into bed, his arm wrapping around her waist. 'I love you.'

She nods and closes her eyes, listening to his breathing, in sync with hers, trying to focus on the feeling of his hands placed just so on her skin, the feeling she has missed for so long.

But she can't sleep. Not even with Ciaran's fingers gently tracing patterns on her back. Not even after his breathing slows, his eyelashes fluttering as he falls into his dreams.

She reaches across to her phone, her focus set on only one thing: the forum.

It shouldn't be long. Another confession is due now that she and Ryan have been found. And everybody knows it. There are thousands upon thousands of people logged on to the forum. Watching. Waiting.

And Emilia waits with them in the dark, horror turning her stomach over and over as she waits for the sound. If she had said something, if she had told the truth, might they be found? Could she have prevented this? Could she have saved two people from what is to come?

Emilia's hand flies to her mouth, her stomach turning as what they have all been waiting for finally comes.

The sound of the slamming of a door.

And two more names.

17th November, 10 a.m.

'The latest victims of the Confession Room murderers have been found in a warehouse in East London. Patrick Hose, a thirty-nine-year-old man from Oldham, was discovered by an early morning walker. Beside him, unconscious but alive, was twenty-two-year-old Rosie Johnson. Miss Johnson's family have asked for privacy at this difficult time and they will not be answering questions from the media –'

Emilia stabs the mute button on the remote then flings it across the room with a strangled cry.

The news reporter is still speaking, their mouth moving silently before cutting to images of each victim.

When will this end? When will the police piece it all together? How? The perpetrators are always so careful: hiding their faces, avoiding and disabling CCTV, covering every track that they have left an imprint on. Making the surviving victim keep their secrets.

Emilia throws up her arms to cover her face, her cheeks flushing as if the eyes of the world are upon her, heavy with judgement. If she had gone to the police straightaway, run inside that station without hesitation and told them every detail she could remember, if she'd told Ciaran the truth that night, maybe they would have found them by now. And two people's lives wouldn't have changed. Patrick Hose would still be alive.

What did he do for them to target him? She frowns. Does it matter? Whatever the reason, their twisted version of justice shouldn't be happening. They shouldn't be getting away with this. Yet they are. And they will. But when will they call on her? When will they make her keep to her promise?

Her parents drop round every day, her dad sitting awkwardly on the sofa, waiting for Emilia to speak, her mum finding any small job to do around the house, anything that will allow her to linger, watching Emilia closely.

Emilia sits up abruptly, the words of Rosie's family ringing insistently, a bell repeating its pattern over and over. *They will not be answering questions . . .*

It's the same answer given by them all. The same rule drilled into them before they are set free: *You do not remember anything. If you say a word, there will be repercussions.* Emilia has never felt more alone. But . . . in truth, she is not alone. The surviving victims have all lived through the same thing, all reiterating the same lie in order to keep the truth hidden. But maybe if they all spoke up, they might be believed. The killers can't target all of their loved ones at the same time, and the police could protect them. If they warned their families and then told the truth, they would be kept safe.

A tear runs down Emilia's face as she faces the possibility that until now she hadn't allowed herself to consider.

If they all spoke up, maybe they could bring this to an end.

Emilia glances over her shoulder, fear almost paralysing her as she stares down the long road which is quiet. But not peaceful. A strange tension hangs in the air, the same tension that vibrates in the atmosphere of her home. A signal that something terrible happened here. Something violent.

She hasn't left the house since she returned home. She has been too frightened, felt too watched. But now she is here, on Isabella's road. The last time she was here, she was nothing more than an online sleuth, trying to uncover the truth of a case. Abandoning her own job to investigate another — a job she's not sure she'll ever be able to go back to. And now, she is part of the very fabric of the Confession Room. When true crime aficionados talk about this case in the future, they will speak her name.

Emilia steps forward, bracing herself, and knocks firmly on the door.

The house remains silent. There is no movement in the hallway, no voices bellowing for someone to answer the door. Emilia glances up at the two windows at the top of the building, both shielded with thin white shades. She squints — was that . . . ?

Yes — there, at the window, peeking through a small gap to the side of the curtain, is Isabella.

She gives a little wave. Isabella disappears, the curtain closing abruptly.

Emilia knocks again, even louder this time. They need to speak. They need to acknowledge what is happening, what they're both being forced to suffer.

'Isabella?' she calls out, craning her neck again to check the road. It is still quiet. 'Can we talk, please?'

The door jolts open. But it isn't her peering through the small gap. It's an older woman, a woman Emilia recognizes from the car on the day of the vigil, and from the news. Isabella's mother.

'I'm sorry, but Isabella doesn't want to talk to anyone about what happened. Not any more.'

Emilia steps back, down one step, away from the door. But her eyes shift up to the window. There she is again, peering down. She must be just at the top of the stairs. Listening. Hearing everything.

'I just really hope she's okay.' She pauses, meeting Melanie's eyes with a small, sad smile. 'I've been having dreams – nightmares – but I think they're actually memories. I'm thinking of going to the police and –'

Emilia stops at the sound of footsteps, thundering down the stairs. Isabella appears, flying around the corner and coming to a standstill behind her mum, her hair falling in her face. Breathless.

'Mum, it's okay,' she says, placing a hand on Melanie's shoulder. 'I can speak to Emilia.'

Melanie swings around, her brow furrowed. 'Darlin', I don't think that's a good idea –'

'I know her, Mum, don't I? It's fine.'

Isabella meets Emilia's eye and forces out a smile. But as Melanie turns back to face Emilia, her back to her daughter, Isabella's eyes harden.

'Okay . . .' Melanie steps backwards, allowing the door to swing towards her. 'Come in, Emilia.'

'No, Mum – it's okay,' Isabella says hurriedly, reaching around her to grab a coat that is hanging behind the door. 'We'll go for a walk.'

'Isabella –'

'It'll be good for me. I need some air.'

She places a quick kiss on her mum's cheek and then stalks out of the house, hooking her arm through Emilia's and tugging her away down the path to the pavement.

They remain silent as they walk down the road. But as soon as they turn the corner, away from Melanie's watchful gaze, Isabella grabs Emilia by the scruff of her coat, her eyes gleaming with anger.

'What the fuck do you think you're doing?' she growls.

Emilia's mouth sets in a hard line, her eyes also turning cold. 'We need to talk.'

'There's nothing for us to talk about –'

'You know exactly what we need to talk about. We need to talk about what we're going to do. We need to talk about what we know!'

'I know nothing.' Isabella releases Emilia, her hands dropping to her sides in curled fists, scuffing her boot against the ground, the sole scraping rhythmically against the stone.

'How can you just act like I don't know what happened to you in that room? As if I haven't just been through the same thing –'

'Lower your voice,' Isabella snarls.

'As if I didn't do what you did!'

'Please stop!'

The words die on Emilia's tongue as Isabella lifts her hands to cover her face.

'Isabella, I –'

'Why are you doing this?' she whispers. 'Why are you dragging me into whatever you think you need to do to forgive yourself?'

'People will keep dying if we don't do something! We

have no idea how long it will take for them to make a mistake or for the police to find them. We can't just let this carry on! And if we spoke up together, we could just –'

'Maybe they deserve it.'

Emilia falls still, the tips of her fingers still tingling with adrenalin, but her mind stalling at Isabella's words. The very words that have been quietly echoing inside her as much as she has tried to block them out. Maybe Ryan deserved it.

'You . . . You don't mean that.'

'I do.' Isabella shrugs. 'You didn't even know yours. Why do you care? He did something horrible and now he's gone. Now he will never be able to hurt anyone again. They aren't choosing innocent people. Gregory . . . he was a monster. He hurt me more times than I can count. And he would have carried on doing it. They deserved it –'

'Did I deserve it?'

Isabella stalls, her face turning blank, eyes empty and mouth open, as if her mind is buffering, analysing what has been said and what it implies.

'Did I deserve to be put in that room and forced to kill someone?'

'I don't –'

'You helped them.' Emilia's eyes sting as the memory floods through her: the woman standing in the garden, staring at her through the darkness. The unlocked back door. 'Did I deserve that?'

'Emilia, I –'

'I helped you. I found you. You begged me to take you to the vigil and I did because I thought it was important. And you . . . you tricked me.'

'Pretty soon they'll ask you to do something too –'

'And I'm terrified! I don't know what they'll ask me to do, but I don't know how I'll be able to do it. The thought of helping them kill another person –.'

'I know. I felt the same. But you know that you don't have a choice. You know how dangerous these people are. It was the last thing I wanted to do. And I tried to warn you. That's why I told you they were choosing their victims from the forum itself. I felt sick knowing that I was part of the reason you were there. Especially when . . .'

Emilia narrows her eyes. 'Especially when . . . what?'

Isabella tilts her head, her chin lifting up towards the grey sky. 'I didn't think you'd do it. An ex-police officer . . . I didn't think you'd be able to do it.'

'So you thought unlocking my door was a death sentence –'

'That isn't fair –'

'And you still did it!'

'My family don't deserve to be killed instead of a stranger!'

Silence covers them, a low-hanging cloud, smothering them with pressure.

'I know that what I did was wrong,' Isabella says, meeting Emilia's eyes with a desperate plea in her gaze. 'But they said that if I didn't do it, they would come to my house and take my younger brother.' Her lip trembles. 'He's only fourteen, he's just a baby. He doesn't deserve that. Not to save someone I don't know. Not even someone who helped me. I'm sorry. I have to protect my family. I'll do anything.'

'Listen,' Emilia says, reaching out to touch Isabella's

hand. She winces. 'I know that you felt like you didn't have a choice. Like you don't have a choice now. But if we reached out to Joseph Henley and the three of us told the truth together, maybe we could stop them. And the police would protect our families.'

Isabella pauses, staring at Emilia through wide eyes, like a lost child. Emilia's heart begins to lift: maybe she's getting through to her. Maybe this is it –

But, no. Isabella begins to shake her head, slowly, resolutely.

'I can't do that.' Her face crumples as she tries not to cry. 'I just can't. What if they hurt your parents? Could you live with that guilt?'

Emilia's stomach drops. 'I –'

'We need to stay quiet, and eventually the police will find them, or they'll stop.'

'You think they're going to stop?'

'They can't go on forever.'

'Isabella, I –'

'Please just think about what you're asking me to do. What you'll be asking Joseph to do. They gave us instructions. There are rules.'

Emilia steps backwards, away from Isabella, away from her panicked stare.

'What if I do it on my own?'

'If you do it on your own, you'll be making that choice for all of us. That isn't your choice to make. And you'll be putting our families in danger.'

'No, I –'

'I've kept quiet this whole time,' Isabella continues. 'I've done what they've asked. Joseph Henley killed his own brother. You're going to ask him to risk the truth coming out? We've all got a reason for wanting the other person dead, right? And my confession . . . I said I would kill him if he ever touched me again. If they release that and the footage of me doing it, what's your expert opinion? The police are just going to let me go?'

Emilia doesn't say a word, her mind scrambling for answers to an unanswerable riddle.

'And your guy. Ryan Kirkland. He said he hurt his ex-girlfriend. Was that you? Someone you knew?'

'No.' Tears stream down Emilia's face. She wipes them away with the back of her hand, her skin stinging in the cold air.

'So what? Who was he?'

Emilia shakes her head, her hands lifting to cover her ears as anxiety swells in her chest.

'Who was he, Emilia? What did he do?'

'They said he killed my sister!'

Isabella covers her mouth, her fingers splayed in horror. 'What?'

'My sister was murdered. About a year ago by a stalker. They never found him. And . . . they said it was him. They had evidence and I . . .' Her voice fades away, her words strangled.

'And what was your confession? Did you confess to wanting to kill him?'

Emilia desperately tries to clear the lump that is stuck at the back of her throat. 'I said . . . I said that if I ever found out who did it, I would kill him.'

She meets Isabella's gaze, and there is an expression in her eyes, a heady mix of sadness and satisfaction.

'That's one hell of a motive . . . Right?'

Emilia hangs her head. Isabella is right.

'I won't say anything,' she whispers, the words hanging in the air.

'Thank you.' Isabella reaches for her, pulling her into a tight hug.

Isabella lets her go and slowly backs away, holding her gaze for a few steps before she swings around and hurries back towards her house, turning the corner and disappearing from sight without looking back.

Emilia stands paralysed, suspended in the moment. The moment she decided that to lie was better than to tell the truth. The moment she decided that the lives of the survivors and their families were more important than the lives of any more victims.

The moment she realized that the Confession Room had manoeuvred them all into an impossible situation, too frightened to make the first move. They had been playing chess, thinking three steps ahead while the victims could only consider what was directly in front of them.

And here she was, unable to move. Defeated.

Checkmate.

19th November, 5:45 p.m.

The crack in Emilia's ceiling is bigger than it was before.

She narrows her eyes, squinting up at it from her position on the sofa – flat on her back, her hands clasped over her chest.

In the old house, the one she shared with Sophie, there had been something similar. 'We should get Dad to come and fill that crack,' Sophie would say, glancing sideways up at it. 'So why don't you ask him?' Emilia would respond, to which Sophie would flash back a wry smile. 'Maybe I will,' she always replied. They both knew that Sophie would never do it. Small tasks like that would just pass her by – Sophie was big-picture focused. A dreamer. It was Emilia who pondered over details. Maybe that's why Sophie knew so little about the man who was following her, because even when it was important, her mind simply couldn't take in the detail.

But now, here, where she lives alone, it's as though her house is cracking open, pulling itself apart knowing what she has done. She tries to force him from her mind but he is always there. Ryan. His reassurance and kind words when she first woke up in the Room. His fear. But then Sophie appears and she is overcome with anger. With righteous justification. But then just as quickly as it arrived, it shatters. How can she justify what she did? How can she even attempt to convince herself that her killing him has made anything better?

The phone rings loudly, the jaunty tone setting her on edge. The night she was taken to the Confession Room it had rung over and over, the string of notes underscoring her horror. She needs to change it. Anything else will do. Anything but that fucking tune.

Emilia turns on to her side, reaching her arm awkwardly over her head to stretch towards the side table. The tips of her fingers brush against the phone and it tips, clattering to the floor.

'Oh, fuck off,' Emilia mutters. She sits up and reaches down for it, her heart lifting at the sight of his name.

'Ciaran, hi,' she whispers.

'How are you feeling? Did you sleep well last night? I'm so sorry I've been so busy again.'

'It's okay. I know it's important.'

'Did you get my package yesterday?'

Emilia's eyes slide over to the hamper she found on her front doorstep: flowers, her favourite chocolates, trashy magazines.

'Yes.'

'God, I miss you.'

Emilia's breath catches, her heart suddenly feeling too big for her chest.

'I could come over tonight after my shift?'

She would give anything to see him. To have him hold her and kiss her, and stroke her hair, and tell her that he's going to look after her. That he'll keep her safe. But she knows that he'll ask her questions. He'll want answers. Answers that she cannot give. And she doesn't deserve his love. Guilt shudders through her as Ryan's face, full of terror, appears once again in her mind. If Ciaran knew what she had done, would he still love her?

'I've missed you too. I really have. And I'm sorry I haven't been messaging that much . . . it's just been hard.'

'Please don't apologize,' he says, rushing to get his words out. 'There's nothing to be sorry for. I know how hard it must be. I still feel so horrible for pushing you for answers and I promise I won't ask you anything else. We don't have to talk about it, not unless you want to.'

'It's okay . . .' Emilia presses her lips together. Should she ask? Or should she stay quiet? 'What's happening with the investigation? Any closer to catching them?'

Ciaran sighs. 'Actually, something just happened with that . . .'

Emilia's breath catches. 'What is it?'

'Wild took me off the case.'

'She did what? When?'

'Literally just before I called you. She wasn't happy with how close I was to one of the victims. She thought it'd be better for me to go back to other work.'

'Oh . . . I'm sorry.'

'It isn't your fault. It's me. It was consuming me already and then once they took you, I . . . I would have ended up doing something stupid. I could have jeopardized the whole thing.'

Emilia nods slowly, relief fluttering through her like butterflies.

'Come over when you're done,' she says.

'Are you sure?'

Emilia smiles widely. He sounds so happy. So relieved that everything hasn't changed between them.

'Yes, I'm sure,' she says quickly. 'As long as . . . as long as you understand that I can't talk about what happened. I can't, Ciaran. I really can't –'

'I understand, Emi. I promise I won't try to make you.'

She hadn't realized how desperate she was to see him, how much she needed to have him close to her again. 'Okay.'

'I can't wait to see you. I love you, Emi. You know that, right?'

'Yes. I love you too.'

'See you later.'

The phone call ends and Emilia drops the phone to the floor as her head collapses into her hands. She cries: big fat tears of guilt and love and shame.

She tries to ignore the feeling deep inside her. The gentle fluttering of butterflies turning violent, their wings smashing against her insides. What was it she read once? Butterflies are nothing but anxiety. We've been conditioned to think of them as positive, but really they are our bodies responding to stress. They are nothing but a warning sign. A glaring red light telling us to go no further.

But she can't let the guilt consume her completely. If this is the decision she has made – to remain quiet, to remain the victim – then she has to get on with her life. And she needs Ciaran. And he needs her.

She flops back and stares up again at the crack in the ceiling.

It isn't any bigger. It's just her imagination.

Her body tenses as that familiar tune blares up at her from the floor.

But she smiles, her muscles relaxing. It will be Ciaran, calling to ask what takeaway she wants him to bring. She leans forward, reaching once again for the phone –

It isn't his name on the screen. It isn't his photo smiling up at her. Nothing but a black screen and *No Caller ID*.

She grabs it, her throat tightening, the butterflies thrashing around, desperate to escape.

'Hello?' she says, trying to keep her voice steady.

Silence.

'Hello? Who's –'

'Hello, Emilia,' comes a low growl. Terror floods through her. But it isn't the initial silence or the no caller ID – it's the tone of the voice, robotic and distorted.

It is them.

She stops breathing as everything slows, the butterflies falling completely still – collapsing instantly to the floor.

Why are they calling? What do they want?

'Hello?' she whispers in response, unable to summon any other words or protestation.

'We said that we would call on you.'

Emilia pinches the bridge of her nose as tears of fear burn in the corners of her eyes. She screws them shut in an attempt to block out the phone, block out their strange, alien voice. Block out everything. This can't be happening. It must all be a bad dream, a nightmare.

'Talk to us, Emilia,' the voice mutters. 'Staying silent won't help you.'

'Please leave me alone,' she cries. 'I'll stay silent, I promise I won't say a word. Just leave me alone.'

'But we need your help. And you promised that you would help us. You said that you understood the rules.'

'I said that I would never help you –'

'You told us that you would do exactly as we said. So that's what you're going to do.'

Emilia's vision blurs, the room spinning violently, tipping off its axis. She blinks up at the ceiling, willing the world to fall still. But all she can look at is the huge crack, spreading rapidly before her eyes, her life tearing itself in two: before the Room; and after.

'What do you want?' she whispers, her voice breaking.

'We've left a gift for you outside.'

'A gift?'

'Yes. In the hedge to the left of your gate, you'll find a package. Go and get it.'

'Right now?'

'Yes. Right now.'

'Okay . . .'

She stands slowly, staring at the front door. What if this is a trick? What if they're just on the other side and as soon as she steps out, they grab her?

'We're waiting, Emilia.'

She inhales sharply. 'Where are you?'

'You don't need to know that. But we told you we'd be watching you . . . Looked like quite the conversation you were having before we called.'

Her skin turns cold. They were there, just outside while she was talking to Ciaran. They could see her. And she had no idea. If they had called on her just a few days ago, they would have been met with journalists around the house, all focused on the most recent survivor. They've been waiting – waiting to use her when the glare of attention has turned to someone new.

She rushes towards the door, tugging it open and bursting out into the freezing air.

'Good girl,' the voice says. 'Now . . . go fetch.'

Emilia's feet curl against the cold ground. She hasn't put shoes on. But she just needs to get whatever they've left. Grab it, rush back inside. Close the curtains.

She runs, pelting across the path towards the gate.

The hedge to the left, the hedge to the left –

Yes – there it is.

An envelope has been balanced just so in the branches, in the spaces where there were once green leaves. She reaches for it, taking it in her shaking hands. It is thin. Almost as if there is nothing in it. But there – in the corner – there is something small. Textured.

She stares out to the road, squinting to see down to the nearest streetlamp. But the lane is cloaked in darkness. Where are they? Can they see her right now?

'You can go back inside,' the voice says.

Emilia's legs move without her commanding them to do so, her body trying to escape their watchful eyes. Just because she cannot see them, doesn't mean that they can't see her.

She slams the door behind her, her heart hammering as she searches the room. What if that was a distraction? What if they snuck inside while she was out there?

'Open the envelope, please.'

Emilia crosses to the kitchen and clutches the edge of the counter, her knuckles turning white. She slides her finger under the flap and it comes away. She turns it over and shakes.

Her eyebrows knit together as she stares down at the contents.

A face gazes up at her. A photograph of a man. Mid-forties, if she had to guess, salt and pepper hair, short, standing in a bar, holding a beer. He's smiling. He looks . . . normal.

And there, next to the photograph, a tiny clear plastic bag. And inside – white powder.

What is this . . . ?

'The man in the photograph is Harris Keaton,' the voice says. 'Tonight he will be in a bar called the Dandy Fox. It's in the City. His employer, Laughton and Kemp, the investment fund, are having a leaving party there tonight. You will go there and convince him to leave with you –'

'I can't –'

'It shouldn't be hard, Emilia. You might want to buy some cigarettes – he's a smoker. Get him to leave with you. We don't care how you do it: be coy about it or offer it on a fucking plate. Either way, he won't say no. Then bring him back to your house. Offer him a drink. Spike the drink with that powder.'

A tear splashes on to the photograph. Harris Keaton continues to gaze up at her, head thrown back in a laugh. So unsuspecting.

'It won't take long to work,' the voice says.

'And . . . and then?'

'Well, isn't that obvious? Then we'll collect him.'

The room spins again, the counter rocking back and forth, the man's face blurring.

'And Emilia . . . Don't do anything stupid. Remember what we told you: we won't hesitate to hurt somebody you love. And your parents aren't the only ones you love, are they? Ciaran Jones seems like he's very important to you.'

Emilia shakes her head frantically, her hand clamped across her mouth to stifle her rising scream.

'We'll be watching.'

19th November, 8 p.m.

The crowd outside the Dandy Fox is three people deep: groups of men in their after-work uniform, suits with loosened ties and unbuttoned collars; women balancing on one foot then the other, freshly reapplied lipstick staining the rims of their wine glasses.

Emilia stands on the pavement opposite. Her hands are clasped in front of her as she searches the many faces for the man in the photo. Harris Keaton. She rubs her palms down the sides of her dress: they are clammy, even in the winter chill.

He isn't there. At least, she can't spot his face in the crowd.

I can't do this, she thinks. *I can't.*

She hasn't dressed up in so long: the fitted black dress is alien, the heels – which she wore so easily for years – uncomfortable. Painful, even. A long cream coat is tossed casually over her arm, as if she has just left her office and darted across the road for a quick one. She has created a whole story in her head: why she is there, who she is. He won't recognize her, will he? Surely she'll just be another face in a packed bar? But her face has been all over the news, on the front of all the papers. So . . . there will have to be Plan A and Plan B. In Plan A, she is just an interested stranger: high-flying City girl, here for a drink after a busy day at work. In Plan B, she will have to be Emilia. Drinking away the trauma of what she has been through. Searching for comfort in the arms of a stranger.

I can't do this.

She looks down at her phone, the response from Ciaran still open on the screen:

> Don't worry, I understand. Spend
> tonight with your parents and I'll come
> over at the end of my shift tomorrow.
> Sound good? Love you x

A loud laugh rings out across the road, above all the other noise, and Emilia pushes her phone back into her handbag.

Inhaling deeply, she quickly looks both ways and then steps into the road, her eyes fixed on the door. She'll look inside first, and if he isn't there, she'll just have to wait outside with a cigarette and keep searching.

The door opens as she reaches for it and a group of men push their way outside, each of them briefly looking her up and down before moving on. She waits, her foot tapping impatiently on the ground, her arms wrapped around her. But the last in their group, a younger guy – he looks out of place – stops, holding his arm out to gesture inside.

'After you,' he says, holding the door open.

'Thank you,' Emilia says with a smile.

But as she meets his eyes, bright and blue, Ryan's dead stare bursts into her mind.

She rushes past him, into the warmth of the bar, pulsing with bodies.

'You're welcome,' the man says, glancing over his

shoulder at her. But she daren't look him in the face again. It will be Ryan looking back.

Emilia scans the bar, taking in the way to the toilets, the fire exit, the stairs to another room on the upper floor, her mind automatically searching for an escape route. What if they are here? Are they watching her right now? Is she in danger?

The room is heaving, every table filled, people standing in all the spaces in-between. She scans every face as she moves through the crowd, pushing and sliding between bodies, some waiting for drinks, others simply standing wherever they've been able to find a space. The atmosphere is electric. A year ago, Emilia would have loved this. She would have fed off the feeling in the air, surrounded herself with friends, laughing and singing into the night. But now? That same atmosphere is pulsating with menace, thick and heavy, pressing down.

She reaches the bar and turns, leaning against it to survey the room. The man closest to her turns his head, appraising her, his gaze burning as it shifts down her body to her legs and then back up. She flashes a brief disarming smile. He looks away quickly, calling out to the bar staff, acting as if he had never even glanced her way.

Emilia bites her lip, dropping her head in frustration. Why did she smile at him? Why do we do this? To appease? To deflect? To make sure that we don't make them angry? Is that what Sophie tried to do? Did she try to pander quietly to Ryan when she should have responded with outrage? Lashed out with violence?

No. Don't think about Sophie.

Do not think about Ryan.

'Can I get you something?' the man asks, leaning towards her.

'No, thank you,' she says, not even glancing his way. Instead, she turns, and leans in towards the barman.

'Could I have a gin and tonic, please?'

'Coming right up,' he says.

She waits, pointedly keeping her attention away from the man. Her leg shakes, energy pulsating through her.

'Here you are,' the barman places the drink down in front of her. She reaches into her bag and slams a ten-pound note down on to the bar.

'Thanks,' she says, turning quickly to search the crowd one last time before heading to the exit. He isn't in here. And sitting at the bar is just asking for trouble. It's asking for questions.

The cold air hits her as she steps through the doors to the outside. Emilia inhales sharply, tugging her coat on awkwardly, passing the drink from one hand to the other.

Slowly, she moves away from the doors, through the mass of people standing just outside, and heads to the right, towards the benches that line one side of the pub. More people have gathered there, so she walks past them, methodically taking in their faces. But as she reaches the last bench, her slowly sinking stomach lifts – is that him?

Yes.

There, beyond the benches, where a few people are standing apart from the crowd, some staring at their phones, others huddled over a cigarette, is the man from the photo. Harris Keaton. The next victim.

Who is he? Why are they targeting him? Is he a hateful, violent man? Dangerous? He looks just like any other man spending his Thursday evening drinking and laughing with friends. But they – the man and woman – would argue that that is precisely what makes him dangerous. That is what helps men like him and Ryan, and Gregory, and all the others, hide in plain sight.

Emilia takes a steadying breath, straightens her spine, lowers her shoulders.

She can do this.

She has to do this.

Exhaling quickly, she strides towards him then slows down as if she is coming to a natural stop just feet away from him.

She sneaks a quick sideways glance at him. But he doesn't look her way. He is reading something – scrolling through some kind of website.

Emilia opens her bag and pulls out the cigarettes she bought earlier from the corner shop next to the station. She slides one out of the packet. It feels strange between her fingers, sending her back to her nights at university, the sting of tobacco as it hit the back of her throat, the rush, the smell of it in her clothes and hair the following morning.

She coughs lightly, readying herself. But panic is taking hold of her voice. The words which are ready, perfectly formed, remain strangled at the back of her throat.

'Excuse me?' She forces the words out through gritted teeth.

He lifts his head, meeting her eye for a moment before glancing around him to check if she is speaking to somebody else. 'Yeah?' he responds, one eyebrow arched in a question.

'Could I borrow a lighter?' she asks, forcing her tone to soften. She holds up her unlit cigarette.

'Sure.'

But he doesn't move towards her. He stays where he is, feet planted, his chin tilting forwards.

She crosses over to him in two short steps and waits as he pulls the lighter out from the inside pocket of his dark blue tailored suit. The lighter sparks and he waves at her to lean in. She already wants to run away, something about him and his expectant stare triggering shivers of revulsion inside her. But she can't run away. She is meant to leave with this man – take him back to her house. Her stomach churning, Emilia meets his eye, placing the cigarette lightly between her pursed lips. She leans in slowly with a small smile, never breaking her gaze. The cigarette lights and she inhales deeply, holding down the cough that wants to burst out of her after years of never tasting a cigarette. Instead she sighs as she breathes out the smoke, as if it is the greatest pleasure.

'Thank you,' she says softly, looking at him sideways, her hand tucked under her chin. 'I needed that.'

'You're welcome,' he says.

They stand beside each other in silence, both staring up at the cloud-covered night sky.

'It was so packed in there,' Emilia says, breaking the quiet before it becomes too awkward and he makes his excuses and moves away. 'I was gagging for some fresh air.' She glances at the cigarette and flashes an ironic smile.

'Funny, that,' he says with a low chuckle. 'Although . . . same. Needed to get away from all the work lot for a moment.'

'Don't you like them?'

He pauses, looking away from her and down at his foot which he scuffs against the pavement. 'No, I do . . . it's just . . . you spend all day with these people and then socialize with them once, twice a week as well. And a leaving party like this – it's like the whole company comes. It can get a bit much.'

'I get it . . . No wife to go home to?'

His chin lifts abruptly, not sure how to take her question. But Emilia doesn't look away, forcing a suggestive, flirtatious smile.

'No . . . no wife. Not any more.'

Emilia licks her lips, holding eye contact for one moment longer before looking up at the sky again, taking another drag of her cigarette.

'How about you?' He inches closer. 'Boyfriend? Husband?'

'No,' she says, ignoring the image of Ciaran that immediately filters into her mind. 'Neither.'

'Why?'

'Why?' She smirks at him and he turns to fully face her, his hands hooked into the pockets of his suit. 'What kind of question is that?'

'Well, a woman like you . . . why wouldn't you have a partner?'

'Many reasons. Besides . . .' She tucks her hair behind her ear, her fingers tangling through the ends. 'There's more fun to be had when I'm single.'

He exhales loudly, his mouth shaped in an 'oh'. Chewing the bottom of his lip, his eyes dance over her face and she raises her eyebrows. But after a moment, his gaze narrows.

'You know, your face is so familiar.'

Emilia's stomach plummets, her breath catching. 'Oh, not that "I've seen you before" line –'

'No, really . . . I just can't place it but I've definitely seen you before . . . You're not famous, are you?'

'No, I'm not famous –'

'Wait.' He falls completely still, his eyes widening. And there it is, the moment Emilia had been dreading; the look she had been praying wouldn't happen. Recognition.

'Are you Emilia Haines?'

Emilia's protestations die on her lips. Every emotion is churning inside her: anger and frustration, sadness and embarrassment, absolute outrage at the complete lack of self-awareness of this man in front of her. But there's no point denying it. He has recognized her – and any arguments to the contrary will only push him away. Plan A is no longer possible. She'll have to go with Plan B.

'I am,' she whispers.

He straightens his head, his eyes shining with a strange expression Emilia can't quite pin down. Intrigue? Interest? No . . . it's triumph. He's pleased that he was right. So unaware of what she must be feeling, only interested in the fact that a survivor of the Confession Room is in front of him, and that he recognized her when seemingly nobody else did.

Her eyes fill with tears. But she doesn't attempt to pull them back or blink them away as she normally would. She lets them fall, allowing her mouth to crumple with emotion, her hand lifting to cover her face.

'Oh shit,' he whispers. 'Are you . . . are you okay?'

Am I okay? Emilia thinks, exasperated.

'I'm sorry,' she says, blinking up at him through her wet lashes. 'I . . . I came out tonight because I've been at home ever since it happened and I just needed to be around people. To have somebody to talk to –'

She wraps her arms around herself, allowing herself to cry. The emotion real, albeit targeted. For a purpose. He moves even closer, his hands extended, unsure whether to comfort her or back away. So Emilia steps forward, into his space. He pauses – shocked – his eyes falling on to her mouth. Her stomach turns. Is he aroused by this? Is a vulnerable woman, a crying woman, some kind of sick turn-on? She is desperate to push him away but instead she rocks her head forward on to his shoulder and, just as anticipated, he places his hands on her back. He makes hushing noises but it seems unnatural, as if he has never made an effort to comfort another person in his life.

'I'm sorry,' he says. 'I didn't mean to upset you. It's just . . . I've been following the case since the beginning and recognized you. I'm sorry if you were upset.'

Emilia sniffs, pulling away slightly to look up at him again, their faces only inches apart, her eyes wide and innocent. 'It's okay. I know you didn't mean it in a bad way. Besides . . . it's been nice talking to you.'

He nods, his hands not leaving her back, his fingers pressing into her spine and her waist. 'You too. You've made my night a lot better, that's for sure.'

She glances away purposefully, her eyes circling down to the ground with feigned shyness before returning to him. 'Well . . . I'm going to head home now but . . . I don't suppose you'd like to come with me?'

He doesn't say anything. Instead, he simply looks at

her, his head tilted, his fingers scratching at the day and a half stubble on his jawline.

A sudden pang of guilt hits Emilia square in the chest. But she doesn't have a choice. Who knows what they'll do if she doesn't follow their instructions? These aren't normal people. This wouldn't just be breaking the rules. This would be going against two people who can murder without a second thought. Two people who have convinced themselves that they are doing some good in the world. Two people who know where her parents live.

'What do you say?' she urges. 'I could really use some . . . company.'

He blinks slowly, as if he is processing what she is asking. But then he nods firmly. 'Sure. I'd love to . . . Can I have a swig of your drink?' His cheeks flush red. 'Need a bit of Dutch courage.'

She smiles and holds out the drink. 'Sure.'

He takes it, gulping loudly, his eyes bulging as he raises his chin up to the sky.

'Finish it – I don't want any more,' Emilia says, dropping her cigarette and stubbing it out with the ball of her foot. 'Shall we go?'

He nods again, eagerly, placing the glass down on the nearest bench and mirroring her action of letting his cigarette fall to the floor. It lies there, smouldering. He taps the screen of his phone, glancing quickly at the time, then steps purposefully towards Emilia, into her space once more.

But Emilia is frozen, her eyes fixated on his phone, the image on his Home Screen still shining out from between his fingers. Two smiling faces, heads pressed together, gap-toothed grins and tousled baby hair.

'You have children?' she asks lightly, even though a wash of darkness is descending over her, like shutters coming down, blocking out the sun.

He frowns, but then follows her gaze down to his phone. 'Oh . . . yes. George and Maisie.'

'How old are they?'

'They're six and four now . . . Do you have children?'

Emilia shakes her head. 'No.'

'Would you like to?'

She forces her mouth into a smile, swallowing down a fresh batch of tears. These tears wouldn't be helpful. 'I've always wanted to, yes. Maybe one day.'

His eyes stay on her, his expression confused, as if he doesn't know what to do, how to bring this conversation to an end and return to their previous, more enjoyable one. 'Shall we go, then?' He holds out one hand and points across the road with the other. 'The taxi rank is this way.'

She nods. 'Yeah . . . Actually, I'm going to quickly go to the toilet. Is that okay? Just before we grab a taxi.'

'Okay . . . I'll wait here?'

'Meet you in two.'

Emilia flashes a smile at him and then turns back towards the entrance to the bar, walking as quickly as she can towards the doors. Her feet are aching, her heart racing. Her stomach churning with nausea.

He has children.

Two young lives who to some extent or another are dependent on him. Love him. He is the only father they will ever have. And he could be ripped from them in the most violent way in less than a day.

She heads straight for the toilets at the back of the bar, on the right. She bursts through the doors, pushing past a group of three women gathered around the mirrors, and slides into a stall, locking the door behind her.

She throws down the lid of the toilet and sits down, her hands raking through her hair, swallowing over and over again to force down the feeling that she is about to be sick at any moment.

He has children.

If he is taken, if he ends up dead at the hands of the Confession Room, his children will never be the same people they would have been. The people they would have turned into, grown up to be, will cease to exist. And it will be her fault.

She can't . . . She can't do this.

The nausea in her stomach is suddenly taken over by something else. Something far more powerful. Rage.

She will not do this. But what about her parents? What about Ciaran? How can she keep them safe?

She holds her breath, squeezing her eyes shut as her mind races. She'll go straight to her parents' house and tell them she wants to stay the night. And she'll keep watch. She'll call Ciaran. If she suspects anything, she'll call the police.

Even if she follows their rules, she can never predict what they will do. So she can only think about what she will do.

And she will not do this.

She can't.

Emilia lifts her head, her gaze boring into the back of the stall door. She exhales, her breath shaky, but her mind certain. There's just one challenge left: she has to get out of here without Harris seeing her.

She opens the door and approaches the sink next to the three girls who are still there, laughing and gossiping, making pouty faces in the mirror. One glances her way, taking in her puffy red eyes, but she quickly returns to her friends. Emilia washes her hands quickly, wiping them on the back of her coat, and approaches the door. But she pauses, her hand poised just millimetres away from the handle. What if he's waiting for her just the other side of the door? How will she get rid of him? Will she pretend that she feels sick? She's changed her mind? What if he really is a monster like the man and woman claimed? Will he follow her? Has she put herself in an entirely new kind of danger?

'Girls,' she says, spinning around.

Their conversation comes to a sudden halt and they all turn to face her.

'You okay, hon?' the girl closest says, her heavily mascaraed eyes wide with anticipation.

'Do any of you work at Laughton and Kemp?'

Another nods, the brunette. 'We all do.'

'Do you . . .' Emilia hesitates, unsure which action would be riskier. Opening the door and hoping he isn't there, or trusting these three girls. Trust the women, she says to herself. Think of all the times in the past that drunk strangers in the toilets of bars and nightclubs have become her firm one-night-only best friends. 'Do you know Harris Keaton?'

The third girl rolls her eyes. 'Everyone knows Harris Keaton. What's the creep done this time?'

'Is he being a pest again?' the blonde asks, her mouth turning downwards into a scowl.

'No, nothing too bad. It's just . . . to get away from him I made the excuse of going to the toilet. I was going to sneak out the back way but I'm just worried that he might be waiting right outside. Could one of you –'

'I'll check,' the brunette interrupts. 'Don't worry, darling. We've got you.'

'Thank you so much,' Emilia says, stepping away from the door, seeking sanctuary back towards the stalls.

The brunette opens the door abruptly and steps out. The door slowly closes behind her as she peers into the crowd then swings around, pushing her way back inside.

'I can see him outside the front,' she says to Emilia. 'So yeah . . . if you go out the fire exit and sneak off down those back streets, he shouldn't see you.'

'Thank you so much.'

'I swear, they should have fired that arsehole months ago,' the blonde says.

'Has he done something bad?' Emilia asks, unable to stop herself.

'He's one of those guys, you know . . . one of those weirdos who seem to think that women are the cause of all his problems. Our friend Georgia once went out with him, he seemed lovely at first, but after she said she wasn't feeling it he said that she had led him on and that she owed him. Owed him! Can you believe it?'

'Quite a few women have complained about him but nothing's been done,' the third girl says, rolling her eyes.

The brunette nods. 'He won't be happy when he realizes you've gone.'

The four of them fall into silence, all nodding slowly, understanding. 'Go on, love,' the blonde says. 'Leave now before he comes inside.'

'Thank you again,' Emilia whispers. She smiles at them gratefully and pulls open the door, lowering her head to shield her face from the entrance as she turns quickly towards the right, towards the shining beacon of the fire exit.

She glances over her shoulder, her heart pounding as she checks to make sure he isn't behind her, that the footsteps closing in are just in her imagination. She pushes down on the bar to the fire doors and they swing outwards, cold air rushing in, taking her breath away.

There is a road directly ahead of her which curves away to the left. She can go down there and then loop down towards the busy main road. Wait there for a taxi. Head straight home.

She steps out through the doors and on to the pavement, peering around the corner, to the side street where not so long ago she was standing with Harris Keaton, ready to follow their instructions. He isn't there. Like the girl said, he must be waiting right outside the front doors still.

Just do it, she mutters to herself. Run.

Run.

She glances a final time over her shoulder and down the side street then pelts across the road, intently focused on the route that will take her into the distance. Her heels are pounding into the tarmac, her feet screaming, on fire, her breath loud and panicked.

She keeps running, not looking back until she is out of sight.

There is nobody behind her. Nobody following her.

How long will he wait? What blame will he apportion to himself? Any at all? No. The blame will be entirely on her shoulders. She'll be the bitch who led him on outside a bar and then decided to abandon him.

A group of men and women walk towards her, heading towards the Dandy Fox. But they pay no attention to her breathlessness, her flustered face. They just manoeuvre around her, talking loudly.

Keep moving, Emilia, she says to herself.

She begins to walk, her feet moving rapidly beneath her, the lights of the main road appearing on the horizon. Relief rises up inside her, from her feet up towards her head –

A loud noise echoes out from inside her pocket. That jaunty ringtone.

Her phone.

No Caller ID.

She gasps, her legs moving faster and faster, until she is sprinting towards the lights. She looks back – are they following her? Chasing after her? Is that van going to appear out of nowhere and grab her, pulling her inside?

No. Nobody.

She is alone.

She reaches inside her bag to clutch the small plastic bag filled with white powder. She glances sideways, to the hedge lining the road, and throws it away, her heart pounding.

Her knees buckle beneath her and she crouches down, not caring that anyone walking past will be able to see her. Her head hangs low and she presses her palms into the rough ground.

The phone rings out again.

Emilia's fingers scramble to press the button and swipe the command to turn it off. The screen turns black, the call extinguished.

Do they already know that she has gone – that she has refused to follow their rules?

Emilia sighs, her tear-strewn face stinging in the cold. It's useless. She won't have stopped them. They won't move on to somebody else. They chose him. And they will take him.

Maybe for someone who bought into the preaching of the Confession Room, it could seem that Harris Keaton deserved to end up there. And maybe no matter what, that will be the ending to his story. But . . .

His children. Those children with their sticky smiles and innocence will not be without a father because of something she does. She can't watch the news in the morning and know that he is there because she helped them.

But the harsh truth is everything that happens to him, and whoever ends up there with him, will still be her fault.

The innocent who stay silent are still guilty after all.

20th November, 5 a.m.

Emilia hasn't moved all night. She has stayed locked in this position on the sofa beneath her parents' living room window, knees tucked up to her chin, staring out into the night. Waiting. For what exactly she doesn't know. For them to come and hurt her parents. For them to call. For lights to blaze in through the window, their masked faces appearing on the other side of the glass.

She had raced to her parents' house, fear thrilling through her, expecting the worst when she arrived: a broken window, a door forced open. She stepped inside, her breathing shallow. But her parents were asleep – their chests rising and falling peacefully as they lay beside each other, Mimi curled up at their feet.

She was sure that the phone would ring again. But it has stayed silent. Two missed calls and nothing more.

Her dad's laptop is beside her – the Confession Room fixed to the screen. Every time it goes into hibernation, the image turning black, she runs her finger frantically over the trackpad. She can't miss it. If a post goes up, she has to see it. She needs to know. Did her rebellion make any difference at all?

They snatched Emilia just minutes after the confession was posted. So if they were planning on taking Harris Keaton in the midnight hours, the post naming him should have gone up by now. But it hasn't. The forum is

251

silent. But there are thousands of people on there, just like her, watching expectantly. The system has always worked the same way. Once a survivor and a victim are found, it's less than twenty-four hours before the next victims are named. So why haven't they posted? Did she really make a difference?

Or have they simply changed the rules?

Emilia straightens her back, her eyes watering as she once again squints into the distance, searching for movement in the growing light. Why can't she calm down? Why is adrenalin still running through her? It's relentless, this level of fear. The fear of the unknown, the unpredictable. The fear of two people who are seemingly capable of anything.

A door slams.

A new post. Is it them?

Is it him?

Anonymous 01

We've given enough warnings. And even with a head start, you haven't been able to stop us. No more. But the killings will not stop. The confessions will now come when it's already too late.

Good luck.

Emilia stares at the screen, her shoulders curling inwards as she brings her trembling hands to her forehead.

They've changed the rules.

Is she the only person in the world who knows that Harris Keaton is their next victim? What if he isn't any more? Maybe they weren't able to capture him without her. But no matter who it is, now nobody will know until they are already dead.

Has the next victim already been killed? They haven't confessed yet, so maybe there's still time.

Emilia grips the edges of the laptop, her knuckles turning white. Maybe this is her chance. Her chance to stop them.

Isabella's scared, frustrated face appears before her.

If you do it on your own, you'll be making that choice for all of us. That isn't your choice to make. And you'll be putting our families in danger.

Isabella was so fearful of what might happen if they tell the truth. And Emilia felt the same — her parents are everything to her. But she can protect them. She'll make sure that the police keep them safe. If she doesn't do something now, there will be more deaths, more victims. Just like they said: the killings will not stop.

Maybe they deserved it . . . That's what Isabella said. And that's the thought that crossed Emilia's mind last night when she was with Harris Keaton: maybe he deserves this.

She shakes her head furiously, anger bubbling up. Nobody deserves this. Who are they to do this to people? To act as judge, jury and executioner? When she ran away last night, she made the decision: she cannot be a part of this. And she won't be.

No more.

She stands quickly, running to the front door. She peers through the small glass window to her car, her eyes darting around the dark, searching for their looming figures in the shadows.

She can make it.

She opens the door and runs, pelting to the back of her car, throwing open the boot. She pulls out the holdall that she takes with her on jobs, growling with frustration as the handle catches on the umbrella next to it. She yanks it free and races back to house, her footsteps echoing beneath her.

Crossing the threshold, she closes the door quietly behind her before making her way back to the living room and setting her holdall on to the floor.

If she goes straight to the police and reveals she knows more than she has admitted, she'll be taken to an interview room, and it will take too long for her to give them the information that they need. Hours maybe. But if she figures it out here, she can have it ready for them. Quickly, without hesitation.

Because her insistence that she didn't remember anything after she was removed from the Room was a lie. Ciaran was right – he knows her so well. She has always had a good memory, taking in the smallest detail. Her investigative mind didn't shut down with fear, didn't collapse under the pressure. It was heightened. So maybe . . . maybe she can figure it out. Not who they are. That one is trickier. But *where* they are . . . maybe that she can solve.

She digs deep inside the bag, moving aside her camera and binoculars, until finally she grips the edge of the map. This will be easier to remember if she works on paper. Pulling it out, she flicks through the pages, searching for the location she needs.

There! There it is –

The police station. The one she ran to when they let her out of the van, Ryan's body discarded on the road.

That's the end location. That's where she needs to work back from. If she follows her memories in reverse, it should lead her to the Confession Room.

Emilia pulls out a thick black marker from her bag and neatly marks an X on the map on top of the police station. She marks a second X a short way down the street where they stopped the van.

They travelled for approximately twenty minutes. That she is sure of. She knows, because she made sure to count. Steady, rhythmic, focusing on keeping the time.

The van never felt as if it was travelling at speed. And they wouldn't have wanted to do anything to attract attention. And on motorways, there are regular cameras, automatic number plate recognition . . . No. They kept to the country roads. Between thirty and forty miles per hour if she had to guess.

Flipping over the map, she makes a quick calculation, her handwriting unwieldy as she sets out the equation.

Distance = speed multiplied by time.

She reaches for her phone, opening the calculator. Tapping quickly, her mind racing, she presses the equals button and then scrawls the result on to the map, circling it wildly.

13.3333 miles.

That's the furthest they travelled in any direction. Retrieving her compass, she measures the scale on the map, and quickly calculates again before stabbing the needle into the X, her hand sweeping round in a steady circle, the pencil scratching against the paper.

She looks down at the map, the hairs on the nape of her neck standing on end.

Somewhere within the perimeter of that circle is the Confession Room.

But now she needs to rely on something not as reliable as mathematics; not as straightforward as an equation. Human memory. It is known to deceive and misguide, to inflate some details and diminish others. But she has spent her entire adult life focusing on the detail. Every minute element. Scolding herself for missing anything. Priding herself on her precision. If anybody can remember with accuracy, it's Emilia.

She closes her eyes, forcing her mind to delve back into its memory, to a place where, until now, she has refused to let it travel. She has blocked the path, refusing to acknowledge that if she searches hard enough, the answer might have been here all along.

Focus, Emilia. Focus.

When they stopped near the police station, the back of the van was facing the station. So they had turned left before coming to a standstill.

Before the left-hand turning, they had travelled straight for a while . . . But they'd stopped for a minute or so. She remembers thinking that they must be at traffic lights. She drags the pen down the road, coming to a four-way junction. She crosses the junction with her pen.

What happened before the traffic lights? She blinks rapidly, searching her memory. There was something . . . something happened that sent Ryan's body sliding across the van, his cold bound hands colliding with hers.

Yes. That's it. A sharp right turn.

Emilia searches the map, her eyes following the streets as they twist like offshoots from the main road.

There it is – a sharp right turn, almost sending them back on themselves but taking them into the country lanes. And there – there is the point where the road swung away to the left in a wide arc.

She smoothly draws a line on the road, her pulse building – she's remembering, she knew she could remember –

She stops suddenly, the force of her abrupt movement pushing the pen through the paper and on to the wooden floor beneath.

There's a fork in the road.

One path leads east. The other north-east.

Which way was it? What direction did they come from?

Emilia's hands clench and release, her fingers curling into fists and then releasing as she tries to remember.

She frowns, her whole body falling still. She was so sure that she would be able to do this, that it was all there, hiding inside her. She hangs her head, pinching the bridge of her nose.

What was it that Ciaran used to say to her? Where memory fails, allow logic to take over. There is an answer to this. There always is.

She pushes the lid back on to the marker and takes a deep, steadying breath. Allow logic to take over.

The road twists back and forth, steadily worming its way east before abruptly turning towards the south and finally emerging to join a dual carriageway.

A dual carriageway.

Here it is. That's the answer. They never travelled on a

big road like that. She is as sure of it as she was before. They never travelled that fast. And the roads were quiet – there wasn't the sound of other cars rushing past them.

Her eyes dart quickly to the other option: the road to the north-east.

This one continues straight for a number of miles, the country road cutting through fields and farmland. It comes to an end, running directly into another country road. A smooth turn to the right or a shorter, sharper turn to the left.

Yes – this is it. This is the road they took.

And that sharp left turn – that wasn't too far into the journey. It was when Ryan shifted from the centre of the van to the other side, his body slamming against the metal. Emilia had winced, her hands flying up to her ears to block out the sound. She had to remind herself to keep counting. Keep the time. Keep your mind.

From there it was straight – just bends in a meandering road but no turns. Nothing except the one turn that led them out of wherever the Confession Room is hidden. And that . . . that was a left turn.

Emilia's pen comes to a sudden halt. With a wavering hand, she marks the page with an X.

She stares down at it, the colours of the map blending together before her eyes, the lines and markings swerving together like a kaleidoscope.

Is that it? Is that where it is?

She rushes to the laptop,

Her eyes dart from one side to the other, and she circles the coordinates. Then, carefully, she types them into the search bar.

The location loads, the map on the screen mirroring the one spread out on the floor. Holding her breath, Emilia leans in, swiping her finger until the mouse is hovering over another symbol:

Street View.

She clicks and the image buffers. At first it is blurred, a small circle whirring in the centre. But suddenly it is crystal clear. Moving even closer, her nose just inches from the screen, Emilia narrows her eyes. The image is showing a thorny hedgerow and the edge of a road. No kerb. She moves the mouse, clicking slowly on the arrow on the bottom right of the screen. The image rotates. More of the road appears, and then more, until she is staring down a narrow country lane that hits a dead end probably no more than a hundred metres further down. She keeps clicking. Click – more hedgerows. Click – an evergreen towering above. Click.

Emilia holds her breath. There, between the tree and a long line of bushes on the other side, are two iron gates. Partially hidden with overgrown plants, nature attempting to take over. But they are there. She closes her eyes, placing herself back in that van, her eyes covered, her hands bound.

Concentrate, Emilia.

A sound echoes just next to her ears. So real it could be right next to her, in this room: the slow creak of an electric gate.

Emilia sits alone in a small interview room, the door propped open, the sound of a clock ticking setting her nerves on edge. The room feels small, alien, so distant from when she was on the other side of the table, asking the pointed questions instead of attempting to answer them.

She had called the police immediately, desperation pulsing through her as she said that she needed to speak to officers straightaway and that they needed to come to her parents' address. She couldn't leave – they were in danger. Wild arrived with another detective and Emilia trembled as she braced herself to tell the truth. There would be consequences. But they couldn't get in the way of the truth. They couldn't get in the way of what was right.

'I know where it is,' she whispered. 'I've found the Confession Room.'

Wild had jumped into action. Emilia had rushed to explain how she had figured it out and as soon as she showed Wild the map, the location on her screen, she was out of the room like a shot, an urgent message going out to all officers. The armed unit deployed immediately.

Wild asked Emilia to come to the police station and after some reassurance that uniformed officers would remain with her parents, Emilia agreed, relief pulsating through her. They are safe. And then she was led to this room and told to wait. She had wondered if a detective would join her, begin asking her questions, begin attempting to piece together why she had withheld this information for so long. But that hasn't happened. She hasn't even been placed under arrest. She has been alone ever since, with nothing but her imagination, her mind travelling along those winding roads, racing to find them before they escape.

She closes her eyes and images unspool behind them, vivid and bright.

Police race down the narrow lanes, but the surrounding countryside is not set ablaze with blue light. They manoeuvred through the traffic of the town with the sirens wailing, but now they are closer they are travelling in silence, the only sound the roar of the engines as they speed around each bend.

The cars pull over abruptly, some officers decamping further away and blocking off the lane. Others, all armed, approach the gates, eroding iron towering above them. Some of them clamber over, others finding a way through a slight gap in the hedgerow further down.

They make their way silently across the space leading up to the farmhouse, their boots squelching through the mud, the loose shingle shifting beneath their feet. If they'd had a choice they would have waited for the cover of night. But no time can be wasted with the Confession Room. Not with these people.

They reach the house, gathering around the various ways inside – the door at the front, one at the side and another at the back – all ready for a coordinated, sudden entrance.

Three, two, one –

'Police!' they shout, the rams battering against the doors in unison.

They rush inside, the unit to the front making their way upstairs, the units from the back and side filtering to opposite sides of the building.

Nothing.

'Any location of the basement stairs?' a voice cries from the centre of the house.

Emilia opens her eyes, blinking slowly in the bright fluorescent light of the interview room as she remembers the feeling of the man's grip as it burned into her skin. He had tugged her up a set of stairs, her feet stumbling beneath her, yanked to standing again by the binding at her wrists. Then there was a short walk, the air close and dank. Then the cold, fresh relief of outside.

She closes her eyes again.

Their footsteps thunder across the building and then down the narrow set of stairs into the darkness of the rooms hidden beneath. A short corridor: then a room to one side, monitors on the desk, the screens black; and a large pane of glass – the other side of the two-way mirror.

Then at the end of the hallway, a heavy metal door, a steel bar drawn across into the wall, locking it from the outside.

The officer at the front grasps the bar and pulls, the metal creaking as it refuses to move. Finally, it gives, shrieking like nails on a chalkboard as it judders open. The officer thrusts one hand against the door, pushing it open, his other hand aiming his weapon.

Tears spill from Emilia's closed eyes, through her lashes and down her cheeks, pooling around her mouth.

There it is.

The Confession Room. The countdown suspended from the centre of the ceiling, the numbers frozen at sixty seconds. The mirror, gleaming. Discarded boxes in the corners. The iron half-moons hammered into the walls on opposite corners.

Emilia opens her eyes. That is where her imagination ends the story. That is where she is unable to even try to predict what might happen inside that room. Will they be there – the man and the woman? If they are, will they be alone? Or will there be victims chained to the walls?

And will they be dead or alive?

The door bursts open and Emilia lifts her head, anxiety flooding through her, her entire body humming.

'Ciaran?' she whispers, not believing it.

But it is him standing at the door, the colour in his face drained away with worry, his eyes red and tired. He rushes towards her, dropping to his knees as his arm wraps around her waist, his head turning towards her, his mouth pressing a warm kiss against her neck.

'I heard that some units had gone out to a suspected location of the Room . . . And then someone said your name, said you were here . . . What's going on, Emi?'

She avoids his insistent gaze, instead looking down at the floor, at the stain on the carpet just between his feet. How is she going to tell him that she lied? And even worse – how is she going to tell him what she did?

'I figured out where they've been taking people . . .' She takes a deep, shaky breath, her chin trembling. 'I lied when I said I didn't remember anything.'

Ciaran's breathing falters, just for a second, his face contorting with confusion. 'You promised . . . you said that you didn't –'

'I know, and I'm so sorry.' He drops his hands from

around her waist, one lifting to his forehead, his eyes partially hidden behind his fingers. She reaches for him, her heart falling as he flinches at her touch. 'I didn't want to lie to you but I was scared.'

'Scared of what? Scared of them harming your family? Your parents have officers at their house now. You would be protected. We would protect you – they couldn't hurt you again.'

'You don't understand –'

'So explain!' He drops to his knees. 'I'm right here . . . It's me, Emi. You've always been able to tell me everything. So, tell me.'

'I want to, but –'

'But what?'

She shakes her head. 'You can't be the first to know the truth,' she whispers. 'I wish I could explain, but I can't.'

'The first to know the truth about what?'

Emilia's chest tightens at his sad, confused eyes. She reaches out a finger, tracing his stubble-covered chin with a sigh. 'The truth about what really happens in that room.'

Ciaran's expression freezes as her words hit him, a blow that takes a second or two to feel.

'Ciaran, I –'

The door opens, air rushing out of the room. They both look round, Ciaran peering over his shoulder to face the door.

It's Henry. And just behind his shoulder is Inspector Wild. Her face is completely still, neutral as she stares down at Emilia and Ciaran, but Henry's expression is stern, almost cold.

'Emilia, can you come with us, please?' Henry says. 'We have some questions for you if that's okay?'

Ciaran rushes to his feet, his gaze darting from Henry to Wild and back again to Emilia.

'What's happening?' he asks, his voice strained.

'Ciaran, it's probably best if you leave. You shouldn't be here.'

Emilia rises to her feet, her hands raised to her mouth, as if in silent prayer.

'What happened?' she whispers. 'Did you find the Room?'

'We'll explain more during your interview, Emilia.' Wild steps to one side and points towards the door. 'Come with me.'

'Wait –' Ciaran holds out his arm, blocking the door. 'What's going on? What did you find at that farm? Penny –'

'Ciaran, I am telling you now as your superior that you need to leave,' Wild interrupts, staring at him impassively. 'You were taken off this investigation for a reason and right now you are actively impeding it.'

Ciaran shakes his head, lifting his hands up in a silent question. She wishes she could explain. She wishes she could give him the answers to all his confusion. But she can't say anything.

Wild walks away, stepping out of the room and waiting to one side.

Emilia takes a step forward, her feet shuffling on the carpet. They are heavy, as if a weight is bound around her ankles. A chain . . . just like before.

Ciaran watches her silently as she moves past him. She doesn't want to look his way, but she is pulled to him as

265

always, a magnet drawn to its opposite. His eyes are full of the secrets he knows she is keeping from him. She wants to whisper that she is sorry. But she won't. Not with Wild there listening.

Instead she breaks away from his once comforting gaze and walks out, leaving him behind, all alone in that room.

Emilia is sitting back in her chair, desperately trying to create as much distance as she can between herself and Wild on the other side of the table, DS Brennan at her side. But the tension between them is still unbearable.

'Okay,' Wild says. 'Let's go.'

Brennan leans across the table, reaching for the recording device. He pushes a button firmly. A loud beep sounds, signalling the start of the interview.

'This is the first interview under caution of Emilia Haines.' He pauses briefly. 'I am Detective Sergeant Brennan and with me in this interview is Detective Inspector Wild.'

'Emilia,' Wild says, shuffling forward in her chair. 'We firstly want to thank you for the information you gave this morning. I know that it must have been difficult for you to do so, but –'

'Did they find the Room?'

Emilia bites down hard on her bottom lip – she shouldn't have interrupted.

'They did find the Room, yes.'

'And the couple?'

Wild pauses, her face still calm. She shakes her head. 'They weren't there, Emilia.'

'They weren't?'

266

'No. And they had removed everything.' Wild sighs, blinking rapidly. 'Well, everything except the latest victims.'

Emilia gasps, her hands flying to cover her ears. 'Victims?'

'Yes. A man and a woman. Both chained to the wall.'

'Alive?' Emilia whispers the hopeful word, even though she already knows the horrifying truth.

Wild shakes her head abruptly. 'Dead.'

Harris Keaton's face appears, hovering in the space between her and Wild.

'Do you know who they were?'

'We'll talk about that in a while,' Wild says. 'First, I'd like to show you something.'

Emilia bites her tongue, forcing down the many desperate questions she has about who they found in that room, the words choking her. She was too late.

Wild opens a laptop and places it in front of the recording device, facing outward so that all three of them are able to see the screen. The forum is there, its stark white background shining out at them, *The Confession Room* hanging from the top of the page, taunting her.

'As officers arrived at the location this morning and found the Room empty except for two bodies, a new post went up on the forum, Emilia,' Wild says. She begins to scroll, her perfectly manicured nails clicking on the trackpad.

She stops, zooming in on the post so it is enlarged on the screen.

Emilia squints, her eyes racing over the confession. Have they named Harris? Who was the woman? She stalls as the words click into place.

This isn't a confession.

We wished you luck and it seems that our wishes may have served you well. This is the end of the Confession Room.

But the end comes with a price. Because somebody broke the rules.

Emilia Haines: the consequences of the below are all because of you.

The Confession Room has not been what it appears. And it is time to reveal the truth. It is time to reveal who the real monsters are.

Emilia's eyes linger on her name – that sentence turning her cold from the inside out.

'As you'll see,' Wild continues, moving the screen downwards, 'below the post are several links.'

Emilia leans in even closer, her teeth chattering against each other.

Rosie Johnson – murderer

Joseph Henley – murderer

Isabella Santos – murderer

Emilia Haines – murderer

Emilia stares at the screen, her mind unable to process how one word follows on from the other. Everything inside her has fallen still, the room turning inconceivably quiet – the storm swirling around her.

Wild clicks on Emilia's name and they are transported

to another site with a black screen, a play button suspended in the middle of the screen. A video whirs for a moment, and then the room appears. And there, standing just feet away from Ryan, is Emilia. Her arms raised, holding the gun.

'Is that you, Emilia?' Wild asks, a gentle voice for a pointed question.

But she can't answer. She tries to breathe in, but she can't. She can't watch this, she can't do this —

A loud bang blasts through the laptop speakers. Emilia cries out, covering her eyes, but too late. Ryan's body slams into the wall behind him, instantly collapsing as life vanishes in a moment.

Wild pauses the video and jabs her finger at the screen.

'That's you — isn't it, Emilia?'

She nods slowly, tears streaming down her face. She can't deny it. It is as clear as day. How had she been so stupid?

'Emilia Haines, we are arresting you on suspicion of murder, perverting the course of justice and assisting an offender. You do not have to say anything. But, it may harm your defence if you do not mention when questioned something which you later rely on in court. Anything you do say may be given in evidence.'

All of the oxygen in Emilia's lungs is forced out of her, as if she has been punched in the stomach. Winded. She falls completely still, her mouth hanging open.

They know everything.

The world knows everything.

20th November, 11 a.m.

Emilia comes to the end of the story and she collapses backwards in the chair, exhausted, the emotional toll of the truth grinding her down. She feels as though there is nothing left of her, nothing more than dust and bone.

After watching the video, Wild and Brennan informed her of her entitlement to a legal representative. She peers at him sideways now, her mind flashing back to all the interviews she had conducted where the suspect shook their head defiantly, believing that refusing a lawyer would make them look innocent. But it doesn't make you look innocent. It simply makes you look foolish. He must be in his fifties, his eyes weary as he looks down at his notebook, his pen poised. They spoke briefly, just for a few minutes before coming back into the room together, and he advised her to say nothing. She told him that she would be telling them everything. He simply shook his head, a disappointed sigh escaping his lips. 'I've given you my advice,' he muttered.

She told them everything about what happened, and the man and woman, describing them as much as she could without having seen their faces. Everything except approaching Isabella Santos. All that would do was show that she had considered telling them earlier, and that Isabella had refused. Is she in a room down the corridor?

Maybe she's being interviewed directly next door, just on the other side of this wall. Is she answering any of their questions? Or is she staying silent, repeating no comment like a record, the needle sticking? Every time Emilia says something, her lawyer sighs, as if it's disappointing him all over again that she is choosing to speak.

'Emilia,' Wild says, tucking one ankle behind the other, her posture still perfect after almost an hour of sitting on a cold plastic chair. 'Did you have any contact with the man and woman you've described after they left you on Wheelhouse Avenue?'

The room seems to shrink, the walls inching inwards. Do they know about Harris Keaton? Did the man and the woman record the phone calls? If they did that might be a good thing for her – it would show that she was threatened; it might help prove that they were being forced to follow the rules.

She rubs her eyes with the back of her hand, the skin sore. With a sigh, she nods.

'Yes,' she mutters.

'How did they contact you?' Brennan asks, his shoulders curving forwards, his forearms extending to the centre of the table.

'They called me from a blocked number. The voice was disguised. Distorted.'

'And what did they want?'

Emilia swallows. 'They wanted me to help them,' she whispers.

'Help them do what?' Brennan asks.

'H-help . . . h-help them abduct their next victim.'

Brennan and Wild exchange quick glances with each other, Wild's face still neutral, the image of professionalism. But Brennan's cheeks are flushed, his gaze unfocused, as if he hadn't expected that admission to leave Emilia's lips.

'Who was the victim?' Wild presses.

Once again, faces appear in front of Emilia, each of them a swift, unexpected blow. Harris. His two children: George and Maisie. Her face crumples. She collapses her head into her hands, her shoulders shaking as she is consumed by sobs, coming from deep inside her.

'I know this isn't easy for you,' Brennan says – good cop to Wild's bad. 'But we need you to calm down and answer our questions. Who did they want you to help them abduct?'

Emilia's chest aches as she tries to catch her breath, willing his name to form in her mouth.

'Was it Harris Keaton?' Wild says, her voice calm.

Emilia's breathing hitches, her cheeks flushed with emotion. 'Was it him?' she whispers. 'Was it him inside the Room this morning?'

Her eyes dart from Brennan to Wild and back again as she implores them silently for the answer.

'Yes,' Wild says bluntly. 'It was him.'

Emilia lets out a broken wail. 'I tried. I tried to stop it! Who was the woman?'

'Her name was Lucy Platt. She worked at the same firm as Harris Keaton – there were allegations of assault.'

Another two people dead. And she could have stopped it. She could have saved them.

'Why didn't you call the police straightaway?' Wild says, leaning forward, her elbows pressing into the table.

'I told you. They threatened me – they told us that they would –'

'They said that they would hurt your families. But that's the consequence you risked when you came to us today, identifying the location. So why didn't you do it earlier, when it could have saved Harris Keaton's life?'

'I really wish I had. But until last night I was too scared. I just couldn't do it. You don't understand what these people are like. I was terrified of them. They'll do anything to get their own way –'

'And you agreed to help them.'

Emilia clears her throat. 'I didn't help them,' she says firmly, wiping her tears away roughly with the knuckle of her index finger.

Wild stares at Emilia for a moment, then runs her finger over the trackpad and the frozen video appears once again, the image still there: Ryan's body on the floor, Emilia's hand still raised, the gun turning upwards from the recoil.

She minimizes the window, navigating to a nameless folder containing several coded files. 'Since Harris Keaton was found early this morning, officers went to retrieve CCTV to show his last movements.' Clicking on the first one, she returns her gaze to Emilia's face, one eyebrow arched. 'Who is that?' She jabs her finger at the screen, her scarlet red nails bright against the black and white of the CCTV image.

It's the bar – the Dandy Fox. But it wouldn't have been difficult to track down where he was – everyone from Laughton and Kemp knew he was there. The timestamp on the top right-hand corner indicates that the image was captured at 8:23 p.m.

'What were you doing there?'

Emilia tears her eyes away from the image. 'They asked me to go there.'

'What did they want you to do?'

Wild shifts slightly in her seat, inching closer towards the table, her stare fixed and unblinking. Emilia sniffs, her eyes blurring, as if her mind is trying to block out the question, block out everything, even the memory of him, their brief encounter erased forever. But it isn't working. He is there, his face as clear as theirs across the table.

'Before they released me from the Room, they told me that they would call on me. That survivors of the Room were expected to help.'

Wild and Brennan glance across at each other again, fleetingly, a small nod passing between them. Either they are noting a question to ask the others, or somebody has already admitted to something.

They look back at Emilia, and Wild nods at her to continue.

The explanation spills out of Emilia, one word chasing another, faster and faster as she tries to get it over with. But as she finishes all she can think is that she actually did it: she followed their instructions, like a kicked dog scared of its master, until the final step. How could she do that? If she hadn't seen the photograph of his children, would Harris Keaton have ended up drugged on her living room floor?

Her eyes blur again, her brain taking control: don't think about it. Block it out.

'Now, here you are approaching Mr Keaton and you stand outside chatting with him for approximately fifteen minutes. Just under.'

'Yes.'

'What did you talk about?' Brennan asks.

'I asked him for a lighter.'

'Are you a regular smoker?'

Emilia drops her chin, staring down at her hands which are wringing together in her lap, her thumb scratching at a piece of loose skin on her index finger. 'No. On the phone they told me he was a smoker. So I . . . I bought a packet of cigarettes from the shop next to the station. It's an easy way to approach someone.'

'So you had given it some thought? How you would approach him?'

'Yes.' She pulls at the loose skin and it tears away, stinging sharply. She winces. 'I'd thought about it. I had to.'

Wild nods and plays the video. They watch in silence for a few moments: Emilia and Harris close together, their heads lowered. Then Emilia begins to back away, eventually turning and walking quickly towards the bar, disappearing inside.

'See,' Emilia says. 'This is where I went inside to try to get away. I realized that I couldn't do it. I just couldn't. I told him that I needed to quickly go to the toilet before we headed back to mine.'

'Why the sudden change of heart?' Brennan asks. 'You had gone so far in approaching him.'

'I saw a picture on his phone – a picture of his children. And when I saw their faces, I just . . . I knew that I couldn't. I couldn't be directly responsible for him being taken to that place.'

Wild sits back in her chair, her upright composure being replaced with a new body language, arms crossed,

275

chin jutting forward. 'This is where it gets interesting, Emilia . . . There's no more footage of you at this bar. You disappear inside, and then – nothing.'

'I rushed to the toilets, then I went out of the fire doors at the back.'

Wild pauses, scrutinizing Emilia's expression, her smooth skin crinkling with concentration. Tearing her eyes away, she turns to the laptop and presses play once more.

'If you could watch Mr Keaton please, Emilia,' she says.

Emilia nods, forcing her tired eyes to concentrate, to focus on the small figure of the man on the screen. He stands in the same spot for some time, occasionally glancing at his watch. But then he moves closer to the door, coming to a stop just outside. He peers through the arched window, past the security guard partially blocking his view.

Suddenly he moves, pushing through the doors and into the bar.

'He followed you in,' Wild says. 'Presumably to find out where you'd gone.'

'I didn't see him. When I came out of the toilets, I didn't look to see if he was still there.'

'And this is where things take a turn. You see, just like you, Mr Keaton enters that bar and doesn't come back out.'

Emilia's muscles turn rigid. 'What do you mean?'

'He goes inside and then he does not come out.'

'What about inside? Surely there's footage of him inside?'

'When we retrieved this CCTV from the bar we asked

276

if there was footage of the back exit to check if he left that way. There isn't a camera out there. The only camera they have covers the bar itself,' Brennan answers. 'There's another one pointing down the corridor to the toilets but it hasn't been working for months.' He shrugs. 'You know how it is.'

'So . . . what happened to him?'

'You tell us,' Wild mutters pointedly.

'I don't know!' Emilia cries. 'I left and that was it! I went home and then drove to my parents' house, terrified that they were following me; I stayed up all night terrified that they were going to arrive at my house and do something horrible, and then when their last post came, I decided to figure out where they were to try and stop them!' She inhales sharply, her shoulders rising and falling. 'I don't know what happened to him.'

Wild sighs, shaking her head, and turns back to the laptop. The CCTV footage opens again but this version is zoomed in on Harris and Emilia as they were standing outside down the side street, their bodies and faces now blurred. Wild presses play and a short clip begins.

Emilia looks slowly from Wild to Brennan. 'I don't understand what I'm looking at.'

Wild taps and the sequence plays again. Emilia lifts her arm and Harris takes something from her, throwing his head back before passing it back again.

Her drink. He asked for a sip of her drink.

Emilia's stomach drops as realization hits. They think she spiked his drink, there at the Dandy Fox, and then he was abducted from the back.

'Wait . . . you don't think that –'

'Why did you give him your drink?'

'He asked me for it! After I asked him to come back to the house he asked if he could have a sip for Dutch courage – he made a joke out of it!'

'Okay,' Wild says, as if she is offering a concession. 'If you didn't use the flunitrazepam in that drink – where is it?'

'Where's what?'

'The drug. The very strong sedative you were going to use to knock a man unconscious so he could be abducted. You say you didn't use it.' She lifts her hand, palm upwards. 'So where is it?'

Emilia closes her eyes, her mind flashing back to the sound of her feet thundering down the road, terror roaring in her chest. Her arm flying outwards to throw the small plastic bag into the hedge. 'I threw it away.'

'Well, that would be convenient, wouldn't it?' Wild lifts her hand to her chin. 'If the plan had been for Harris Keaton to go home with you, and for you to use the drug against him there, why did you take it with you?'

'I . . . I took the photo and the powder and put it in my bag. I didn't want to just leave them in my house.'

'Or is the more sensible conclusion that there was never actually a plan for you to go back to the house? The plan was for you to give him the sedative there. After all, why would they trust that you could get him back to your house? Surely it would be easier to simply tell you to go to a location, a location where they knew without doubt he would be, and for you to slip the drug into his drink?'

'But that isn't true. And I never gave him the drug. They got to him another way.'

278

'Mr Keaton had traces of flunitrazepam in his system when he died.'

The room turns silent, the sound of the recorder suddenly loud in her ears, white noise rushing in like the tide.

'He had what?'

'At some point in the hours before his death, flunitrazepam was administered to Harris Keaton.'

Emilia's mind races, her eyes flying about the room, searching for an explanation. 'One of them must have been there all along. And we wouldn't know – we have no idea who they are.'

'Or maybe, if we're throwing theories around, you spiked his drink, pretended you needed the toilet knowing that he would eventually follow you to the back of the bar where there's no cameras, and he was picked up there by the people behind the Confession Room. Is that what happened?'

'No! I told you – I was going to take him back to my house, but I changed my mind. I couldn't do it. And why would I do that? It was already a huge risk simply showing my face. Why would I drug him in public? What if something had gone wrong?'

'Why would you do any of this when you could have simply come to the police?'

'You don't understand!' Emilia shouts, her temper finally breaking. 'And you never will! Unless you're snatched from your house and chained to a wall in a room, not knowing if you will ever come out alive. You don't know how it felt to be given your freedom but on condition that you obey.'

'Emilia, I'm just doing my job,' Wild says, holding her hands up in feigned defensiveness. 'I have to challenge you with what the evidence is indicating. And the evidence points towards you willingly killing the man you believe murdered your sister, and then working with the man and woman behind the Confession Room to murder another man.'

'But that isn't true! I didn't want to kill Ryan. I was forced. And I know that it seems like I made the wrong choice. With Ryan and with Harris. But I didn't feel like I had one. I'll live with what I've done always . . . but I tried. I really did try to save them.'

Emilia stops speaking, unable to utter another word, and suddenly all of the pent-up anger and confusion, her frustration at not being believed, is replaced with an overwhelming guilt. She could have done more. She should have done more.

She drops her head into her hands and she cries. Uncontrollable, soul-shaking sobs, from deep inside her, from the dark place where regret and shame and hatred hide their faces. But now they are there, their ugliness emerging into the light, refusing to stay hidden any longer.

20th November, 1 p.m.

'Okay, Emilia: in you go. You'll be held here until a charging decision is made.'

Emilia lifts her head, blinking into the bright white light. Brennan gestures at her but she is so exhausted after the hours spent in interview, it takes her a moment to recognize what he is asking her to do. Her breath catches in her throat as the world stops spinning and what is in front of her falls into focus.

A cell. Six feet by six feet. White painted concrete walls, yellowing with age. A camera hanging from one corner. A thick metal door.

'I . . .' She turns to look at Brennan and he frowns at her, his eyes darting to the custody officer standing on Emilia's other side, keys in hand. 'I don't have to go in there, do I?'

Brennan raises his shoulders, his face torn. 'Given what she's been through, surely –'

'We have to keep them separate,' the custody officer says. 'So she has to go into a cell – Wild's orders.'

'Maybe I should speak to the sergeant –'

'You can, but she's busy booking someone else in.' The custody officer places a hand on Emilia's shoulder. 'If you go in for now and we can chat to the sergeant. Go on – you'll be fine. You've been in lots of these before.'

Emilia nods, unable to react, unable to argue back. All her senses are prioritizing one thing: the small cell just feet away from her. She shuffles forward, removing her shoes. Stepping inside, she moves quickly to the bed and sits down, swinging around to face the door. She brings her knees up to her chest and hugs them tightly, her chin resting on top. Breathing in shakily, she expels the air through her teeth in a low whistle.

The custody officer tugs on the door and it slams loudly. The lock clicks into place.

Emilia whimpers. The walls are so close. Her eyes are drawn to the camera, its light glowing red. She flinches as the camera in the Confession Room runs through her mind unbidden, its hateful eye taking in everything that she did, her shame recorded in perpetuity. Heat washes over her, sweat pooling in her chest under her top, the fabric sticking to her skin. She presses her face down into her knees, her eyes squeezing shut.

Her hands fly up to her head, her fists pressing into her temples.

She just needs to calm down. This isn't the Confession Room. She isn't trapped. She's with the police. At the station. She is safe –

A loud bang sounds from outside.

A gun.

No – it wasn't a gun. It was just a door closing. She is safe –

No. No – she isn't safe. She needs to get out! They're going to hurt her –

She throws herself off the bed, falling to her hands and knees before staggering forward, launching herself at the door with all her might, fists hammering against the unforgiving metal.

'Let me out!' she screams.

The walls close in, inching towards her.

'Please! Let me out! You can't just keep me in here! Please!'

Welcome to the Confession Room.

'LET ME OUT!'

Black spots flash across her vision, her head spinning, her legs unsteady and weak. And suddenly the floor is rushing up to meet her, an instant stab of pain and then darkness.

'Emilia,' a voice says, breaking through the heavy fog. 'Emilia, can you sit up, please? Can you hear me?'

She tries to open her eyes but they feel heavy, weighted down, so heavy it is as though she will never be able to open them again. Her face scrunches in on itself, eyebrows lowering, nose lifting, mouth twitching. A ray of blinding light rushes in through a small gap in her eyelashes and she winces. But her eyes blink rapidly, finally opening to stare up at the greying ceiling, three faces hovering above her.

Brennan, the custody officer and a new face are there. Emilia narrows her eyes, trying to focus on the third person. Her face shifts into focus.

'Jenny.' Emilia's eyes flood with tears – her best friend is here. But the rush of relief is tinged with shame. What will she think of her now?

'Jesus, Emi,' she huffs, her face wrinkled with concern. 'You scared the living shit out of me.' She pushes her hand underneath Emilia's shoulders. 'Come on, sit up.'

Emilia tenses, allowing some of her weight to be taken

by Jenny, and by the other custody officer whose face is wrinkled with concern. Probably worried that she'll be blamed.

'You feeling okay?' Brennan asks as Emilia sits up, her back aching.

She nods. 'I just feel a bit shaken. Did I hit my head?'

'No,' the custody officer says quickly. 'Your arm flew out . . . your shoulder took the brunt of it.'

Emilia nods, turning back to Jenny. 'I can't be locked in that room. Please.'

'We're not going to lock you in, Emilia.' She stares sideways at the officer and then glances out into the custody suite, bustling with people and energy. 'And anyone who thinks I'm saying that because you're my friend,' she says in a loud voice, her tone pointed, 'can think again. That's come from Holden.'

'I was just following orders,' the officer says, in a low, defeated whisper.

'I know,' Jenny says. 'You can go back to whatever you were doing before.'

The officer nods and glances quickly at Emilia before rushing away, staring at her feet.

'You can go too,' Jenny says to Brennan. 'I'm sure you're very busy.'

'Thanks,' he says. He nods at her, then raises a hand to Emilia, his face a bewildered mix of sympathy and annoyance. Jenny watches him leave, her hand still pressing into Emilia's back, her touch firm and strong.

'Ciaran's been messaging me non-stop,' she whispers. 'He's so worried about you.'

'I hate myself for doing this to him. To you as well . . . I'm so sorry.'

'Don't say another word,' Jenny says.

'Sorry. I don't want you to get in trouble –'

'I didn't mean it like that, you lemon,' she says, smiling sadly. 'You've nothing to be sorry about. I don't know what's gone on but I do know that you're one of the best people there is.'

Emilia sighs. She isn't so sure about that. She isn't sure of anything. She doesn't even know who she is any more.

Jenny stands, pulling at the material of her trousers which has gathered around her knees. She holds out her hand and Emilia grabs it, groaning quietly as she is pulled to her feet.

'When did you last sleep?'

'Wednesday night. Last night I stayed up . . .'

'So maybe you should try to get some rest. We'll wake you if they call you for more interviews. And we won't shut the door, I promise. But I'll have to get one of the lads to sit outside. I know you're not going to do anything stupid, but –'

'No, I know. You're doing your job. Thanks, Jenny.'

Emilia turns back into the cell, the flat, thin mattress atop a shaky metal frame not really inspiring a desire to sleep. But maybe once she lies down the exhaustion will quickly overcome her. And she'll face the open door.

Jenny smiles at her, warm like afternoon sunlight, and then walks quickly out of the room. 'Grant,' her booming voice calls out, as clear as if she was right beside her, 'can you come and do an offender watch at cell eight?'

Emilia takes three slow steps towards the bed. It's so low it only reaches halfway up her shins. She folds herself on to it, wincing as her weight drops on to her shoulder. Then she turns over quickly, away from the wall which looks too familiar to the walls of the Confession Room, the dirtying white paint causing small bubbles of anxiety to pop in her chest. But as she turns on to her right, she sees the door wide open, and a police officer – Grant – sitting on a chair just a few feet further away, a cup of tea clutched between his fingers.

He catches her looking and raises his mug towards her. 'Want one?'

She shakes her head, her hair rustling against the plastic of the mattress. 'No, thanks.'

'Let me know if you do.'

'Thanks,' she whispers, her voice breaking at this small act of kindness.

She wants to close her eyes, she wants to sleep, but for now fear fixes her eyelids in place, her mind constantly searching for confirmation of where she is, who is around her, that the door is still open. Until even her terrified senses are not enough to withstand the pressure of a body wracked with fatigue, and her eyes, heavy and aching, finally close.

But still she dreams, the terrors arriving quickly.

She dreams of the Confession Room.

The mug is warm between her hands, her fingers clutching at the fading china.

'It's perfect,' Emilia says, taking another small sip. 'Thank you.'

'If I can do anything, it's make a banging cup of tea,' Grant says, lowering his chin to watch her from beneath his eyebrows.

She smiles, the warmth of the emotion reaching down into her chest. She is finally feeling a bit more normal. Although normal is relative. All that it means at this point in time is that her body is not utterly consumed with terror, her nervous system reacting to every sound, every strange smell, every sensation registering as alien and unsafe. It means that she has had a small amount of sleep, interrupted by being called for three further interviews through the evening and into the night, the same questions asked of her in different ways, pieces of information they have gathered from elsewhere being drip-fed to her, sprung on her at the opportune moment. It means that with each tick of the clock, she is getting ever closer to her twenty-four hours being over, and a decision being made. Will they let her go? Will she be charged? She closes her eyes, either outcome feeling overwhelmingly too large. Either option not changing the fact that life will never be the same: one way or the other everything will be different. She will be different. Until the man and the woman are found, she will live in constant fear. And everybody – from people she has always known to strangers in the street – will think of her differently. The old Emilia is gone.

Movement at the top of the corridor catches Emilia's eye and she tenses, anticipating danger, both real and imagined.

It's Jenny. And there, just behind her, still wearing her heels, is Wild.

'Emilia,' Wild says. 'We need you to come with us.'

A strange feeling of acceptance washes over Emilia – it's

time. Now she will know. She sets her mug of tea down on the floor with a clink then, groaning, she stands, lifting her hand to grip her shoulder which is still aching, the skin now black and blue with deep bruises.

She follows them out of the cell, smiling at Grant as they walk past him, wondering what he is feeling at this very moment. Does he look at her and feel conflicted about what and who she is? Victim or liar? Survivor or murderer?

They reach the custody desk and Emilia braces herself to finally find out her fate as Jenny breaks away, taking her place behind it. But Wild does not stop – instead she veers away, taking the corridor to the right, and turns abruptly into the interview room. And there is someone waiting for them, his notebook in hand. The Detective Chief Inspector – Henry.

He looks as tired as Emilia, his face drawn, the weight of the past twenty-four hours sitting heavily astride his shoulders. 'Good morning, Emilia.'

She glances awkwardly at Wild who is staring at her, a frown fixed to her face. 'Good morning, sir,' Emilia replies. She holds her hand out towards the chair she has been sitting in for every interview, the seat hard and unyielding. 'Should I –'

'Yes, sit, please.'

But Henry and Wild do not follow; they stay standing, Henry shifting from foot to foot, Wild continuing her furrowed blank stare. Emilia waits, her heart racing. What are they going to tell her? Why does this all feel so strange? She has been through this process so many times, with so many people, the outcomes always the same. Charge or release. Remand or bail. So why does this feel so odd?

'Emilia, we're going to explain the decision that has been made,' Henry says, 'but we've brought you into this room because we need to speak to you. There's some things that have happened while you've been at this station that you need to be made aware of.'

'Okay . . .' Emilia sighs. 'Sir, I'm really sorry, but you standing there above me is making me very uncomfortable —'

'Of course,' he says quickly. 'Wild — let's sit.'

'Yes, sir,' she says.

They both sit opposite Emilia. She presses her lips together, the dry skin cracking, the tangy taste of iron on the tip of her tongue. Whatever has happened, it's something big.

'Why don't you explain what's happening with her arrest, Wild?' Henry says. 'And then I can . . .' His voice fades away, his sentence incomplete, hanging in the air unfinished.

'Of course,' Wild says. She shuffles to the edge of her seat, her hands pressed together, pointing towards Emilia. 'Emilia, you're going to be released on conditional bail pending further enquiries.'

'Bail?' She glances back and forth between them. 'I'm not being charged?'

'No,' Wild says. 'This case, all of the moving pieces . . . we need more time to consider the evidence. And for the CPS to consider what is in the public interest.'

Emilia's arms turn cold, her skin covered in goosebumps. The public interest. Of course . . . For any prosecution to continue, a case must pass two tests: there must be enough evidence, and it must be in the public interest. But what is that balance in a case like this? Should the people who made it out of the Room be punished? Or should they be forgiven? Where does that leave the dead, if the people who pulled the trigger go free?

'Okay . . .' Emilia looks away from Wild, turning to focus on Henry with wide, pleading eyes. 'So what's the other thing?'

He sighs, rubbing his forehead, the skin wrinkling and stretching. 'Emilia, since those videos were released, the videos of each victim being killed, there has been a significant reaction. As you'll probably be able to understand, a lot of people are . . . upset.'

'Angry,' Wild says.

Henry throws a withering glance in her direction. Wild lowers her gaze, sucking in her bottom lip.

'Yes, people are upset and . . . and angry,' Henry continues. 'There's already been a protest this morning. With people on both sides. But some people – and we will be coming down on them – some people have acted out.'

Emilia frowns. 'Acted out? What does that mean?'

'Well, in your case . . . Ryan Kirkland's mother has found your address.'

The colour drains from Emilia's face, her eyes blinking rapidly. 'What has she done?'

'She and a group of others have encamped themselves outside. They've graffitied on the door, on the entrance . . . even on the pavement outside. She's demanding that you pay for the murder of her son.'

Emilia's mouth trembles, her teeth chattering uncontrollably. She grips her hands together, her nails digging into her palm, pressing harder and harder to inflict some pain, anything to serve as a distraction from the information that is cascading towards her.

'So, we can't bail you to your address.' Henry leans forward, his fingers stretching towards her across the table. 'We'll bail you to your parents' house and we'll make sure there's police presence nearby. And the same goes for Isabella. They found her address too.'

Emilia freezes. 'Isabella?'

'Yes. She is going to be bailed to a family member. Her mum and her siblings are going to stay there too. They couldn't remain in their home.'

'What about the others?'

Wild coughs. 'Sorry,' she says, staring at the floor. Her eyes are watering. A chill runs down Emilia's spine. Is Wild crying?

'What about the others?' she asks again, each word dropping like stones into water, each ripple growing bigger than the last.

'Rosie Johnson, the last survivor, the woman who was taken directly after you, is missing. We've been unable to locate her. We are assuming that as soon as the videos went live she made a run for it.'

Henry swallows loudly, dragging his eyes to Emilia, her mouth open, her gaze full of questions. She doesn't say anything: part of her isn't sure what more to ask; the other part full of fear.

'Joseph Henley is dead.' He shakes his head slowly, his hands clasped to his chest, over his heart. 'He committed suicide.'

Emilia lets out a shaky breath, her mind falling completely still, completely quiet. 'Wh-when?' she stammers.

'Just after his family saw the video,' Wild says. 'He was at home with them. He ran upstairs with a knife and locked himself in.'

'No . . .' Emilia cries, her face crumpling with pain. 'Please, no –'

'Emilia,' Henry says, moving off his chair and around the table to kneel in front of her, his hand gripping hers. 'I didn't want to tell you this now. It's too much.'

'No, it isn't enough! It's no more than I deserve –'

'Don't –'

'It's my fault! It's my fault he's gone! They all stayed quiet and I just had to come to you! I just had to tell the truth, do what I thought was right! I knew what the consequences would be and I still did it!'

Isabella's voice echoes in her ear, the memory springing up from deep inside her. *Joseph Henley killed his own brother! You're going to ask him to risk the truth coming out?*

Emilia lets her head fall into her hands, her sobs ringing out of the interview room and into the custody suite.

What has she done? What should she have done? How can this be real?

Isabella warned her of what could happen. And now it has come to pass. She wanted to save people – to make sure that nobody else's life would be taken. But now Joseph Henley is dead. Rosie Johnson is missing. She didn't even manage to save Harris Keaton and the poor woman who was taken with him, who would have been set free – now she is dead too.

And her and Isabella? Their futures are balanced in the hands of a baying crowd. Some calling for mercy. Others for blood.

21st November, 1.30 p.m.

Emilia stares out of the window of her childhood bedroom, her heartbeat pounding in her ears. Even though the Confession Room has been abandoned, the forum completely silent, she hasn't been able to stop herself from keeping sentry. What if they still choose to retaliate? What if it isn't over?

She takes a steadying breath, cracking her knuckles as she backs away to lie on the single bed. She props her laptop on her chest and opens the internet, navigating to the news. She shouldn't look – she knows that taking in what is being said is like taking in poison – but she can't help it. She has to know.

There, on the main page, are their faces. Isabella, Joseph, Rosie. And her. A bold headline written beneath the photographs: *The Confession Room Killers?*

Pressing her lips together, she takes a slow, calming breath and clicks on the headline.

There is an article setting out all the details. She scans it, chewing on the inside of her cheek, but then scrolls back up to the top, ready to click away. Enough for now. But there at the top of the page is a video: a news presenter standing on the streets of London – maybe outside Westminster – holding out a microphone, speaking to passers-by.

'What do you think about what's been revealed about the murders that happened inside the Confession Room?' the presenter asks.

An older man and woman crowd around the micro-phone, him lowering his head towards it. 'I think it's appalling,' he says. 'All this time those people acted like they had been innocent in the whole thing. And they're making the excuse that they were being threatened. They could have said something, though! They told the police nothing and didn't help, knowing what would continue happening –'

'And, and,' the woman interrupts, pulling the microphone towards her, 'those poor people, the ones who were killed, their families deserve justice for what was done. Justice.'

They disappear suddenly, replaced by another woman, young, her long auburn hair pulled back in two French braids. 'I feel sorry for them. They didn't ask to be put in that position. They didn't ask to be taken. They didn't have a choice. Just leave them alone and let them get on with their lives.'

'You don't think that the victims deserve justice?'

'Justice for who? Don't the survivors deserve justice for what they were put through? Why does nobody care about justice for them?'

Her face disappears, replaced once more by a woman holding a sign. Emilia gasps, her mouth hanging open. Ryan's mother. Pippa Kirkland. The sign has a photo-graph of Ryan, their slogan, *Justice for the Victims of the Confession Room,* scrawled across it.

'Mrs Kirkland,' the presenter says. 'May I first express my condolences to you for the loss of your son.'

'Thank you,' she says, her lip trembling.

'Since the videos were released you've been campaign-ing for the people who survived the Confession Room to be prosecuted.'

'Yes. And they should be. I can't understand anybody who argues that they shouldn't. Emilia Haines believed that my son killed her sister. And I'm sorry for anyone who goes through that kind of loss, but my son was not a murderer. And now, instead of being left in peace, we have the police investigating him for something he would never do. He wouldn't hurt anyone. And she took him from me!' Her voice breaks and she stares down at the ground, her face contorting with emotion.

The corner of Emilia's mouth curls upwards with a strange sort of satisfaction. She hadn't expected the police to look into the Confession Room killers' insistence that Ryan killed Sophie. But the investigation has been reopened, after all this time, after all the months of no leads. Maybe Sophie will get justice after all.

'What about the people who created the Confession Room? The people who put your son there in the first place? Would you agree that it's them who deserve to face justice?'

'Yes, but not just them,' she cries. 'It was Emilia Haines who pulled the trigger. It was Emilia Haines who murdered my boy. It's Emilia Haines who should be punished. Lock her up and throw away the —'

Emilia turns off her phone, the screen turning black — Pippa Kirkland's voice coming to a sudden halt. Pressing it to her chest, she stares up at the ceiling, her mind racing. Their words bounce around her head, the opposing opinions colliding against each other, each side trying to consume the other.

'Did that boy really kill our Sophie?' her dad had asked when she first came home, in a horrified whisper.

'I . . . I think so, Dad,' she had muttered. 'He had a

295

photo of her. Taken in secret. And he had talked about hurting a woman called Fiona online.'

'Fiona?' her mum interrupted, heavy with emotion.

'That's what he called her. Sophie, Fi . . . Fiona. Until she died and she was in the news, he thought that was her name. But he wouldn't tell the truth. I don't know what actually happened –'

'We'll never know now.'

Emilia's response died on her lips, the guilt hurtling through her all over again. 'You know that I didn't shoot him because of what they said he did to Sophie, right? Whether it was him or not . . . I did it because otherwise they would have killed me –'

'We know that, love,' her dad said. 'We know . . .'

'I didn't want to lie to you. But I had to!'

They both nodded silently, their eyes spilling over.

Emilia sighs, slamming the laptop shut. She's only been here a couple of days but the tension is palpable, her parents not knowing what to do or say, unable to navigate this new version of their lives or the new version of their daughter.

Her phone vibrates, long and low. A phone call.

Ciaran.

'Hi,' she whispers, already finding comfort in just the thought of his voice. He has spent hours talking to her, reassuring her that he believes her, that it will all turn out right in the end. Justice will be on her side.

'Emilia,' he shouts, his voice panicked, 'you need to lock all the doors and windows now – make sure your parents don't go out –'

Are they here? Are they all in danger?

'Ciaran, what's going on?'

'Your parents' address! It's been posted on the Confession Room! There's officers on their way –'

She throws herself off her bed, her phone clattering to the floor, and races out on to the landing. Her mum is crossing the hall, heading towards the front door.

'Mum, no!'

She thunders down the stairs, darting forward to throw her weight against it just as it opens, slamming it shut.

'Emilia, what are you doing?' her mum cries.

'Your address – it's been posted online! Lock all the windows. Lock the door!'

She spins around, the hall blurring around her as panic rises up, bubbling towards the surface. 'Where's Dad?' she shouts.

'He . . . he went to the shop to get a paper –'

'Call him! Now, Mum!'

Her mum rushes into the kitchen, searching for her phone. 'David!' her voice rings out into the hall. 'Someone put our address on the internet – come home now!'

An engine roars from outside, and Emilia rushes to the living room. Her mouth drops open. There, standing on the pavement outside, is Pippa Kirkland, wearing that same T-shirt, Ryan's face stretched across it, his smile distorted. She has three others with her, two men and another woman, their eyes narrowed as they turn to face the house.

Emilia drops to the floor, her heart racing. They can't get inside – can they? Would they try? What on earth are they hoping to achieve?

'Mum?' she calls out, desperately attempting to project her whisper. 'There's people outside. Ryan Kirkland's mother.'

Her mum rushes into the hall, her eyes widening as she

takes in Emilia crouched down on the floor beneath the windowsill. A loud series of bangs echoes through the house. She's pounding on the front door.

Emilia stares at her mum, shaking her head slowly.

'Don't move,' she whispers.

Her mum steps backwards slowly into the kitchen, the phone pressed to the side of her face. 'David,' she says, her whisper full of terror. 'There's people at the house!'

'Emilia Haines!' a roaring voice shouts. 'We know you're in there!'

Emilia tucks her knees up towards her chest, curling her head downwards to shroud her face. If she ignores them, they'll just go away. If she ignores them, they'll leave her alone.

The pounding comes again, loud and relentless. Mimi runs from the kitchen to the front door, barking loudly, hackles raised.

'Come out here now, you bitch! You need to look me in the face and say the lies you've been telling the world!'

Rage swirls in her stomach but she forces it down, her nails digging into her shins.

The pounding stops, the shouting fading away. Are they leaving?

Emilia uncurls herself, turning on to her knees, readying herself to peer over the windowsill.

A brick flies through the window and she crouches down, throwing her arms over her face as glass shatters over her head.

'Emilia!' her mum screams from the kitchen, her hands covering her mouth in horror.

And suddenly the undiluted fury inside her cannot be

contained. Emilia scrambles to her feet and rushes towards the front door, and Pippa Kirkland spots her, moving away from the living room and darting back up the front path to the porch.

Emilia glares at her through the glass. 'I didn't have a choice – there was a gun pressed to my head.'

Pippa's face flushes with anger. 'You did have a choice. And you had the choice to not spread lies about what my son did –'

'Your son murdered my sister.'

'You're a liar! You're the killer, not my boy, not my Ryan!'

'I'm not, he –'

'Emilia!' her mum shouts. 'Stop –'

'He was a murderer. And nothing you say will ever change that.'

'You're going to go to prison for the rest of your life for this,' Pippa snarls, spit flying from her lips and landing on the glass between them. 'And my Ryan – my Ryan died an innocent man!'

Emilia spots the cross hanging from her neck, the chain swinging just in front of Ryan's eyes. 'God knows what he has done –'

'You bitch!' she cries, pounding against the door once more. 'You fucking bitch! You'll pay for this! You'll pay for this!'

Emilia turns her back, pressing her spine to the front door before dropping to her knees, Pippa's screams still vibrating through her, only stopping as the sound of a police siren wails down the road, the blue lights flashing in through the glass.

25th November, 9 a.m.

Emilia's computer pings and she glances over to the other side of her bed where it is lying discarded. She has been opening it every morning, desperate for any scrap of news on the police search for the man and woman, but quickly finds herself unable to go any further, unable to face what the world might be saying about her. It's as though she is no longer a participant in the events, but simply a witness. With nothing to be done.

She sighs, tucking her legs in towards herself, finding a small comfort in the foetal position. She can't even face looking outside any more – there is a police car parked outside for their protection, but all it does is serve as a reminder that she is a target. Journalists come every day, hounding her parents as they leave the house to go to the shop or to get some fresh air.

'How does it feel knowing that your daughter believed she was killing Sophie's murderer?'

'Do you think she wanted to kill him?'

'How do you feel if it was him? Are you happy that he's gone?'

Her parents try to ignore them, but her mum has stopped leaving the house. And her dad returns as though he has seen a ghost, his face pale and drawn. And they try to speak to her but the conversations feel hollow. Did they really believe her when she insisted that pulling that trigger was to save her own life, rather than to take his? Did she even believe it? When her finger moved, pulling back on itself to let the trigger fly, clattering into the hammer which forced the bullet out of the barrel, travelling faster than she could imagine, killing him instantly – when that happened, was it fear that made her do it? Self-preservation? Or was it anger? Rage? Was it love?

She throws her arm across her face, her elbow wrapping over her head, cocooning herself in the dark. She doesn't know what it was. But does that mean she deserves to be punished? Should she have to spend the rest of her life locked up in a prison or always looking over her shoulder, terrified of what someone might do in the name of vengeance? In the name of justice? Why should she be the one having to live this way? Why should her family be the one with police parked outside the front of their house for protection? Where are they, the man and the woman? The Confession Room was theirs, the entire sick scheme was their doing. They're probably on the run, or hiding in plain sight, but they should be the ones facing the wrath of the public. They should be the ones paying for everything that has happened – for the chaos that they orchestrated. She has been reaching out to the police liaison officer every day, asking questions – have they found anything? Anything at all? But she walks the fine balance between victim and suspect: if the police have found anything, they're not telling her. The helplessness is overwhelming.

She sits up suddenly, gazing at her laptop which stares back at her. She blinks slowly – she has spent the past year watching people, monitoring them, researching them. Finding them.

She grabs the laptop and rushes to the desk. She doesn't need to be helpless. Why is she allowing herself to lie around in this house, waiting for the outcome to the case against her, when she could be trying to figure out who they are? Why has she already given up? If she helps the police find them, it's not only justice for the victims, for their families – but for her and Isabella too. Maybe then they could move on, away from the vitriolic glare, away from all the questions.

Somewhere in everything they said, in what they told her, there will be a key. There must be. And when she finds it, it will unlock everything.

But where to begin?

She closes her eyes, allowing them to appear in the dark. Their shadows reaching towards her, one tall, one smaller. The masks covering their faces. She shudders, her eyes immediately springing open, her heart racing.

No. She needs to stop being scared. They haven't retaliated – they've gone quiet, their heads to the ground. Whoever they are, it seems they've disappeared along with the Confession Room. But they are the ones who should be afraid; they are the ones who should be looking over their shoulder. They can't stay hidden forever. She won't allow it.

She shuts her eyes again, this time tight as a trap. Once again they appear, closer this time. He was very tall – close to two metres. He was broad, his black top taut against his body. She was much smaller, only reaching the centre of his chest. Maybe five foot two, five foot three at the most. And their voices: their voices she could recognize anywhere.

Their relationship . . . When she first saw them in the Room, she had thought there was none. But then they mentioned their daughter. And as he was getting Emilia out of the van to release her on to the road, the woman barked something: *stop playing with her*. And it wasn't just impatience behind those words. Or fear that they would be caught. There was jealousy there. Just a shimmer of it in her tone, but there all the same.

They are together. A team – in every sense of the word. Partners. Parents. Parents to a daughter.

A rush of adrenalin pounds through her, the tips of her fingers tingling. They spoke about their daughter. The woman's voice changed, turning warm then sad before finally being consumed with anger, the man bringing her rant to an abrupt end. What was it she said? Emilia presses both fists to her eyes, her knuckles digging into the sockets as she wills herself to remember. The woman's masked face appears, her mouth, visible through the open slash in the material, moving passionately.

You should know more than anyone why we do this, Emilia. The monster who took our daughter did it without thinking twice. Just like your Sophie. And the police did nothing. They did nothing!

Emilia's hands drop, hanging limply down by her sides as the woman's voice echoes deep inside her mind. *They arrested that boy, sure, but then they let him go. They set him free! Not enough evidence. And we were meant to simply get on with our lives? No. No! It should have been us who killed him –*

She frowns as the woman falls still. That was when the man interrupted. *Quiet*, he muttered with a glare.

But . . . she said one more thing, didn't she? Didn't she say one more sentence, the man then repeating his demand for silence with a shout that had bounced around the room, slamming violently against the walls?

Yes. She did.

He shouldn't have been able to do it himself.

That's it, Emilia thinks, her eyes springing open, the cold winter light streaming through the window warming her face. That is the key.

The woman gave too much away.

If she hadn't felt the need to parade their ethos in front of Emilia, if she hadn't insisted on rallying against Emilia's cries that what they were doing was wrong, and would always be wrong, Emilia would be ignorant. But now that this memory has risen to the surface, she knows things. She knows that they had a daughter. A daughter who was killed, and the person they believe did it wasn't charged. Arrested, but never charged. And he killed himself. She never said it explicitly, but what else could those words have meant? *It should have been us who killed him*, she said. *He shouldn't have been able to do it himself.*

So that's who they need to look for. A couple, either married or partners, a daughter who passed away. And a man questioned about the crime who committed suicide soon after.

Emilia rubs her finger furiously on the trackpad, the screen turning bright, and clicks on the internet. She breathes in deeply, then exhales slowly, cricking her neck from one side to the other.

Okay, she thinks, staring at the empty search bar. *Let's begin.*

The faces on the screen gaze out at her, their cheeks pallor-grey, their eyes full of sorrow. She moves closer, unable to look away from the photograph of the husband and wife, dressed in mourning, all in black.

Joshua and Amanda Reign. Mother and father to murdered fourteen-year-old Lacey Reign.

Emilia lets out a shaky breath.

Is that them?

She moves still closer to the screen, not even allowing herself to blink as she scrutinizes their eyes, their mouths, their height difference. She is a little taller than his chest-height, but she could be wearing heels. And the man in this photo, Joshua, looks a little leaner than the man was in the Confession Room. But time has passed. This article says that Lacey Reign was killed five years ago – a person can change a great deal in five years. They can put on weight. Lose some of their stature. Become a murderer.

She scans the article again, her eyes searching for the sentence that had caused her to pause, her breath catching in her chest. She has looked at so many articles about so many poor parents who have lost a daughter and she has immediately moved on, but as soon as she read this sentence she realized that there was something there: this one was different. This one could be them.

Her eyes land on it and that feeling stirs inside her again, in the place below the chest, in the very centre of the body where all emotion lives and is stirred up, rising out before submerging once more.

A suspect, who has not been named by the police due to his age, was interviewed but released shortly after without charge.

The woman had called the person who was arrested a boy, not a man. She wouldn't have done that unless he was young, young enough for him to process in her mind as a child. And this suspect was kept anonymous due to his age.

Emilia's eyes dart around the room, searching for her phone.

Where is it? Where on earth has she left it –

She rushes to grab it from the floor beside her bed and unlocks the screen, navigating quickly to his name.

'Emi,' Ciaran answers, his voice as warming as the sun still shining on her through the glass. 'I was going to call you after my shift. How are –'

'Ciaran, I need your help with something,' she says, interrupting him.

'What's wrong? Has something happened?'

'Are you in the office? Are you at your computer?'

'Yes . . . Why? What's going on?'

Emilia sighs, the familiar pang of guilt stabbing in her chest. 'I need a favour.'

'What is it?'

'I need you to look up a case for me . . . a murder investigation.'

'Why?'

'Please can you just do it?'

'You can't just ask me to break the rules and not tell me why!'

'I've been searching for the couple who were running the Confession Room.'

'Oh no, Emi –'

'And I think I might have found them.'

'I can't do this. If you think you've found something, you just need to go to the team. Go to Wild and tell her what you think you know.'

'I will, I promise. I'm not going to do anything stupid, and I'm going to go to Wild straightaway and let them do their jobs, but I need to know for myself if this last piece of the puzzle is correct. If it isn't, they might not believe me and then there's no point to any of this.'

He sighs. 'What do you need to check?'

'There was a suspect in the murder investigation of a girl called Lacey Reign. Were you working in homicide at the time?'

'I think I remember her name . . . was she young? A teenager?'

'Yes! She was fourteen.'

Tapping echoes from his end – he is searching on his computer.

'No, her case was before me.'

'Well, somebody was brought in for questioning but released without charge. I just need you to check if he's been brought in for anything since, especially recently.'

'How will this help you?'

'It just will.' She swallows loudly. 'I know I ask too much of you, and I lied to you and I absolutely don't deserve you. But I need this one last thing. Please.'

Silence. Ciaran doesn't respond at all – in fact he is so quiet that Emilia squeezes the phone to her face, her cheek burning. Has he gone? Is this it? The swift kick that will send their friendship – their relationship, whatever it is – shattering into a million tiny pieces, too damaged to ever be repaired?

'Ciaran?' she says, a waver in her voice. 'Are you still there?'

A hitched breath through the receiver sends a shiver of

relief through her. 'I'm here,' he whispers. 'And . . . I'll do this for you, Emi. But I need you to promise me something.'

'Okay . . .'

'Once I do this, you'll go straight to Wild, you'll tell them whatever it is that you think you've discovered, and you'll let them get on with their investigation.'

'I will,' she says firmly.

'But really, Emi – you need to step away. You've been blaming yourself for everything, taking on too much responsibility, too much guilt, and if these people aren't found . . . if they're never found, I don't want you to think that it's your fault. And I know that you will. Just like you did before. With Sophie.'

Emilia holds her breath, fighting an urge to bite back. To exclaim that Sophie *was* her fault, that she could have done so much more. That she should have protected her: the police should have protected her. But she doesn't. Instead, she lets go, exhaling the rising anger like blowing out a match before the flames lick your fingers.

'I will. I promise.'

'Okay.' He clears his throat. 'Give me two minutes.'

There is a gentle thud and Emilia closes her eyes, imagining Ciaran as he sets his phone down on the desk beside him. His fingers clattering on the keyboard tap rhythmically in her ear, followed by pauses as he reads, the whirring roll of the mouse as he scrolls downwards.

'Emi? You there?'

'I'm here,' she whispers.

'About four months after he was questioned in the investigation for the murder of Lacey Reign, the boy in

308

question was given a warning about following a girl home from school. He was told that if he continued to behave that way, he could be arrested and charged with stalking offences.'

'Anything else?'

He scrolls again and Emilia waits, her entire body, inside and out, falling still as she waits for some piece of information that might confirm the truth. Is this the case she is looking for? Is this the daughter she is looking for? Are they the parents she is looking for?

'Ah.' He sighs. 'Well, if you were hoping to speak to this guy, it's bad news, I'm afraid.'

Her eyes fly open, drawn instantly to the photograph that is still displayed on the screen of her laptop: the parents of Lacey Reign – their mournful faces and downward gaze. She shivers.

'Why?'

'Because he killed himself days after he was given the warning.'

'He's dead?'

'Yes . . . I'm sorry –'

'This is the information I needed. This was the key. Thank you, I've got to go –'

'Emilia!' Ciaran says, his voice a warning. 'Straight to the police. Nothing stupid. Okay?'

'I promise. Bye. Thank you!'

She ends the call, the phone falling from her shaking hands and to the floor. But that photo is still in her sight, her eyes narrowing, anger rising up again, stinging the back of her throat.

Got you.

25th November, 2 p.m.

Wild and Brennan stare at her across the small kitchen table. Emilia finishes speaking and searches their faces for a reaction, waiting for their response. Any indication that they have heard her – that they understand. But their faces are both unreadable.

She jabs her finger at a piece of paper on the table between them, the photo printed on it in black and white.

'This is them,' she says again, her finger moving from the woman's face to the man's and back again. 'Joshua and Amanda Reign.'

Wild tips her head back to look up at the ceiling, letting out a prolonged sigh. 'Emilia, I worked on that case as a sergeant, before I moved up. I remember these parents. I remember how devastated they were about Lacey. And you're saying that they created the Confession Room, they started killing people because . . . because why?'

'I told you . . . Because they believe that the police didn't do enough and that they'll continue failing to find perpetrators. That's why they made the confessions before anyone had even been killed. Remember what they said in that final post, after they asked me to help them with Harris Keaton? "No more warnings" . . . "Good luck". That was to you – to the police. It was a taunt. Because they believe that you will never find them. And they chose to abduct people like Lacey's killer. Obsessive, violent, disturbed men.'

'But what about the people chosen to kill?'

'They chose people who have been affected by this type of man. But also people who had all made a similar kind of confession.'

'That you would kill them if you had the chance,' Wild says, her eyes tinged with disgust.

'Don't look at me like that,' Emilia says. 'It's an expression. Everybody uses it and don't pretend that you never have! I never imagined that someone would cage me in a room and force me to actually do it.'

She stares at them both, her eyes wild, her whole body burning.

'So you think that the reason they chose the victims and the reason they chose you and the others to be the killers, is because they wanted justice for what happened to their daughter,' Wild says.

'Yes – they see themselves as giving justice to people. Joseph Henley wrote that he hated his brother and his life would be better if he was dead. Isabella wrote about Greg's violent ways, his controlling behaviour, how she wished he would stop. And Hayley . . . Hayley said that she wished her boyfriend would be kinder. That he would stop listening to these online voices who claim that women should serve their men. She wished that he would change.' She presses her elbows into the table, her trembling fingers raking through her hair. 'Like I said before . . . the woman said that the boy who murdered their daughter shouldn't have been able to kill himself. That they should have been the ones to do it.' She holds her hands out towards them, palms up, her head shaking slowly. 'Don't you see? They chose people they thought would feel the same way as them. They chose us because they truly believe in their own kind of justice: an eye for an eye. The victim should be the one to pull the trigger.'

Wild rests her chin in her hand, the fingers curled up and over her lips. She sighs, glancing down at the photo.

'Why didn't you try to figure out who they were before?' Brennan asks. Wild narrows her gaze, her eyes veering up from the photograph to watch Emilia carefully.

'I . . . I don't know. I couldn't think. Not the way I usually would about any other case. I couldn't let myself remember. Not until today. Not until I forced myself to go back there. I couldn't find video footage of them, or anything that I could use to identify their voices, but I'm certain it's them.'

'They never did any direct press,' Wild says. 'Everything went through the officer in the case.'

'This is them. The man and the woman behind it all. I just feel it.'

Wild continues to watch her with an unblinking stare. 'Thank you for bringing all this to our attention,' she says, pushing her chair back to get to her feet, the metal legs scraping on the rough floor.

Emilia scrambles to her feet. 'You'll bring them in for questioning? I mean . . . if you can find them. They might have run away.'

Wild glances at Brennan who is taking a large gulp of his tea, and he stands quickly, setting the mug down with a heavy thud.

Wild picks up her notebook, the pages littered with

hurried notes. She then snatches up the photograph, sliding it carefully behind the cover. 'We'll take care of it, Emilia.'

They turn and file out of the kitchen, and Emilia follows them along the corridor to the front door.

Please let the police find them, she repeats in her mind. *Please.*

6th December, 8.45 a.m.

Emilia shields her face, turning away from the window even though the glass is tinted. The crowd on the road outside the police station is less tightly packed than when she saw it on the news, but there are still people here, holding up their signs demanding justice. Ryan's mother is still there. Ciaran says she has been there every day.

The car turns in to the side road that runs around the back of the station, coming to a gentle stop outside the gates. They open and the car crawls forward. Emilia leans over to stare out of the opposite window. Are any of the crowd moving around this way? What will happen if they realize that she is here? That today is the day a decision is being made on whether to charge her and Isabella? Maybe they already know.

The gates close behind them and she sighs. The past couple of weeks have been strange: she has been both completely consumed by what is happening, and protected from it. Wrapped tightly in her cocoon, shielded from the glare of the public, from the opinions and the attacks. She hasn't been able to leave her parents' house till now – there are still journalists outside, and the occasional protester, Ryan's face plastered across their chest, even though they have been warned not to come to the address. But inside the house, she is safe. After the first week of spending hours watching out the window each day, waiting for something to happen, the anxious terror in her stomach had settled. They've really gone. They've stopped – choosing to hide instead of seeking retaliation like they'd threatened. Maybe that's all the threat was – an empty promise. So she was finally able to take advantage of what she had been given – a place of hiding.

But now it is time to face the consequences. She was told that she needed to return to the station, and suddenly the bubble surrounding her popped – the world beyond the boundary of her parents' house becoming clear once again. And it is changed.

Even the police station looks different to her now. She throws open the door, stepping out into the bright winter light. It towers over her, its grey walls looming above them, blocking out the sun. This is the place where she spent so many years working and living her life, but it is entirely transformed. Does anyone inside those walls even know her any more? Do they understand her? Do they think she deserves protection? Or punishment?

The custody sergeant peers at her over the top of the computer screen. But it isn't Jenny. Emilia frowns, her heart tumbling. Is Jenny not here because she isn't on shift? Or did they specifically ensure that she wasn't here because she's friends with Emilia? She feels a rush of nausea and presses her knuckles against her tightly clamped lips, swallowing rapidly as she forces herself to exhale slowly, her breath trembling out of her.

'Ready?' the custody sergeant asks. But he isn't looking at her – he's staring at Brennan who is hovering just behind Emilia's right shoulder. Emilia turns the other way, searching the custody suite.

'Detective Brennan?' Emilia whispers. 'What happened with the information I gave you and Inspector Wild?'

'Let's focus on you for a moment, Emilia,' he says, staring straight ahead. He won't look her in the eye. Her stomach turns again, dread settling in – a heavy weight threatening to pull her down. 'We're ready,' Brennan says, nodding at the sergeant.

He tilts his head so that his entire face appears over the screen. 'Emilia Haines, you are being charged . . .'

A rush of white noise enters Emilia's brain, the room plunged into a chaotic silence. The sergeant's mouth is moving, his face completely blank as he speaks in a monotone and rattles off her charge, the allegations against her, but she can't hear a word. All she can hear is those four words, over and over again, a ghostly taunt: *you are being charged.*

She had spent all this time haunted by the thought that she would be charged with Ryan's murder. That despite everything they were put through, they would be forced to bear the burden. But now that she is faced with it, it's clear that deep down she trusted it would never actually come to pass. That they would see her and the others for what they were: victims forced to do unspeakable things or face unspeakable consequences. But they haven't.

Her vision sways, the desk violently tilting to the right. She's going to go to prison. She's going to have to face a trial. But what defence can she give? What defence in law will protect her?

Brennan is peering into her face, his eyes full of an

impatient concern. Like a parent worried for their child but sick of their emotional tantrums. 'Emilia – do you understand the charge that has been brought against you?'

She nods. 'You've charged me with murder.'

Brennan shakes his head. 'Weren't you listening? Emilia, the murder investigation against you has been dropped.'

The white noise comes to an abrupt stop, the only sound her pulse as it throbs in her temples. 'What?'

'You haven't been charged with murder. You've been charged with perverting the course of justice, which as you understand is still a very serious offence.' He looks down at his feet. 'The CPS decided that it wasn't in the public interest to charge you or any of the others with murder or manslaughter. You were victims of that room. But not coming forward when you were released is an offence. Actively lying to the police and misleading the investigation is perverting the course of justice.'

Tears spring to her eyes and she lifts her hands to cover them, but they stream down her cheeks nonetheless. No murder charge ... not in the public interest ... But a charge of perverting the course of justice? After she was the one who came to the police? She was the one who figured out where the Confession Room was; she was the one who went against their instructions and broke the trust of the others, all to try and stop it from happening again. Yet now she has to face a charge of perverting the course of justice? It isn't murder – but it carries a life sentence all the same.

'Is there anything you wish to say?' the custody sergeant asks. 'I do have to remind you that anything you do say may be given in evidence.'

She shakes her head. Her mind blank, unable to muster the words even if her voice was able to speak.

'The decision has also been made to remand you to custody until your trial as there is substantial reason to believe that you will fail to surrender to court should you be bailed.'

Emilia's head is ready to explode. They are remanding her. She isn't returning to her parents, and she isn't going home. The next time she steps outside it will be to climb into the back of a prison van.

'This isn't fair,' she whispers.

'Emilia, you were in our position once,' Brennan says. 'Think of what you would do.'

She glares at him, her anger boiling just under her skin. 'If only you could have done the same.'

A door opens, creaking loudly, and Emilia swings in the direction of the sound. Someone has come out of one of the interview rooms to the side, their heels clacking on the floor as they turn to close the door behind them.

'Inspector Wild,' Emilia shouts out to her. She spins around, startled.

'Emilia, not now,' Brennan says.

'No, please,' she says, shrugging him away, stepping around him and taking a few steps towards Wild before he blocks her path. 'Inspector Wild, please can I talk to you quickly?'

Wild sighs. 'Of course. Follow me.'

She turns, immediately heading back to the room she just emerged from. 'Quickly, Emilia – I don't have much time.'

Emilia rushes forward and into the room, past Brennan who stares after her wearily before trailing behind.

'No, don't worry,' Wild says to him, holding out her hand. 'I'll speak to her alone.'

Emilia stares at her back as she closes the door. It clicks shut and Wild turns slowly towards her.

'I need to ask,' Emilia says in a rush. 'I need to know. Have there been any leads? Have you questioned the Reigns? I watched the news, I waited . . . But there was nothing. Nothing was announced about anyone being brought in for questioning.'

'Emilia, why don't you sit down?' Wild says, gesturing to a chair.

'No,' she responds bluntly. She pauses, taking a calming breath. 'What happened with the Reigns?'

Wild pulls out a chair, folding herself into it elegantly, one ankle tucked behind the other. 'We located them, at their home address where they have always lived, and brought them in separately for questioning.'

'So what happened?' Emilia folds her arms, her fingers gripping her elbow.

Wild tilts her head, looking up at Emilia through her lashes. 'They were released with no further action. There is no evidence to suggest that the Reigns are behind this other than your word.'

'Even with everything I found? What about the farm? Surely it has a connection to them?'

'That farm has been derelict for years. It was abandoned, all of the animals slaughtered. Anyone could have been using it. It has no connection to Joshua and Amanda Reign.'

'But what about everything else? Everything else I showed you?'

'What you showed us was randomly pieced together bits of information that fit your memory of what happened. Your story. And the timing of your story was very convenient.'

'What do you mean?'

'I mean that at the very time you knew police were considering whether to charge you or not, and public opinion had turned against you, you suddenly remembered information about what was said in the Confession Room which you had never mentioned before. Maybe you thought that if the people who orchestrated this were found, you would be off the hook.'

'That isn't fair. And it isn't true!'

'We cannot charge two innocent people – people who have already suffered – just because you have pulled them out at random.'

'But I haven't pulled them out at random. The people from the Confession Room had a daughter who was killed. And –'

'Emilia, we are keeping the Reigns under investigation, but there is not a shred of concrete evidence which would allow us to charge them.' Wild stands, one hand rising to rest on her waist. 'We are doing everything we can to find whoever did this. And if anything further comes up that directs us towards Joshua and Amanda Reign, then of course everything could change, but as it stands, there is no case against them.'

Emilia whimpers and drops her head, unable to look at

Wild any longer. Unable to face her outright disdain, her complete lack of understanding.

'My . . . my parents,' she whispers, staring down at her hands as tears drip on to her lap. 'What if the killers come back?'

'The families of the survivors will continue to be watched by the police. We're not letting any of this go just because you've been charged. The investigation is continuing and your families will be protected. Now, I need you to return to the custody suite, and they'll get you ready to be transferred to Holloway.'

Emilia attempts a nod, but her head is heavy, a weight bearing down on the back of her neck. She bites her lip in a desperate attempt to stop herself from crying – she doesn't want Wild to see her like this, not again, not now. But she can't help it. She is crying for everything that has happened, for everything she has lost. The past, and the future.

She follows Wild out of the room, her feet dragging across the floor until she reaches the custody desk. But she can't look up at Brennan or the sergeant. She continues to stare at the ground as they explain what will happen next, and as they speak, tears course down her face, the pain in her head now all-consuming. Even as they place her in a cell to wait, as she leaves the station to get on to the van, even as she realizes that Isabella is there also, her eyes full of emotion, before they both clamber on and the door slams on their individual compartments, and Emilia's breathing tightens, her eyes squeezing shut to block out the claustrophobic space, the handcuffs bound tightly around her wrists, even as shouts come from the crowd outside, and she flinches as a hand bangs on the glazed windows – the same thought is going round and round in her mind, like a spinning top, faster and faster.

They're letting them get away with what they did to us and we're going to be punished.

They're letting them get away with what they did to us.

They're letting them get away with what they did.

They're letting them get away.

9th July

Eight months later

'Before we turn to the verdict, I want to thank you once again for your service over the past five weeks in what has been a trial at the very centre of the public stage,' Judge Watson says to the jury, her round glasses perched at the end her nose, magnifying her eyes so that she appears even more owl-like. Wise and all-knowing.

Emilia likes her. She liked her from the start of the trial when she peered at them from her bench, high above them in Court One of the Old Bailey, and there was kindness in her eyes instead of disdain. She has watched her carefully throughout the trial, taking in each of the judge's reactions: her displeased frown as the prosecution insisted that there was no reason for either of the two defendants to remain silent; her dead-eyed glare as they proclaimed that there was no possible defence to keeping the information from the police for so long.

'You understand, don't you, Miss Haines, that to successfully argue the defence of duress, the harm that you were so afraid of would have to be imminent?'

The prosecutor's tone had sent a rush of anger through her. But she forced herself to remain calm, poised. Reacting would have no effect on him, but it could only do her harm.

'I understand that, yes,' she had said. 'The fear of harm was always there. We never knew where they could come from. They abducted me from my house.'

'But the harm was not imminent, was it, Miss Haines?' He raised an eyebrow, as though he was impatiently explaining something to a small child. 'Once you were released from the Confession Room, you would agree that there was no constant gun to your head, forcing you to remain silent?'

'It was.'

'If that were true, Miss Haines, how did you have the time to investigate the location of the Confession Room and report back to the police?'

'I –'

'If you were able to do that without coming to immediate harm, then surely you could have done it sooner?'

She hadn't been able to respond, and a deep feeling of dread began to stir inside her. Her eyes had darted quickly to the jury. Some of them were nodding, their eyes gleaming with conviction; but others were shaking their heads, however subconsciously. The dread in her stomach was briefly smothered: they were torn. To convict her they would have to be unanimous.

But they'd returned now with a unanimous verdict. So one way or the other – the doubters had been converted.

The public? The public were a different story. As soon as the press revealed that they had been charged with perverting the course of justice, they were divided. Some were appalled, insisting that Emilia and Isabella should have been allowed to continue their lives unpunished; others thought the prosecution had not gone far enough – that they were being let off lightly. As though a perverting the course of justice conviction would just be a slap on the back of the hand.

But it doesn't matter what the general public believe. It doesn't even matter what the judge – the arbiter of law – thinks. The jury are the judges of fact. The jury are the ones who matter. What do they believe?

'Right . . .' Judge Watson glances down at her clerk and nods. The clerk adjusts his gown, tugging it forward just as he has done multiple times a day, the material sliding off his suit beneath. As he stands, Emilia's stomach turns and she glances sideways at Isabella, who meets her eye and sighs. It is time.

'Isabella Santos and Emilia Haines – please stand.'

They both rise, their faces close to the glass. A low hum of whispers comes from the public gallery to the left above them, followed by a hush. But Emilia hasn't been able to face looking up there and seeing the devastated faces of her parents. Or Ciaran's bewildered dismay. If she looks at them she will cry. And she can't bear the thought of the other people in the gallery, the onlookers who have been queuing from the early hours to get a coveted seat, seeing her crumble. She will not give them that. Nor will Isabella. She hates it too – after the first day they came to an agreement: no looking up at the public gallery.

'Can the foreman please stand,' the clerk says, his voice clear as a bell in the towering expanse of the room.

The man in the furthest seat to the left of the front row clambers to his feet, his movements slow and stiff. He clasps his hands in front of him but he can't seem to keep them still, and his fingers tug and pull at each other, the energy emanating out of him all the way to the dock.

'On the charge of perverting the course of justice against Isabella Santos, have you reached a verdict upon which you are all agreed?'

The man moves his head in a single firm nod. 'We have.'

'And what is your verdict?'

Emilia turns her head to look at her friend – because that is what they have become, after the blame slowly melted away: friends. The only two people who will ever understand each other. But Isabella has closed her eyes, mouthing words silently down to the floor. She is praying. Emilia holds her breath.

'Guilty,' the foreman says.

Isabella lifts her head, her mouth agape. And Emilia . . . Emilia can't breathe. She can't comprehend what has just happened; she can't understand how this jury have decided that Isabella wilfully got in the way of the police investigation. She felt like she had no choice – that much was completely clear. The courtroom spins, and a migraine – a daily occurrence now – creeps around her temples to the front of her forehead.

'On the charge of perverting the course of justice against Emilia Haines, have you reached a verdict upon which you are all agreed?'

He nods again in the same exacting movement. 'Yes, we have.'

Maybe there's still a chance for her. Isabella kept quiet the entire time. But Emilia came forward and told the truth.

'And what is your verdict?'

Emilia winces, holding her breath, as if she is readying herself to be plunged into a cold sea. The courtroom jolts to a stop, suspending itself in time –

'Guilty.'

She gasps as the verdict slams into her, freezing cold, taking her breath away, so powerful that it's as though she is kicking against a current, unable to break through the surface. Everything beyond the glass is blurred – the murmurs trickling down from the gallery, the words of the clerk, the foreman once again taking his seat. Her hands fall forward and she holds on to the wooden ledge that runs around the dock. Her forehead thuds heavily against the glass and her head spins, the migraine turning the screws on its vice-like grip. She tries to breathe, desperate to focus back in on the room, back in on what the judge is saying, on the comments of the barristers, on Isabella. But she can't. She is frozen, only able to stare down at her fingers – the knuckles which have turned white.

'Emilia . . .' A whisper comes from behind her. She lifts her head slowly to look at Isabella who shakes her head, her mouth still open in disbelief, tears falling so fast down her cheeks that they are streaking in one clear line and dropping to her feet.

Emilia's eyes dart out through the glass to the courtroom. Everyone is standing as the judge departs, returning to her chambers to consider their sentences. The defence barristers are cutting through the benches, making their way to the docks to try to offer advice. And the noise in the public gallery builds suddenly, no longer silent or speaking in hushed whispers, but now speaking openly, leaning towards each other with excitement on their faces, as though they have just watched the finale of their favourite show – five weeks of entertainment leading to the ultimate climax.

But the front row of people are entirely different. To the left sit Isabella's family, her mum sobbing, her hands clutching at her head, her body rocking back and forth. Isabella's younger brother is standing above his mum, staring out into the courtroom, not speaking. A sister sits beside their mother, her face consumed with anger. And to the right are Emilia's parents. Her mum is talking rapidly, her confusion written all over her face, looking to her husband for some kind of reassurance. A mistake has been made, that's all. But her dad is paying her no attention: instead he is staring down at Emilia, and as she finally meets his eyes he says three words, her heart tumbling. *We love you.* She blinks rapidly, wiping away tears with the back of her hand, her face burning under the intense gaze of one more person.

Ciaran.

She blinks up at him, and for a moment the room falls silent, the world becoming still in his warm, sad eyes. The man who has stood beside her through everything, even when she didn't deserve it. Even when she asked too much. Even through this. She sniffs and his face breaks. He is crying. His hand trembles up to his face and tears fill her eyes as he mimes their familiar old routine: pointing to his eye, his heart, then to her. *I love you.* She nods, lifting her hand also: eye, heart, pointing to him then holding two fingers aloft. *I love you too.*

She collapses back into her seat, the bench vibrating beneath her. The world shifting.

The glass throws her reflection back at her, the court-room still in focus beyond, and her eyes flicker between the two: her tear-strewn cheeks; the jury chatting amongst themselves; the anger in her eyes; the clerk checking the files; her face painted in sorrow; the prosecutor turning to the bench behind him, shaking hands with Inspector Wild.

This is justice?

She shakes her head, her hands curling into shaking fists.

This is justice.

Epilogue

Emilia was sentenced to five years' imprisonment; Isabella to eight. The judge said that while she felt empathy for what both of them had been through, their lies directly led to three more people dying. That the reach of the Confession Room was extended because of their inaction. Isabella's sentence was more severe because Emilia had eventually come forward. But her coming forward hadn't been enough. Not to avoid prison completely. Not like she'd hoped. Emilia had thought that maybe once the sentencing was in Judge Watson's hands they would be let off lightly. But that wouldn't have pleased the public. That wouldn't have satisfied their hunger.

And then that was it: just like that, it was over.

No more victims. No more names. No more posts.

The trial at a close.

The Confession Room silent.

~~Until now.~~

The End

I delete the last line, and release a sigh. I've finished.

Tears sting my eyes and I smile – an overwhelmed laugh bursting from me.

I've *finally* finished.

I roll my neck in a wide circle as I lift my hands off the

keyboard, my bones creaking. My time in prison did my body no favours: I feel old now, more restricted, as though the two and a half years I spent inside a cage clipped my wings, and even though I have been set free – I've been free now for as long as I was imprisoned – I'll never be the same. Not on the outside. Nor on the inside.

A loud thud clatters from somewhere behind me and I look round quickly. Did that come from inside the house?

Shaking my head, I return to the laptop. They can't hurt me. Not any more.

I scroll upwards, staring at the thousands of words as they fly past, the story I have been telling myself finally fully transcribed. Hundreds of pages, covered in my scrawled handwriting, are piled up around my desk, the final page propped up beside my screen. I reach for it and hold it for a moment, the thin paper folding over itself between my fingers. So thin that it's not even able to stand straight – but it's all they would give me. 'This is what we have,' the guard told me. 'Take it or leave it.' I place the final page on top of the closest pile – the one lying just to my left on the floor beside my chair, and breathe out a heavy sigh.

I'd only been in prison a few months when I asked for that first scrap of paper. I thought that it might help me process everything that had happened if I told the story as if through the eyes of another person, an onlooker observing the events unfold. As soon as I was released and I settled into my new home, just over an hour away from my parents, I began to transcribe, reading the story as I went, allowing it to soak in, typing it up in snatches between my shifts at the closest village library, and trying to form some kind of new life after everything that has happened. At the final meeting with my probation officer before my licence came to an end she said that she was proud. And I suppose there is much to be proud of: while I have kept as much of my old life as I can – Jenny visits often and my parents come at least once a week, Mimi trotting beside them, unable to be separated from them after so long – I have built a new life. New friends, a new home in a new place. A new job. I have started over. And I have tried to let go.

I raise my arms high above my head and stretch, my spine clicking loudly, vertebra by vertebra. My hands drop down to hang by my sides, and I scan my desk for the TV remote. I turn in my chair, my eyes searching the room. There it is – on the small sofa, tucked into the corner of the only living space. They said it was a three seater but there's barely room for one.

I cross the room and turn on the television, and am immediately greeted by the newsreader's voice. She has been telling the same story on repeat since this morning, and all the other channels are the same.

'The Confession Room – the forum that led to confessions of murder, the deaths of eight people – was deleted after the killings came to a halt. However, early this morning, a new website appeared, and a confession was posted, mimicking the confessions from the previous case. Police are investigating and this morning Detective Chief Inspector Wild, who led the investigation five years ago, gave the following statement.'

My eyes narrow, focusing like lasers as Wild's face appears, anxiety swelling in my chest like it always does when I think of her. She's Chief Inspector now – a promotion handed over to her like a reward after Isabella and I were convicted, even though the people who actually orchestrated the entire scheme were never caught by the police. We were enough, it seemed.

'The entire country was consumed by the case five years ago and we are taking the new confession very seriously. Any person who chooses to post in this way – even if the post in question is a hoax – will be met with the full force of the law and we will do everything in our power to ensure these people face the justice that they deserve.'

I turn away from the television, my eyes flickering back to my second screen, where the new Confession Room is open, the new post highlighted as always in bold.

Anonymous 01

Have you missed us?

It's been a long time, so here's something to keep you occupied.

But this is different to last time.

No names. No location.

Just this confession:

Murder.

It's beginning again.

Gravel crunches on the drive, shingle shifting rapidly. I stand up quickly, and rush to the side of the window where I can't be seen. Nobody has said they're coming over: my new friends aren't close enough to simply drop in and only a very small circle from my old life even know where I am: my parents, Jenny, Isabella . . . that's it.

I peer around the curtain – a rolling vehicle is coming to a stop. The door swings open, feet land on the drive with a heavy crunch, and a person appears. They turn towards the house and –

I inhale sharply, my stomach dropping.

It's Ciaran.

Ciaran is at my house.

But why? And how? He shouldn't know where I am.

At first he visited me in prison, and I looked forward to seeing his warm face, his comforting smile. He was the best part of every week. But with each month that passed, seeing him became less of a treat, and more of a torture. All it did was remind me of everything that we could have been if tragedy and horror hadn't intervened. I can never be the Emilia that he loved again. So eventually I asked him to stop coming. I said that it would be best for both of us if we moved on. He continued for a while, but I didn't meet him. And after a few weeks of sitting opposite an empty chair in the visitation hall, he finally stopped.

He disappears from view and I close my eyes, waiting for the sound I know will be coming at any moment. Five, four, three –

He knocks sharply, in his familiar rhythm, like he always did before.

Could I just stay here quietly, and pretend to be away? I could be out. But my car is in the drive. And going anywhere around here requires a car – the only place I'm able to walk is into the woods.

If I stay here, completely still, after a few minutes he will give up and return to his car, disappearing forever.

But what if he simply hangs around, knowing that I can't have gone far? I need him to leave. And the only way to make him leave is to make it clear: he is not wanted here. I walk quickly towards the door, my hand reaching for the handle, but then I stop, my fingers trembling, my breathing heavy in my chest. I breathe in deeply, all the way to the bottom of my lungs. There is nothing to be afraid of. Even though it breaks my heart to have pushed him away, I have to do this. And maybe this way, he will finally let me go. It can be the end for both of us.

I grip the handle and turn, tugging the door towards me.

And just like that, after so long – he is there. Just the same as always. He has barely changed: his hair still dark blonde but now peppered with some grey, his warm amber eyes swimming with surprise.

'Hi,' he says quietly.

'Wh . . . what are you doing here?' I stammer.

He flinches slightly, and my heart drops as his expression changes. I didn't mean to be so cold. But I don't know how else to be when faced with him standing at my door.

'I wanted to make sure that you're okay after . . .' He raises his hands. 'Everything that's happening.'

I shrug, my eyes dropping down to stare at my feet which are curling against the cold wind now blowing through the door. 'I guess.'

'Have you . . . have you seen the confession?'

'Hasn't everyone?'

He nods slowly, not saying anything. His face is

furrowed into an expression I can't read. I used to be able to decipher his feelings so well – they were always so clear to me. Our lack of closeness has rendered us strangers. But that was the point. He cannot be mine, and I cannot be his – not in the way we had hoped, not after everything we went through and everything I did. He deserves more. Better.

'How did you know where to find me, Ciaran?' I ask, staring at him once more. 'You aren't meant to know where I am.'

'I know ... I'm so sorry. I saw the confession this morning and I was terrified that you would be out here alone and watching it all unravel. I was worried.'

'But who gave it to you?' I cross my arms, stepping back slightly to shield myself with the door. 'Was it Jenny?'

He doesn't say anything but it is there on his face, in the lowering of his eyebrows, the subconscious rubbing of his jaw – I guess I can still read him after all.

'She shouldn't have done that. Nobody is meant to know –'

'I know, and please don't blame her. She only gave it to me because I was so worried and she knows – you must know – that I would never do anything that would put you in danger. So are you ... are you okay?'

I don't respond. I can't. I just stare at his beautiful face, my eyes widening as the air between us shimmers with ghosts.

'You know that if you need help, we can give it to –'

'I don't need help,' I say, nodding once, assertively. 'I'm fine ... You really shouldn't be here.'

He steps back, off the doorstep and on to the path,

shifting his weight from foot to foot. 'I'm sorry ... I shouldn't have come.'

'No,' I whisper, my voice breaking, tears stinging my eyes. 'You shouldn't ... I have to go. You have to go. Goodbye, Ciaran.'

I slam the door shut, the sound echoing up to the ceiling. Throwing my back against the rough wood, my heart heavy, I wait for almost two minutes, one hundred and twenty long seconds, as our relationship, everything it ever was and everything we ever wished it could be, clicks before my eyes like a film on a projector. The memories sepia-tinted. And there is no movement on the other side of the door. No shifting of gravel. He must be standing there, his mind replaying everything just like mine. I know what he had hoped ... he had hoped for more than he ever should have. He should have known, he must know deep down, that he could never have me back again. Our relationship was destroyed along with so much else.

The Confession Room left behind many victims.

Not all of us dead.

Finally, he moves, his footsteps tapping against the brick of the porch before crunching across the drive. The car door slams. The engine growls. And then he drives away.

I dart across to the window and stare at the car as it trundles along the drive then takes the sharp left out on to the road, vanishing from view.

I flop down on to my chair, the seat swinging beneath me, spinning me slowly in a circle, my view of the room blurring with tears. I sniff abruptly, shaking my hands out in front of me. This emotion does me no good.

None of this does me any good. Sitting here crying over what I have lost is futile. I must be grateful for what I have.

And I'm grateful for this house. Small, red brick and covered with ivy, a collapsing gate, hidden at the end of a long gravel drive, obscured by trees at the foot of a large wood. The closest village almost nine miles away. Miles away from London. Away from the world. Solitary. Secluded.

I stand, walking out of the living room and into the narrow corridor which leads to the kitchen. Peering in from the door, my eyes are drawn as always to the woods through the window, the trees dense and thick with foreboding.

Bang.

That same loud thud vibrates up through my feet and I turn my head, staring at the door to my left – a door under the stairs. A door that leads to another part of the house for which I am now truly grateful . . .

The basement.

I step through the door and flick on the light switch. A lone bulb dangling from the ceiling glares above me and I descend the stone stairs, my heart pounding. I reach the bottom step and wait. Listening.

Bang.

There it is again. That sound.

At the bottom of the stairs, there is a door straight ahead, bolted shut, and another to my right – also locked, this one with a key. I reach into my pocket and retrieve it, pushing it quickly into the lock. It clicks open and I press the door with my fingers, waiting as it swings open before quickly stepping inside. I lock it behind me. It's funny – my fear of being locked in small rooms has vanished – my time in prison like severe exposure therapy, one that I could not avoid. Did it cure me, though? Or was it just more trauma on top of trauma until the brain could handle no more and simply blocked it out? Either way, the result has been the same.

I sit down at the tiny desk, my leg curled beneath me to cushion the metal chair, and I turn on the computer. This one is old, and bought specifically for one purpose. For the camera. It is a monitor, the image grainy and black and white. But it will do.

Finishing my story had led me to one clear conclusion: the ending was even more unfair than I had realized at the time. There was no justice. None at all.

So I just have to deliver it myself.

I lean in, my brow lowering as I focus in on the live feed.

The man is moving, his arm randomly spasming, lifting off the floor and slamming down again. But he remains unconscious, his eyes firmly shut.

It will be the smell that wakes him.

At first Joshua Reign was perfectly still, but now he is stirring. His nostrils are flaring. His reaction is fascinating to watch. Humans are all the same; all animals reacting in the same instinctive way to a stimulus. In this case: the realization that something is incredibly wrong.

And something is very wrong. He is not in his bedroom, as he should be, but instead in a room made up of four cement walls, a grey ceiling, no windows . . . and the overpowering smell of bleach.

339

He sits up and rocks forward. The room will be tossing violently back and forth, the after-effects of falling unconscious without warning. He clamps his hand over his mouth . . . That will be the nausea.

After a few minutes, his rapidly blinking eyes lift. He looks around, forcing himself to take in the strangeness of the situation.

Why am I here? How did I get here?

He brings his knees up towards his chest and —

There it is. The moment of terrifying recognition I've been waiting for. He stares down at his leg, his mouth dropping open as his eyes take in the shining steel cuff wrapped around his ankle, attached to a chain, tethering him to the wall.

'Hello?' *he calls out, trying to keep the panic from his voice.* 'Hello?'

His face slowly falls as he waits for a response that won't come. There is no worried cry or violent outburst coming from behind the locked door. No aggression. No rescue. He won't even find comfort in the echo of his own voice. The room is too small for that. The walls and ceiling both too close.

There is nothing but silence.

He forces himself on to his knees and then groans as his body rights itself, chest puffing with the effort. He is shaking. Shaking with adrenalin and nerves and the confusion that is keeping him from screaming out, from crying for his mother, from calling for someone, anyone.

This is fear. This is the moment he understands how fear really feels.

He steps forward, one small step into the room, his eyes darting around as he tries to make sense of his surroundings. He frowns, turning slowly in a circle, tangling his legs in the chain.

He focuses first on the corner of the room to the right. There is another bolt fixed to the wall, for another person to be chained to. But it is empty. So instead he turns his attention to what is sitting innocuously in each of the room's four corners.

Four boxes, painted black.

How long will it take him to brave opening one? Some people would launch themselves directly at the boxes, scrambling in their haste to crack them open, like overeager children at Christmas. Others would cower, shrinking away from the unknown.

I had anticipated that he would be the former. But by his reaction to the room, I'm guessing now that he might be the latter. Not so big and brave, after all.

His eyes shift away from the closest box and look up to where a stop-clock is hanging in the centre of the ceiling, its red digital figures frozen, ready to begin counting down.

00:60.

Sixty seconds.

He stares helplessly up, his thoughts written across his features — a story so easily read it is as if I know it by heart.

What will happen after sixty seconds?

And when will it begin?

I glance at the laptop discarded beside me. I took it from their house, used it to set up a new website, to post the new confession. To contact their friends explaining their absence.

I crane my neck to where Amanda Reign is lying on the floor just behind me. Soon I'll need to pull on my black jumpsuit and cover my face, then take her into the room to join her husband. And it can't be long before they'll open the boxes, retrieving the photographs of all of their victims, both dead and alive.

And then it will begin.

Sirens wail somewhere in the distance, but I can't tell if they are real or just wailing in my imagination. Maybe one day, flashes of blue will light up my home. Police will crash in through the front door and I'll be placed in handcuffs once again, returned to the small cell and its years of confinement. And maybe it will be warranted. But it will be worth it.

The Reigns will get what they deserve. I am giving them what they believe in: their own unique brand of justice.

Welcome to the Confession Room.

My Confession Room.

Acknowledgements

As my third novel makes its way into the world, I'm still in absolute disbelief that my childhood dream of being a storyteller has become a reality.

My agent Kate Burke has been a constant support, adviser and friend. I wouldn't be anywhere without her pulling my debut novel out of the slush pile and working her incredible editorial magic on it before sending me out to publishers. Thank you so much for your incisive advice, and for your ability to read my mind and make me laugh. And thank you to everyone at the brilliant Blake Friedmann Literary Agency – your hard work to support my career is appreciated more than I can explain (and I'm a writer!).

As always, thank you so much to the fantastic team at Penguin Michael Joseph. I am still so proud whenever I see that little penguin logo on the cover and spine of my books. Clio Cornish: you are a dream of an editor. Your notes never fail to make my writing shine and you *just get me*. Thank you also to Ella Watkins and Courtney Barclay, my publicist and marketer; Madeleine Woodfield for her support during the publication process; and Sarah Bance, Nick Lowndes and Emma Henderson for the exceptional copy-editing and making my book ready for publication.

The Confession Room felt like a slight steer away from my previous novels, which felt far more firmly rooted in the world of psychological thrillers, while this novel leans more heavily into crime, the trope of the 'serial killer', with sprinklings of horror. This led to the most challenging writing experience of my career so far, but I'm immensely proud of this novel.

I must give thanks to the man responsible for the catalyst of the idea for *The Confession Room*. I stumbled upon it as I read an article in *Crime Magazine*. A man named Allan Bridge had created a project in 1980s New York called The Apology Line. He left flyers around NYC with a number for an answering machine where people could leave anonymous apologies that until then had gone unsaid. And from there, the idea for *The Confession Room* was born. So, thanks to Allan Bridge and his wife, who created a podcast on the experiment in her late husband's honour.

Turning to my friends: thank you to the VWG who never fail to amaze me: you are the most talented and inspiring group I've ever had the honour to be a part of, and this journey as a writer would be one hundred times harder without you beside me. Special thanks to Fíona Scarlett, Neema Shah and Daniel Aubrey for responding to my 'anyone fancy coming with me to Iceland?' message with a resounding, 'Yes!' I had the best time with you all. And, thank you to my Harrogate and festival companion Laure Van Rensburg for your brilliant plotting mind and for keeping me company on multiple train journeys from Kings Cross!

Thank you to my family for their constant and unwavering support. My parents always make me believe that anything is possible, and it is because of that, I feel able to keep pushing when writing feels insurmountably hard. I couldn't physically write without my husband, Daniel, who wrangles the kids away from me when I need time during the day and spends many a night alone on the sofa while I hide away in my office. And, as you can tell from the dedication, my siblings mean the world to me. They spent their tweens and teens entertaining their baby sister with ridiculous games of make-believe, and for that I'm forever thankful. They have also grown into my closest friends who know me better than anyone. For a story that revolves around one woman's love for her sister, I couldn't dedicate this book to anyone else.

And finally, thank you to you, dear reader. Without you picking up my books and immersing yourselves into my imagination, I wouldn't be able to tell stories at all. I hope you enjoy the journey as much as I do.

Loved *The Confession Room*?
Turn over for an extract from
Your Word or Mine

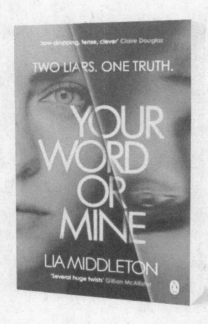

Available to buy now

We both watch as the jury file in. They each take up their places, just as they have for the past ten days, but something in their faces has changed.

They've made a decision.

Do they believe him?

Or me?

My eyes flash to the dock. He is pristine as always, his suit pressed, his dark brown hair slicked to one side, his face cleanly shaved.

'Anabelle, don't look at him,' Mum whispers.

My body jolts at her voice – a gunshot in the quiet courtroom.

'It's okay, sweetheart,' Dad says, his eyes shining with emotion. 'No matter what happens – it'll be okay.'

'Don't say that,' Mum mutters. 'They're going to find him guilty.'

'Can the foreman please stand,' the man who sits in front of the judge says, his voice ringing through the large room and up into the expanse of the vaulted ceiling. I tear my gaze from Dad and look back towards the jury.

The lady who's sitting in the front row, the one who has been taking notes for the whole trial, the one who wears glasses at the bottom of her nose while she's writing, her greying hair tucked behind her ears, stands.

'Have you reached a verdict upon which you are all agreed?'

The lady coughs, clearing her throat. 'Yes,' she said.

'On the count of rape – what is your verdict?'

She looks down at her hands. I inhale sharply, my breath crackling in my lungs as I wait for her to speak.

Guilty. Please let them find him guilty. Please let me put this all behind me.

Her voice breaks and she stammers, but the verdict spills from her lips and ripples through the air.

'N-not guilty.'

ONE

To spare the guilty is to injure the innocent.

Publilius Syrus

1. Ava

Eighteen years later

'You bitch.'

The defendant's rage leaves globules of spit on the glass separating the dock from the rest of the courtroom. His fists are clenched, even in their restraints – a pair of shining silver handcuffs fastened to contain his unpredictable anger. They aren't usually restrained in the dock, but Justin Anderson has a reputation. He is violent: often dangerously so. And his mouth is always full of bitter, hateful words. In his mind it is my fault that the judge has decided to withhold his bail. It is my fault that he will have to stay in prison until his trial. He seeks a victim on which to hang the blame – someone, anyone. Anyone except him. And the prosecutor is always the easiest target.

The guards yank Anderson to his feet and he stands, his shoulders slumped as he turns to leave the dock. 'Bitch,' he shouts over his shoulder in one final attempt to rile me. The door clangs loudly as he is taken down to the cells.

'Thank you, Ms Knight,' the judge says. 'Miss Jones.'

He stands and the defence barrister and I follow his movement like shadows, bowing our heads, just a fraction, as he nods to us and leaves.

The defence sighs as she begins stacking her belongings on top of one another, her hands shaking. She is new. I could tell, even before her reaction to her client's profanities gave her away: the pristine state of her robes, the bright whiteness of her wig. A baby barrister, newly born into this life of prosecution and defence where justice falls like an axe whose blade has become blunt and dull over time. She isn't used to it – not yet anyway.

'Try not to be too hard on yourself,' I say as I reach up to pull my wig from my head, tucking my short hair behind my ears. 'Some people just can't be saved.'

She sighs, her expression pained. She looks so young. So naïve. But soon she'll learn, as we all do. Even the best of people aren't truly innocent.

I push my way out of the courtroom into the long corridor, walking past the short rows of seats where family members sit in small huddles, whispering in hushed voices, whilst the defendant's gaze sits somewhere in the middle-space, their head lowered, their words stroppy or sullen or scared. I've become used to the way their eyes veer towards me as I pass, drawn to the long, black robes – a bull to red cloth.

My phone vibrates and I glance down at the screen.

Message received: Will.

What time will you be home tonight? I have to leave for my dinner by 7. Are you going to your mum's first? Love you x

I met Will during pupillage. I remember seeing him that first day, sneaking a look as we stood next to each other, almost shoulder to shoulder. That evening he asked if I wanted to go for a drink. I took in his warm eyes and truly beautiful face. His kind voice. I said no, like I always did when men tried to approach me – shrinking away from the glare of their attention. But over time I learned to trust him. Over time he became my friend. And last month he proposed, quietly in our flat, just the two of us.

I reach the dark wooden door and balance my phone on

top of my file, but as I punch in the key code to enter, the door swings open.

'Here she is,' Caroline, the advocacy manager, says, stepping out of the room reserved for the Crown Prosecution Service. 'How was Anderson?'

'As charming as always.'

'Silver tongue, that one.' She laughs but then reaches for my arm, her eyes shifting away from my face. 'Ava . . .'

'Is something wrong?'

'There's a first hearing for a Grievous Bodily Harm with Intent in Court One,' she says.

'Okay . . .'

'Jonah was meant to be covering it but he's been pulled into some urgent police briefing at the office –'

'So you want me to do it?'

'Please?'

'Caroline, you know I want to help you but I'm so busy already. I've still got the list in Court Three and I really can't finish late today. I have to go and see my mum and –'

'Come on, the hearing shouldn't take long. They'll just take her not guilty plea and set a date for the trial. And it's in front of your favourite.'

'Gilbert?'

She smiles. 'Gilbert.'

I glance down at my watch – 10:45 a.m. If I get to Court Three by half eleven, maybe I can still make it . . .

'Fine,' I whisper. 'But you owe me.'

'I know.'

'When's it going on?'

'I told Gilbert's usher that I'd grab you and you'd come straightaway.'

'Okay.' I turn away from the CPS room and we begin to

355

walk, Caroline trotting beside me. 'Quickly give me a summary . . . What's the defendant's name?'

'Lily Hawthorne,' Caroline whispers, her eyes darting around for anyone who might be able to hear. 'She's only fifteen.'

'Fifteen?' I mutter. 'The youth court sent her here?'

'Yep, she's very young. Long history of convictions.'

'Is she in custody?'

'No, she's in local authority accommodation with a tag. We asked for a remand to custody but the judge went soft. And the children's home she was in before agreed to have her. I was surprised.'

'And what was the GBH?'

'Stabbing.'

'Why?'

'Something of a teenage crush. He rejected her and she lost her temper.'

'How many times did she stab him?'

'Just once. But to the torso from behind.'

I nod. 'Okay. DNA evidence?'

'Yes. When she was arrested, she was covered in his blood and the knife had her prints on it.'

'Did she talk in her interview?'

'No. She went no-comment but we're expecting her to claim self-defence.'

I slow as we reach the door to the courtroom and glance at the large metal 'One' fixed to the wall.

'Okay . . . And the victim?'

'Forty-three-year-old photographer and entrepreneur. Runs a chain of hotels. She was at his house when she attacked him and —'

A rush of air interrupts Caroline as the door to the courtroom opens outwards.

'Oh good,' Charlie — Judge Gilbert's usher — says. 'You're

here.' He tugs his robe onto his shoulder. 'He's waiting to start.'

'See you soon,' I say, flashing a wide smile at Caroline.

'Good luck,' she says.

Charlie opens the door and I step inside, the courtroom expanding in all directions before me. Dark beams support the high ceiling and the walls are windowless, the room lit by artificial light even in the height of summer.

I glance to my left to where the judge usually sits, but he isn't there. He must have returned to his chambers. And the dock is empty too. I walk forward, towards the front where prosecution and defence share a bench. But as I do so I glance to my left, to the public gallery. Three of the seats in the front row are occupied: journalists – I recognize their faces. And just behind them a man is sitting, his head lowered, but he glances up, his gaze briefly dancing over me.

I freeze.

He is staring down at his lap again now, no longer looking my way, his focus drawn to his phone. But ... that face. Those eyes.

I rush towards my place on the front row and slam my notebook down, opening my laptop. The screen glows. I navigate quickly to the court files, my fingers flying over the keys as I type her name – Lily Hawthorne. The casefile loads and I quickly move the mouse to the summary tab, hesitating just for a moment.

It can't be him.

I click. My eyes quickly scan over the police summary, my brain automatically acting on years of experience, years of having to quickly ascertain key pieces of information –

There it is. The name of the victim.

My stomach plummets.

Michael Osborne.

He has never truly left me. His name has lingered, refusing to fade even after I stripped myself of my own. The last time I saw him, Ava Knight didn't exist. I was a different person with a different name.

I was Anabelle King.

He just wanted a decent book to read ...

Not too much to ask, is it? It was in 1935 when Allen Lane, Managing
Director of Bodley Head Publishers, stood on a platform at Exeter railway
station looking for something good to read on his journey back to London.
His choice was limited to popular magazines and poor-quality paperbacks –
the same choice faced every day by the vast majority of readers, few of
whom could afford hardbacks. Lane's disappointment and subsequent anger
at the range of books generally available led him to found a company – and
change the world.

*'We believed in the existence in this country of a vast reading public for intelligent
books at a low price, and staked everything on it'*
Sir Allen Lane, 1902–1970, founder of Penguin Books

The quality paperback had arrived – and not just in bookshops. Lane was
adamant that his Penguins should appear in chain stores and tobacconists,
and should cost no more than a packet of cigarettes.

Reading habits (and cigarette prices) have changed since 1935, but
Penguin still believes in publishing the best books for everybody to
enjoy. We still believe that good design costs no more than bad design,
and we still believe that quality books published passionately and responsibly
make the world a better place.

So wherever you see the little bird – whether it's on a piece of
prize-winning literary fiction or a celebrity autobiography, political tour
de force or historical masterpiece, a serial-killer thriller, reference book,
world classic or a piece of pure escapism – you can bet that it represents
the very best that the genre has to offer.

Whatever you like to read – trust Penguin.